Reg. U. S. Pat. Office

Frontier Stories

I0659247

T. T. SCOTT, President and General Manager　　　　　　　　　　MALCOLM REISS, Editor

WINTER ISSUE, 1940
Volume 14, No. 9

20c per copy

THIS IS A FICTION HOUSE MAGAZINE

FRONTIER: Published quarterly by FICTION HOUSE, INC., 461 Eighth Ave., New York, N. Y. Copyright 1940 by
FICTION HOUSE. All rights reserved. This issue dated November 1st, 1940. For advertising rates address: THE
NEWSSTAND FICTION UNIT, 9 ROCKEFELLER PLAZA, New York.
Printed in U. S. A.

Mormon Girl

By GEORGE E. MAGEE

The soft-eyed Navajo maid had marked Ben Stridewell for her man. But the trail-scout's heart was given to the Mormon girl who lay captive in Spotted Pony's teepee.

BEN STRIDEWELL watched his twenty big Murphy wagons come lumbering into corral on the bank of Cottonwood Creek and noted with pride the tight fort-like circle with the new canvas tops ruddy in the late sun.

He wheeled his horse as the hum of activity broke out, and rode back to investigate the three straggling wagons that had been following all day.

A tall man, black bearded, and with a sort of wild strength in his bearing, came striding to meet him, with the evident intent of keeping him at a distance. The flat-topped hat, the flowing beard, and the absence of visible arms, marked him as a Mormon.

The instinctive dislike for the man and his manner was moderated a bit as a woman showed between the curtains of the nearest wagon, but Ben spoke without greeting, and to the point. "Better drag your wagons close to ours," he advised shortly. "My scout cut Indian signs today."

"The hand of the Lord—" began the bearded one.

The wrinkled woman looking out of the wagon shrilled, "The hand of the Lord was absent when them Yankee traders beat you out of your good horses, Jediah Smith. Better listen!"

Wheeling on her the Mormon shouted, "Hold your tongue, woman!" And then, his rage-reddened eyes on Ben, "Go back to your wagons!"

Shrugging his distaste for argument, Ben had turned his horse, when a girl, slim, yet tightly rounded, and with merry brown eyes that lighted her face like quick laughter, ran from the wagon to put a hand on his saddle. Standing with her shoulder against his knee as if to hold him, she spoke to the Mormon in a warm, chiding voice, "Your tongue and your manner will lead you into trouble, Jediah Smith."

The Mormon hesitated. The girl turned deep eyes up to ask a smiling pardon of Ben.

In that moment Ben Stridewell knew the meaning of the restlessness that had ridden him so wildly of late. At twenty-five he was wagon master, and had been three times across the trail from Independence to the trading post at Santa Fe. The honor, the money, the adventure, had until lately filled his life. But now, speechless with a rush of emotion that warmed his body like a flame, he stared until the girl colored deeply and dropped her eyes. Fumbling with his hat, the blood roaring in his ears he heard her question, "What have you to say, Stranger?"

He struggled, dry-throated. "Ma'am, I suggested that you run your wagons in with ours. There's signs of Indians about. I expect trouble tonight." His words died, but he was unable to tear his eyes from the girl's face. He was almost glad when the Mormon broke in.

"Get thee gone, girl! A clacking tongue is the curse of woman. Go pray for humility and obedience to those whom God has placed over you. You are sealed. Go!"

A threatening gesture of the Mormon's bull whip stressed the words, and brought Ben tense in his saddle, but a quick warning from the eyes of the girl, and his knowledge of the ways of Latter Day Saints, held him from action. He nodded shortly, "Sorry, Ma'am," and rode back to his wagon. His heart beat loudly, and his hands tensed on the reins. The picture of the girl was a part of his soul.

COOKING fires glowed in the twilight inside the circle of wagons. Tied stock were already settling for the night when Ben rode through the narrow opening left for him.

Men smoked, talking of the day's trip. Women were busy about bubbling pots, and children dodged in and out in a never-ending game of tag. Contentment and happiness covered the scene. It was flattering to his leadership, but it found no echo in his heart. A sealed girl—a girl promised. A girl with laughing eyes going out to marry some grim old man. So ran his thoughts, as he was handed a plate of cornbread and beans.

While Ben ate, a grizzled scout armed with a long Sharps rifle, his waist heavy with a belt of snub-nosed brass cartridges, rode in, and, sliding from his horse, walked with the stiff gait of a tired rider to make his report.

"Them redskins is camped three miles back," he stated. "It's ole Sun Cloud and a bunch o' young braves. They ain't painted so mebby they's jist sneaking 'round fer practice, but . . . Say, where's that outfit I passed this morning? Prettiest gal I ever did see waved at me. Got eyes like a sunny river. Dang! I growed up too quick. Wasted mighty nigh my whole life jiggling men and bulls across this trail. Jist gettin' interestin' now. Dang! You see her?"

Ben grinned at the wordy old man. "I

did," he admitted around a mouthful of dry bread. "I did and I got run off. Her pappy's kind of touchy."

Jide Benette cut his wicked old eyes at Ben, spat a stream of brown juice on the trampled grass, and hinted, "I reckoned it ware worse'n that. I figgered she ware sealed to the old 'un. She don't favor him none. Sure she's kin?"

Without waiting for a reply, the old scout hailed one of the women, "Hi, Liddy, what you got to eat? I'm empty's an Injun's bottle." Finishing his meal, Ben strolled over to where the old man wolfed his food, his head low over his plate, and his wide-bladed knife used as a conveyor.

"You slip over and watch the Mormon wagons tonight," he directed. "I'll scout for you tomorrow. And don't bother the girl, you old reprobate."

Jide giggled at the implied compliment, vowing, "I watch her fer ye, sonny. Say, how'd you like a nice scalp lock? I could make me a dandy outa that Mormon. Take a piece o' har, a piece o' face, and round her off with a mite o' beard."

Ben slapped the stringy shoulder. "You just watch," he laughed, and turned to his wagon bed, as the scout yipped at a gangling boy, "Fotch me a fresh hoss, son. Might do me a 'bit o' ridin' tonight."

Ben climbed into the wagon, pulled off his cowhide boots, looked to his twin guns, jerked the wagon curtains almost together, then lay thinking of the girl. Presently, the clatter of washing the tin dishes died, the fires became red eyes, fast dimming, and the rustle and squeak of cornhusk mattresses told of men and women going to well-earned rest. He slept.

Morning was but a dim promise in the sky when he awoke with a start. An owl hooted. Hooted again. Ben rolled out, pulled on his boots, buckled his gun-belt, and slid out of the wagon.

The owl called again. Ben ducked under the wagon, and crawled toward the sound.

The dim white alkali rim of a buffalo wallow showed before him. From the deep shadow of the depression came the querulous whisper of the scout. "Dang! I reckoned you'd never wake!"

"What's up?" breathed Ben.

"I snuck around and took a look at them Injuns," said the scout, low. "They's all packed up and ready to run. Three young fellers took to the grass whilst I was watching. They headed fer the Mormon wagons. They had knives. There's trouble brewin'. That old Sonny-boy is a tricky cuss. I fit him before. He won't know a thing about what happened in the morning. Probably be miles away, innocent as a bird, and not able to understand a word of English or Spanish. Let's slide over, get under the wagon, and give them snakes a scare."

Ben hesitated. To lose stock or equipment might teach the old Mormon a lesson. The Indians were probably out to do a simple job of stealing. But, of course, some of them might have seen the girl. A lot of bucks get ideas.

"Think we can get ahead of them?" he questioned.

"Shore!" promised Jide. "I ain't one to be caught nappin'. Got lots o' time. Come on!"

Moving with the silent caution of snakes, and keeping their heads well below the lighted horizon, the two wormed through the grass and nodding weeds. "Dang them sunflowers," complained the scout, "allays stickin' up and wavin'. Keep clear o' em."

Ben headed straight for the wagon where the girl slept.

The scout chuckled when he saw that.

SCARCELY breathing, they reached the shadow of the wagon, and lay waiting.

The sharp scent of buckskin and grease came to their plains-sharpened nostrils.

"Close!" warned the scout. "Use yore knife when they jump us."

The words were just spoken when three sleek, dark heads showed in the grass not five yards away. An interchange of chilling guttural whispers came to the men shivering in anticipation under the wagon.

Suddenly the Indians leaped upright. Three gray ghosts ran to attack the sleeping women.

The scout and Ben leaped to meet them.

Breast to breast they struck. Ben's hand grasping for the knife hand of the nearest savage. A chill of fear shot through his body as knife grated on knife. The Indian was left-handed. The usual method was useless. Agile as a cat, Ben bounded back, changing his tactics by swinging a fist at a high-bridged nose.

The Indian grunted his pained surprise as the blow landed. He went staggering back.

Ben leaped for his falling body. As they crashed to the ground, the third Indian landed astraddle of Ben's back. The bite of a knife was already between his shoulders as he struggled to meet this new menace. The blow was delayed. Ben felt the Indian's legs clasp him convulsively, and turning his head, he saw that his foe struggled in the grip of the scout who had a skinny arm around his throat from behind, and was grinning assurance over a dirty shoulder.

"Got him foul," exulted Jide, as the Indian twisted in bung-eyed agony.

Ben tore the gripping legs from his lean waist, and brought down his knife in a skull-crushing blow on the fallen Indian. Then he rolled clear, and quickly aimed a knife to put the scout's captive out of business.

"Leave him be!" panted Jide. "I got a use fer him. I'll send him back to Sonny-boy with his tail draggin'."

The grunts of combat had aroused the Mormons. With a growl of warning to the women, the black-bearded man tumbled from the wagon, clad only in red underwear. His sleep-bleared eyes took in the scene in the growing light. His glance fell on the Indians. The knife of the scout was still fast in the ribs of one. "You murdering hounds," he roared. "You Godless sinners! Get gone, before revenge is mine!"

Ben was stunned by the unexpected attack. But the old scout, who had been tying his prisoner swiftly, now pushed him to the ground, and turned on the Mormon, "Don't valley yore life none, I see," he taunted. "Hope you ain't plumb crazy, but you shore acts it. These devils would'a had yore heart roastin' on a stick, if Ben an' I hadn't been watchin'. . . ."

The girl ran swiftly from the wagon. The first rays of sun were bright in her hair that flowed over her shoulders. Her eyes fastened on Ben, warm with thanks, and something deeper.

On her heels came the woman who had dared to face the wrath of Jediah Smith. She darted wasp-like at the tall man. "You fool! You utter fool!" she shrilled.

"Have you taken leave of all your muddled senses?"

Jediah Smith muttered deep in his beard something about a Christian burial, and turned to jerk a spade from the wagon.

The woman pushed back her gray hair from a face that still showed traces of strong beauty. "He's crazy," she hurried, speaking to Ben, "church crazy. He's taking a dozen women out to Utah. They're sealed to men out there. He forced the girl to go. She's to marry a man twice her age. I can't leave him; he's my husband. . . . You don't know, sir." Her voice broke with emotion. "God help us women," she wailed. "Oh, sir, let us travel with you. I can control him sometimes, but I'm afraid. I'm afraid for the girl. He's . . ."

The Mormon threw down his spade at her words. "The command of the Lord is upon me," he shouted. "I'll have no company with murderers! Get you to the wagon. I'll deal with these."

The eyes of the scout and Ben met as Jediah Smith's wife made a sign to the girl.

The scout drew a quick questioning finger across his throat, his knife held ready.

THE girl, her head high, and her eyes level and fearless, walked straight to the crazed man. She put a hand on his shoulder. "I have a vision from the Lord," she asserted. "It is His command that you travel in safety that His work may be done. All men are His servants."

Ben saw a sly and pitying smile on the face of the woman as her husband's form lost its angry tenseness. With his eyes almost gentle, he muttered, "Blessed be His name. You are His messenger. It shall be done."

"Ain't so loco as he acts," winked Jide at Ben. And then in a whisper, "Dang! Don't reckon she's teched too?"

The face of the girl shone with a light more than the sun as she spoke to Ben, "My name is Vega Spears. May I know yours and your companion's that I may thank you for your kindness to us?"

Ben's voice was deep as he answered. He held his hat in his hand. Yellow curling hair fell nearly to his shoulders. "I'm Stridewell. Ben Stridewell. And this man is Jide Benette my scout. It would pleasure me to have you join us, but I want no trouble. My first duty is to the men who hired me."

The eyes of the girl darkened.

The old scout chuckled. "Man's liable to change his mind about what comes first," he ventured. "When you're ready to pull, I'll ride with you fer a spell, Miss. Ben ain't the whole cheese. He runs the wagons; I run off Injuns. You can figger which is most important."

He halted his garrulity at a glance from Ben, and turned to nudge the captive Indian in the ribs with a moccasined toe, "Hi, Mud-in-the-face," he gibed, "heap big chief, eh? I'm going to take you over to Sun Cloud and tell him I licked you bar-handed. You'll be hoeing corn with the women next season."

The stolid face of the Indian broke into unexpected pleading under this threat. He evidently understood every word. He spoke rapidly in Sioux, his hands tugging at his bonds as he tried to gesture.

The scout chuckled as he listened. He slapped a leather-clad leg, cackling his delight. "This coyote claims he's a chief's son," he translated. "He says he's got two squaws. One is good lookin', the other is a good cook. He'll gimme 'em both if I turn him loose. He was only showing them young braves how to swipe, playin' like. His people have taken many Apache scalps he says, and therefore we should be friends. We have killed two of his warriors, which should satisfy us, and it is going to make it tough on him. He says he didn't intend any harm, but he's probably lying handsome."

Ben Stridewell made one of his swiftly considered decisions. "Let him go," he ordered, his eyes on the old Mormon and the girl.

They reacted as he expected. He knew the ways of Mormons with Indians. They treated them as brothers, and thought of them as one of the lost tribes mentioned in the BOOK OF MORMON.

Jediah Smith stopped his digging, and with calmness in his fanatic eyes, waited the next move.

JIDE BENETTE looked doubtful, but he picked up the Indian's knife and cut the bonds about his feet. Then, jerking him up, he drew the point of the knife swiftly across the bronze throat. "I could shed yore blood, and I have not done so, my brother," he declared with some sarcasm in his tone. "Remember this!"

The face of the Indian lighted at the words. He offered to shake hands when the scout cut his bonds.

Jide stepped back quickly, and slapped him on a shoulder. "Yo're a great chief," he complimented. "Anyway, yo're a great talker. If I find you have spoken with a double tongue, I'll collect yore scalp and spit on it every night. We'll be on the trail when you come to get yore chums. Put yore heart into wailin' fer 'em, son. It might have been you."

The Indian, clothing himself in sullen dignity, stalked away without a backward glance. Once well out of rifle range he turned to make a derisive gesture that is age-old, and ducked out of sight.

The scout whinnied shrilly. "He's plumb even now," he cackled. "He don't feel no shame, nor carry any grudge. Funny fellers, Injuns. But mostly good as their word, which ain't none too good mostly."

With this slightly ambiguous statement, the scout turned to find Ben eyeing the girl with so ardent an admiration that it brought a black scowl to the Mormon's face, and a high color to the girl's cheeks. "Let's git back," he suggested. "I'm prime hungry."

Ben hesitated. The rules of the trail dictated that they be asked to breakfast. He got no invitation, only a glance of apology from the girl. He turned reluctantly away.

Out of earshot, Jide bragged. "You done jist right, Benny. Bet you got a soft spot in the ole feller's heart. What you aim to do about the gal? Dang! Yore eyes bung out comical when you looks at her."

"Don't you ever run out of words?" growled Ben, his olive cheeks and high forehead ruddy, but his lips smiling.

"Not when they're needful," vowed the scout. "They'll travel with us fer a spell now, an' you'll probably have to kill the ole feller. Mebby I ought to sneak over and make a deal with Sun Cloud. Give him a sack of flour to stick a few arrers in yore pappy-in-law-to-be, or whatever."

For a scant second, Ben was tempted.

His whole body longed for the girl. He had known many Mormons. Stubborn, humorless people, bound by iron rules; as well try to change the sun in its course as to argue with one of them. He saw trouble ahead. Only death would free the girl. Death was the way of settling trail differences. Few men would have hesitated. Yet all his training, and his inclinations were against such acts.

"I'll take care of that," he directed. "You look after the Indians."

"That's what I'm thinkin' of," protested the scout. "They'll branch off fer Utah in ten days or so, and that'll put 'em in the Arapahoe country. Them devils'll get yore gal shore.!"

She isn't—" began Ben.

The scout halted suddenly. "Listen, son," he asserted, every trace of his usual slipshod speech absent. "If I ever saw two people called together by the great gods of the plains, it is you and that girl. You need them laughing eyes to make a real man of you, Ben. You take things too serious. You could lick the world with her backing you. You know it. There is only one mate for a man. I missed mine. I lost her because—"

He broke off, unable to continue for the stress of memory. He put a claw-like hand on Ben's arm. "Don't let her go!" he commanded, his eyes gleaming.

The words were but a faint echo of the feeling in the wagon master's heart. He hunched his shoulders as if against a heavy wind, as he strode toward his own people.

BREAKFAST was ready in the wagon-fort. The stock had been turned out for an early feed and a chance at water in a slough high with green rushes. While Ben ate, he answered questions about the night's work but left details to the scout.

While the camp was still clacking with the news of the Indian attack on the Mormon wagons, Ben swung his saddle on his arm and went out to whistle up his horse. Throwing on the heavy saddle, he rode to a little distance where he could see the whole train, and prepared to give the usual orders for starting.

Seeing that most of the women had carried the breakfast dishes to the wagons, he swung his hat and cried, "Catch up! Catch up!"

Teamsters ran to catch horses and to fling harness on their dancing charges.

The Waldon brothers, three stalwart men with their families, who had elected to drive oxen, flailed and prodded at the flanks of their bawling beasts in an effort to beat the more agile horses. The whole family helped. Women drove the hickory pins fast into the bows the moment the great yokes were on shaggy necks. Children tugged with twisting faces at the heavy chains, fastening to the sturdy ash wagon-tongues. They made a game of this each morning. It furnished the competition and the fun to start the day right. This morning the Waldons were ready a moment before the slowest team. A shout of triumph came from their wagons.

Teamster after teamster, after giving a look to lost articles, and checking his family, scrambled up over high wheels, gathered his reins, squared his elbows, and cried, "All set!"

Ben watched until all were ready, and then gave the signal, "String out! String out!"

The lead wagon lurched toward the ford at Cottonwood, and the rest fell in at regular intervals.

There was pride and pain in the heart of the wagon master as he watched. If he had not this responsibility, he would have acted swiftly to take the girl from the Mormons. His troubled thoughts were cut short as he remembered his promise to take the scout's place for the day. He splashed into the ford, lunged up the cutbank on the far side, and rode to a little rise where he could see the lay of the prairie ahead.

He wondered as his eyes swept the thin horizon line, just what was the story behind the three straggling wagons. They would fall some distance behind during the day's march, but he'd make an opportunity to see the girl or the woman soon.

The grass was noiseless under the shuffling feet of his horse. The sky was a blue dome. A meadow lark whistled from a prairie-dog mound. A buzzard swung high in the vault of sky. A ringed necked dove cooed so constantly that the ear refused to hear it.

Then a strange silence fell on the land.

A silence that tells much to a man used to the open. His horse pricked his ears, laying one far back.

Ben turned to look behind him. Far behind him in the East, he saw a line of black dots wavering in the heat that was already making vision tricky. This might be another train, or buffalo working down to water. Probably buffalo, the southern migration was due. A few white clouds had built up in the sky. Their shadows drifted across the grass as if driven by the gentle breeze. There seemed to be no danger in the peaceful scene.

He stood high in his stirrups, squinting his eyes to see the horizon. A yellow plume shot up back of the black dots. The plume darkened to a black cloud, red at the lower edge. He caught his breath. A fire. He held up a wet finger to test the breeze. It was behind the flames. The Mormon wagons were still on the east bank of Cottonwood Creek. Something had delayed their starting. His wagons were safe. He wheeled his horse to gallop back. As he did so, he saw ahead of the fire, the black dots that were running buffalo.

THIS was Indian work. They had probably fallen in with the herd, rounded them up, driven them down the Cottonwood valley, and after aiming them at the Mormons, and giving them a stampeding start, lighted fires to urge them on. Too well, Ben knew the danger from the avalanche force of a thousand head of maddened beasts. They turned aside for nothing.

He was sure that if he were watched from the Mormon wagons—and he hoped he might be—that he could warn them in trail language. He wrote his warning large against the sky by riding quickly back and forth across the trail. That meant danger ahead, but at least they would catch up their horses.

Swiftly he made his plans. Unless they pulled out in time, it would be necessary to turn the herd. Only riflemen could do that, and only at the last moment. Men who had nerve to stand before the thundering menace of the charge, and who could shoot accurately, could pile enough of the beasts to split a run. It had been done before.

His own wagon train, mistaking his warning for them, acted swiftly. Like a jointed snake it swung out and came into the tight circle that is the result of training.

Ben saw the old scout running for his horse that trotted alongside the train. The old man, rifle in hand, swung on bareback, and came galloping to meet him.

Ben's intent eyes told of danger behind when they met. Without a word, the scout wheeled, and they went racing for the Mormon wagons, where the horses were being hastily harnessed.

For a moment, the dip of the creek hid the wagons from their view. When they came up again in the plain, both the fire and the dark mass of buffalo, with a whirling cloud of dust behind, were less than a mile from the wagons.

One thing seemed sure, the Mormons and the wagons were doomed. Ben felt a knife-like burn in his heart as he visioned the girl under trampling hoofs.

It was plain that the Mormons knew the danger of the fire, for that spread into the sky, but the buffalo were not visible from the slight depression in which the wagons stood.

They must be warned and helped. Neck and neck the wirey horses ridden by Ben and the scout surged back by the corralled wagons to shout a warning, although they stood in no danger except from the stampede.

The two splashed into the creek, and came spurring down to where the Mormons still struggled to hitch frightened horses. As they arrived, the bearded man ceased his efforts and threw himself on his knees in the path of the running bison. "Get a gun! Get a gun!" yelled Ben.

The praying man made no move.

Ben jerked his heavy Colts. The scout worked the bolt of his rifle, casting a glance of pity at the cluster of women who huddled behind a wagon.

The thunder of wildly running hoofs, the crackle of the fire, sent the Mormon horses into a panic. They broke across the flat, dragging the wagons with them, just as Ben and the scout plunged by, straight at the spear-point of the stampede, led by a red-eyed bawling bull.

"Stick together," shouted Ben to the women.

"Goo-bye," grinned the scout at Ben, as

he jerked his horse to a stop, and leveled the long rifle at the bull leading the herd.

The roar of the gun was in Ben's ears. He shot with stiff fingers at the following bison.

The bull gave a great bound, and landed on his massive shoulders cutting a bellow in half. Another dropped behind him. Another! And another!

Both men shot as fast as they could load.

The dead buffalo formed a dam. Behind them a rushing mass poured into a tangled jam of heaving, twisting, bellowing bodies that threatened each moment to break the barrier of the dead, and come charging down on the two men and the defenseless women.

The sight was too much for the bearded man. He jumped to run to one side. At the same moment the pressure of the jammed bodies became too great. They divided, leaving only a small plot where rescuers and rescued stood, as they went rushing like a torrent on either side.

Ben was conscious of the trembling of his horse beneath him, and of the husked words of the scout, "Dang! They sure cotched the ole feller. Good riddance! But I didn't think the Injuns would do a trick like this."

Ben slid from his horse, his heart hammering out an assurance that the girl was now his. She ran to meet him. He held her for a sweet moment against his broad chest, and kissed her brow. Then he stood stricken at his own daring.

Jide Benette was busy the moment the last of the straggling buffalo dashed by. He twisted a torch of dried grass cursing the slow sulphur match, and ran forward to light a line of fires to protect their little island.

Ben pulled his shirt and flapped at the flames that ate toward them. Smoke choked him. Flames crackled close; but gradually the fire set by the scout gained against the wind, and the two fires met, flamed high, and died.

Through the clearing smoke Ben saw the men from his wagons riding with wet blankets to beat out the flames that threatened to flank them.

He saw something else also. A horseman coming rapidly across the blackened prairie, and behind him the tops of another wagon train.

THE approaching horseman rode to the clustered women, jumped from his horse, and spoke to the wife of Jediah Smith, "Where's Jediah?"

Ben didn't hear the low answer, but he saw her point to a thing that looked like a trampled shirt crumpled into the beaten grass. All the bright dreams that had flooded his heart in the last swift seconds were now ashes in his heart.

This man had come from another Mormon train.

A wild temptation to grasp the girl, fling her before him on the saddle, and carry her away, tore at his soul. He looked deep into her bright eyes. He saw within them the assurance that she would go willingly.

He fought the urge. The Mormons would never rest until they had gotten her back. Other men had tried to take Mormon women.

Under a stress of emotion that forced him forward, he clasped her rounded arms above the elbow with tensing fingers. "Somewhere, somehow, Vega Spears," he vowed, "I'm going to have you and keep you until God parts us!"

The girl's eyes filled with quick tears. "It is the wish of my heart, Ben Stridewell," she said staunchly.

The Mormon who had ridden to the scene was of a far different type than the dour Jediah. "My name is Gabe Laton," he offered, as he shook Ben's hand. "I want to thank you for what you did. We started that fire, and it got away from us. When you can, ride back and visit us. We're using oxen, and travel slow. Besides we'll be loaded pretty heavy with these extra people. I'll go back and get help to find what became of the wagons and goods. We warned Jediah not to get ahead, but he wouldn't listen."

The Mormon was turning away, as Jide rode in, his face streaked with dust and sweat. He heard a part of the statement. Eyeing the Mormon with no favor, he contended, "Fellers thet let a fire git loose ain't fit fer this country. But, dang, I'm glad it wasn't the Injuns. I hate to be fooled."

Then he nudged Ben. "Make yore play fer her right now," he urged. "You saved her. She's yourn by all rights."

Ben gave the old man a warning glance

as he introduced the two men. The time was not yet. He could only cause her trouble by acting now. There was nothing to do but wait.

Ben's men came back from their quick fight with the last of the fire. They fell on the buffalo with whoops of joy. Hides and meat they could use.

The old scout had been a jump ahead of them. From his saddle hung a dozen long tongues.

The Mormon women followed the tracks of the runaway wagons where they entered the willows along the creek.

Ben watched them go, his heart in his eyes, as he noted how the girl lagged behind. If he had known how many weary days were to pass before he saw her again, he might have taken the scout's advice.

The wide prairie with the burned spot in it, was empty and dark as his heart.

WITHOUT event, except sickness from too much fresh meat, the prairie rolled under rumbling wheels until they reached and passed, Plumb Buttes, Pawnee Rock, and sighted Fort Larned.

Crossing the stream at Pawnee Forks, they made the three day journey across dry country to the Cimarron crossing.

Here the trail divided. It was Ben's inclination to take the North road, because he might see the girl again if anything delayed them.

But a messenger riding on the business of Magoffin Brothers, traders at Santa Fe, warned of possible Indian trouble, and reluctantly Ben turned his train south.

The last chance to see Vega Spears was gone. The Mormons, unless they elected to go to Santa Fe to do some trading, or to send goods to the colonies in· Mexico, would turn north after crossing the river, work along the mountains to Denver village, and strike through the range for Salt Lake. Every day would make new distance between the girl and Ben.

The messenger camped with the train for a night. Ben asked about Susan Magoffin, whom he had seen on a former trip crossing the trail with her weather-beaten husband. A sight to be remembered, for they drove a pair of spanking blacks hitched to a shining buckboard, and Susan, nineteen, and beautiful, carried a lacy sunshade.

Ben remembered her vividly. She had eaten a meal with them. Her brown eyes had been alight with all-encompassing interest. Her laugh, at some tale of the old scout's was like a silver chime.

"Crazy as ever," laughed the messenger in answer to Ben's question, "an' just as lovely, and as much loved. Not a man, white, Mex, or Indian, who wouldn't give his life for Mrs. Magoffin."

The words strengthened Ben's resolve to go to Salt Lake and make his fight for the girl as soon as he could get away from the train. Love, a woman's love, was a real force. A man had only half lived, until a woman loved him.

But it was not until they reached Rio Gallias, afterwards known as Los Vegas, that they heard anything more of the Mormons.

A long-haired trapper, Pete Price, told of coming on the remains of a strong party that had been attacked by the Indians. "I counted thirty skulls," he said, "and I found a trail register blowing around the remains of the wagons. It had forty names in it. The varmints must have taken some prisoners. Happened on the Green River, 'bout six days out of Salt Lake. Looked like Ute work."

The news fired Ben with a new fear and a new longing. He must take up the trail of the raiding Indians. She might be among the captives.

Luck favored him at Ratoon Pass. A company of Mexican regulars met the train with an offer of escort.

Ben called a meeting, and stated his case. Reluctantly they voted to let him undertake· the dangerous journey. Using his pay to buy trade goods from the wagons, and two horses from the remuda of the Mexicans, he was packed and ready, when much to his delight, the old scout decided to go with him.

"Dang!" he protested, fingering his big gun. "Too danged quiet around here! An' Santa Fe'll be worse. I gets me into a fight every time I lands there; but ain't no pleasure fightin' Mexes. They ain't got the spirit. Fraid of gittin' killed. Gimme Injuns!"

The two left the train when the morning stars were still dim in the sky. The wild hurry of Ben was checked by the scout. He knew the country until they reached the waste land on the west side of the Colorado.

Few men, besides the wandering Mormon missionaries, knew that Indian stronghold. And they, only the trail that led twisting away from the only possible crossing of the turbulant, muddy and flood-plagued stream, through a desert cut and fretted by endless canyons going nowhere. Yet there were green and well-watered spots in that tortured jumble of sandstone that had once been ocean bottom.

The Navajos fed their bands of sheep and horses there. The Paiutes lived in the valleys, and the Utes eaked out a thin-ribbed existence on the wind-swept tablelands.

The old scout had a good word only for the Navajos. He had lived with them once more for a winter. His cracked voice told a strange tale as they camped on the second night away from the train. "If she's traded to them Injuns," he piped, "she's lucky. Them Navajos squaws is independent as skunks. They runs the men. An' talk about woman's tongues! Them gal's is hung plumb center. They don't think nothing of telling every move their bucks make. Jist like the danged Mexes. I listened to 'em; an' I tell a man, I left 'em alone. Feller gits fresh with one o' them young squaws, an' they'll laugh him outa camp. Course if they takes a shine to you, that's different. But they'll still talk scand'lus behind yore back. They won't let none o' their men get mixed up with a white gal. Thing to do Ben, is to jist work slow through the country, an' listen to all the gossip. Glad we got plenty trade goods."

THEY headed straight for Green River, striking the trail of the Mormon wagons about fifty miles from where the trapper had placed the attack. From that point they traveled fast, the day's journey limited only by the endurance of their horses. In two days they were on the river, hunting among the burned remains of the wagons for something that might offer a clew.

Ben shrank from the task of identifying the coyote gnawed skulls, but the scout piled them for a marker, and offered the cheering news that none of them had had hair like the girl they sought. "They took most of the young gals prisoners," he summed up. "I'll bet you, yore gal give 'em some trouble."

They turned south on the dim trail of the Indians.

The desert preserves signs well. The Indians had made a long march on the first day. "Scared," said the scout.

The next camp-site told something. Ben picked up a shred of ribbon to which clung a few hairs that might have been pulled out in a struggle. There were no marks of blood. Nothing to indicate that the Indians were mistreating their prisoners. Some spilled flour, a few beans, and buffalo ribs indicated a feast of a kind.

"Them Utes," observed the scout, naming the tribe by the form of their cooking fires, "took a lot of grub from the wagons. Right now, they're feelin' good. An Injun with a full belly is sleepy as a coon. Reckon they'll stay on this side the river till they eat everything they swiped. We ought to hit 'em at the first good camp spot. Days don't mean nothin' to them skunks if they kin eat."

The trail was dim and hard to follow. Hunting parties had branched off at intervals. To cover more country, the men separated, agreeing to meet at a glistening dry lake of salt or alkali, to which all the twisting canyons apparently led.

Ben was guiding his horse carefully down a pitch of smooth sandstone, and watching the slipping pack horse follow, when from a side trail came a girl with a water olla on her shoulder.

She was caught fair, evidently thinking that the noise of the approaching horse had been made by some of her own people. She was dressed in a short skirt of deer-skin, leggins, and a beaded shirt. She was handsome. Her wide black eyes stared at Ben for a second, and then dropping the earthen vessel with a tankling crash, she ran back up the trail, the long braids of hair flying over her shoulders.

Ben was after her at once. She might be some distance from her tribe. If he could catch her alone, he might get valuable information.

She had a little start, and ran like a rabbit, scrambling and dodging over rocks that offered no foothold for Ben's heavy boots. It was not until the canyon ended abruptly at a spring trickling from the rock, that he had any chance to catch up.

There she turned and faced him panting, her breath lifting her breasts under the loose shirt, and a small knife ready in her hand. There was no fear in her attitude.

Ben caught his breath, and standing at a safe distance, spoke in Spanish, "I would talk with you, my sister. See, I come in peace." He held up his hand in the peace sign. "I will not harm you. I am looking for a woman who is lost. Is there a stranger in your tribe?"

The girl spoke softly and quickly in Indian. She evidently understood something of the question, and was trying to answer.

Her face showed good nature, and a quick intelligence.

Ben could make nothing of her words. He came to a quick decision. "How many are your people," he asked.

The girl put her knife back into a beaded sheath, and raised slim hands with fingers wide, four times.

"Forty," nodded Ben, and rushed her.

He got, in the next few minutes, a very fair idea of a cat fight. The girl was wiry as a willow, quick as a glance. Yet there was no savagery in her methods. She did not scratch. She simply twisted out of his arms. Finally, he picked her up and squeezed her breathless.

She lay helpless a moment, her black eyes flashing, and then seeing that he intended no harm, for he was smiling down at her, she answered his smile uncertainly with an inticing quirk of her lips, and nodded at his question, "Navajo?"

Thinking of what the scout had told him, he ordered, "Lead me to your camp." But making the sentence partly a request as he remembered the character the old man had given these comely, if somewhat rebald women.

The girl struggled in his arms, her eyes filled with a shy admiration of his strength. Her lips quivered as she shook her head, and made the sign of a throat being cut.

Grasping her roughly with intent to convince her of his earnestness, he pushed her back down the trail. She gave dark and warning glances over her shoulder, but made no other protest.

The horses had already begun to feed on the scanty brush growing from the canyon wall, and knowing that they would be safe for a while, Ben urged her ahead down the trail, keeping close on her heels.

The girl showed increasing reluctance as they neared the camp.

Ben was soon to know the reason.

THEY came without warning from the dogs, abruptly around a bend in the rock trail and were among the lodges set close to the edge of a cliff.

Instant commotion greeted their arrival. The twenty braves gathered swiftly. They were Paiutes, dirty and dangerous, led by an evil-looking old man who confronted Ben, and spoke harshly in Spanish.

Ben made haste to explain himself. He said nothing of captives, wishing to give them every chance to be friendly. "I'm looking for a woman who wandered away from a wagon train," he explained. "I have other men with me. They will be following me soon. They are well armed, and have swift horses. I come as a friend. Tell me what I have asked, and I will go in peace."

The old man jabbered a harangue to his circle of sullen braves.

They grunted protest, their eyes covetous on Ben's boots and guns.

The girl spoke, using mostly signs.

An ill-favored buck stepped quickly forward to grasp her arm.

The chief knocked it aside with a gruff command. "She wants to go with you," he said. "I would say take her. But this man has traded two prisoners for her. She will not marry him. And she talks too much."

The scowling Indian who had claimed the Navajo girl protested with bitter words and wide gestures. A chorus of approval went up from his backers.

"He says he'll fight you for her with knives," translated the spokesman. "He wants your guns. He says you are a coward."

Ben looked over his challenger calmly. Ill-favored as he was, he was strong and stringy. There was no sense in fighting for the girl. He didn't want her either. But he knew it was deeper than that. This probably meant a chance for life. The least sign of fear, and they'd be down on him like a wolf pack.

He unbuckled his belt, and handed his

precious guns to the chief, hoping they'd be safe if he lived to claim them.

Pulling his shirt for greater freedom of movement, he jerked his heavy knife from his boot, and faced his scowling opponent in the tight circle of watchers.

The brave crouched low, circling like a cat, his knife pointing upward for a heart-searching thrust up under the ribs.

Ben fell into a like attitude, his boot heels padding softly in the sand as he circled. He knew the Paiute method of battle: a feint for the belly, a bound, and a downthrust into the hollow of the neck.

The Indian, taunted by the yells of his backers, made the first flying lunge. Ben made no effort to meet him. He leaped sideways, and slashed down on the Indian's knife hand.

A howl went up from the watchers. They wanted hand-to-hand fighting.

Ben was assured of that when he was pushed from behind, as he tried a retreat to wait for an opening. He felt no fear, but with all his heart, he wanted this trial over that he might be about his business.

He saw the Indian's eyes shift to his booted feet, and he leaped aside just in time to escape a disabling kick aimed at the knee. Gathering himself, tensing his muscles for a supreme effort, he set his eyes on the menacing point of the knife, and leaped to grasp the knife-hand.

The audience grunted. This was something like.

The two men met like fighting cocks. For a long tense second they strained breast to breast, neither gaining an advantage.

Then, despite anything he could do, Ben felt his knife arm bending slowly back. Unless he could resist that, the Indian would kill him with his own knife. His strength was draining. His face twisting with the agony of his effort, and his breath whistling through drawn lips, Ben suddenly let go all resistance, and at the same second came down with all his strength on the Indian's knife hand. He felt the knife strike flesh, grate on a rib, and plunge deep.

With a strangled yell, the Indian staggered back and sank to the ground, jerking at the knife.

The chief jumped between the combatants, handing Ben his guns.

The girl dodged about the bunch of braves surrounding the fallen man, ran to a lodge, and came back with a bundle. She was only a step behind Ben when he backed around the sheltering turn of the trail.

THEY looked at each other for a long moment. Ben had to smile. The girl had gone to rescue a precious blanket. She patted it, and said something in Navajo. Ben shook his head. But he remembered that she had been traded for two prisoners. One of them might be Vega Spears. If he got the girl to the scout who could talk her language, he might learn much. Only this thought kept him from sending her back.

She smiled again, confident now that she was going with him.

She followed him up the trail to where the horses fed, folded her blanket and throwing it on one of the pack-horses, climbed on and waited his orders.

Ben, thinking that she might have an idea where her people were, made a questing motion, and said the word, "Navajos?"

Instant comprehension showed in the black eyes that were by the moment looking at him with greater trust and liking. She slid to the ground, picked up a twig, smoothed a place in the sand, and drew a twisting line, pointing to him and to her.

Ben grinned his understanding. This was the canyon where they sat.

She continued the line farther, indicating a pass by a line on either side, and a simulated shiver with her arms wrapped tight about her to show that it was high and cold. From there the line twisted again, and ran down to a lake, represented by a circle. She clapped a quick hand over her eyes to show that it shone.

Ben nodded his delight. This was the lake where the scout waited.

Across the lake the trail went on. The girl indicating a two-day journey by two fires, and a sun rising and setting. She indicated a camping spot by drawing a willow with big leaves, and there planted the stick with the one word they had in common, "Navajos!"

Seeing that he intended to go, the girl shook out her skirts with a feminine motion that reminded Ben of his sisters, smoothed them down into place over nicely rounded hips, and, her eyes just a little inviting, climbed her horse, and led the way.

They crossed the divide at sunset. Ben had been wondering a great deal about the girl, but had come to the conclusion that she only wanted to get back to her tribe. He saw down in the hollow a small fire, and knew that the scout was waiting for him. Soon he would be able to find out a great deal.

Jide Benette sighted them from a distance, and, drawn by his curiosity at the sight of a woman, came out to meet them.

"What the hell, young feller," he chided, as he caught sight of the more-than-comely Navajo girl. "Changed yore mind already?"

Ben told what he could.

The scout listened, and then turned to the girl with a question in her language.

The words of reply came in an endless gush.

A T the first pause, the old scout yelled his delight. He slapped his leg in vicious glee, and finally sank weakly to the ground shaken by his internal chuckling. "Oh, Dang!" he gulped, wiping his eyes, "Oh, dang! This sure beats my time. She says you are her man. She says she was traded for two other prisoners because she would not marry the man he picked out for her. She says one was a woman with eyes like the stars, and so pale she was probably sick. That is yore gal, all right; but how you going to get loose from this one. She'll never give you up. Want I should cut her throat?"

The Navajo girl put her hand tentatively on Ben's arm as if she sensed the danger in the conversation. She said two English words, "Good man," her eyes very soft.

"What'd I tell you?" said the scout. "Probably every woman in her tribe know them two words, and figure they're enough." Then with his face stern, the old man gazed out over the lake, that on closer view was nothing but hummocks of salt. "Can't cross tonight," he decided. "We'll camp here. What's yore name?" he asked the girl.

With eyes softly cast down, she answered, "Isk-ka-da."

"A fallen star," muttered the scout. "Well, gal, looks like you fell in a bad hole." He shrugged at Ben. "No use

trying to explain to her. You fought fer her. She's yourn. Dang yore yellar hair! Why ain't I younger! I looked fer years fer a gal like this one. Notice she's clean."

Ben eyed the girl with pity in his glance. Her eyes met his, soft and inviting.

"Get wood!" barked the scout at her. "We must eat. Tonight you watch the hosses. Yore back will smart if you do not do it well."

Ben shot an angry glance at the scout.

The old man grinned, but there was no mirth in his eyes. "Had to be done, sonny. If she had nothing to do, she'd be cuddling up to you like a friendly pup. Young fellers falls fer that. We got trouble enough coming up. The tribe ain't goin' to act nice when you brings back a gal they don't want, and tries to take one they do. Dang! I wished this gal hadn't turned up. I was on the trail. I found shoe prints, a man and a woman."

The scout fell silent as Ben watched the girl build a quick fire. She moved about cooking the grub that the scout had set out from the packs, with the grace of a deer. Her oval face was pensive, and at the same time determined. Her manner seemed to say that she had time enough ahead. At intervals, she stole glances at Ben. Each time she did, he felt his heart warm. She was probably nineteen, nicely rounded, her teeth white and even between cleanly modeled lips. Her bearing proud, confident, and warm. They might have been her guests. A lancing thought cut Ben's mind. Her was a fit mate for a wilderness man.

They ate a silent meal. The girl scoured the tin dishes in the sand, and went to gather scanty vegetation to carry to the tied horses.

The scout watched her under shaggy brows. "Good woman," he grunted. "All them Navajos know how to take care of hosses."

B EN awoke at daylight filled with the childlike anticipation of something pleasant about to happen. He was close to the Mormon girl. Soon he would see her. His first glance over the lake of salt hummocks showed the Navajo girl standing with her face toward the distant mountains.

The sun touched the eastern rim of the

valley, and high and clear, the girl sang a welcome to the morning. Ben's eyes smarted suddenly. He lay watching, his heart skipping queerly, while the flush of dawn painted the salt bed with shadows of rose and purple.

The old scout rolled from his blanket, took a chew of tobacco, and sat looking quietly at the scene. He turned to Ben, speaking with a soft reverance. "Sometimes, son," he mused, "God comes so close to man that it fair scares me." And then, as if ashamed of his words, he shouted harshly at the girl.

She raised a hand in answer, and came running toward them, picking dry wood from a flood-gulch as she came.

Pity was in Ben's heart as he watched her. She was going to be hurt.

The scout put the feeling into words: "Funny world, Ben. I kill me an Injun this year, and next time I come by the place, there's a bunch of flowers brung up by his blood."

It became increasingly evident as the scout questioned the girl while they ate a breakfast of jerky and bitter coffee, that he was finding a great deal that did not please him.

"What's the hold-up?" asked Ben, as the old scout's face showed dark with trouble.

Jide Benette kept his eyes down, and drew a finger through the soft sand as he spoke. "She says," he began, hunching a shoulder at the girl who squatted on her heels with her lips slightly parted in an effort to understand, "she says that she refused to marry Spotted Pony, who is chief, because he is too closely related to her. So he traded her off to the Paiutes for a couple o' prisoners they was anxious to git shut of. One of them was the leader of a wagon train. He fought bravely, so the Paiutes honored him, and let him live. So there she is, son. Say we get the prisoners away from the Navajos, which will be some job, the Mormons will still claim the girl. We might try buying 'em off. But we still got to think of Spotted Pony. I knowed him when he was a kid. Mean sort o' feller. I hate to go into that camp. I shore do."

"Let's get going," snapped Ben, impatient at delay.

"Talk don't git nowhar," admitted the old man, getting stiffly to his feet, "but an arrer in the belly gits you somewhars too danged fast. We'll travel slow and come up on the camp at night. That's safest. The gal claims it's two days' march. Her people have found a good country, water, trees, and lots of game. Sounds like the happy huntin' grounds. Might be, fer both o' us. Why don't you take this woman, and turn back. She's a good gal. She'd make a good wife. You could start a little tradin' post and sit easy the rest o' yore life. I'll stick with you, of course, but, dang, I only got a few more years to live. I was settling to trappin' come this fall. . . ."

The girl had filled their canteens from a pot hole in the rocks, and was now making shift to wash her face and hands, and to arrange her hair in the mirror pool.

Jide looked at the sight with strange eyes. "Woman's a woman, wherever she be," she said darkly, and went to throw packs on the waiting horses.

THEY took a dim trail snaking between the hummocks of crystal salt that sparkled jewel-like in the sun. Although details of the range of mountains to which they headed, were clear, it was late evening before they came to the old shore on the other side.

The scout, leaving the care of the horses to Ben and the girl, set about making an elaborate meal. He cut bacon with his hunting knife as he explained, "No use saving grub now. Tomorrow will be a feast, or we won't need any."

Ben and the girl came into the circle of firelight together. He was conscious of every move she made. She squatted, and after a long silent look at the still lighted mountain peaks, she spoke a low question to the scout, her lips scarcely open or moving, as is the habit of the throat-speaking Indians.

The scout straightened; glanced sharply at Ben under his bushy brows, and translated. "She says there is something wrong with you. She wants to know if the Mountain Devils have your heart, or if it is a stone."

Ben struggled with his thoughts. Strange that the scout lost all trace of slipshod speech in times of stress. "Tell her the whole story," he ordered.

"Dangerous," protested Jide. "You

can't tell what a woman will do. She might lead us into ambush if she knew. Right now she is anxious to get back to her people, and just a little scared to boot. She knows they won't be too friendly and she's depending on us."

"Don't see what I can do," shrugged Ben.

"You could give her a kind look," offered the scout. "She isn't just an Indian. She's a young girl, and likely a princess by right. I tell you these Navajos feel deep; and they got more brains than you give them credit for."

Ben turned his eyes on the girl in the firelight. Her shoulders were bowed, her neck a delicate column rising from the V of her buckskin shirt, her oval face outlined by dark hair parted and braided, was interested and alert. Her eyes, reflecting the firelight, were deep with thought, and her slim hands clasped loosely in her lap.

"Better tell her," he commanded. "I'm not taking her help unless she knows."

Jide gave Ben a look of admiration, and slid close to the girl, taking one of her hands in his gnarled fingers. "My daughter," he began in her soft language, "you have asked me what manner of man this is. I will tell you. The moon has shone upon him and blinded him, so that his eyes see only one woman. She is the one whom your people hold prisoner. To this woman his heart is bound. He is helpless. As helpless as if the Mountain Devils had taken the house of his thoughts. I have told him that he should not tell you this, because you might not help us if you knew. I know that you have given your heart to him. I feel a sadness, my daughter, for you are as a lily, and Yellow Hair is a man fit for you. But he speaks with a straight tongue. He wants you to know that he thinks of you as a sister. You understand?"

So expressive was the face of the girl, that Ben could tell almost what the scout said. Now she spoke quickly as if pleading, or extracting a promise. She laid her hand over Jide's heart, and then over her own. Her eyes were steadfast, but her lips trembled.

The old scout recoiled sharply, shaking his head. He protested quickly. The girl gave him a quick sad smile, and then, a

sly humor in her eyes, told a tale that lightened the scout's face. He explained her last words to Ben. "She says that once the men caught an eagle. They tied it to a lodge pole. It struggled until it wore the thong thin and broke it. Two days later it was back, and made trouble by swooping down on the braves and taking their meat. Men and eagles do not know what they want."

"But what did she ask you to do," questioned Ben.

"She has given a promise to help," evaded the scout. "She says you are her sun and moon. Her life is yours, and what you do with it is none of her affair. That's settled. Let's get going!"

The three, busy with their own thoughts, packed horses, and took up the trail. The girl led. The scout brought up the rear, his fine old face troubled, and his lips moving with his thoughts.

G RADUALLY the country changed. The spiny verdure of the desert flat gave way to a mat of upland sage, pungent in the bright sun. As they twisted up canyons, gaining altitude, cypress, and low pines straggled along the ridges. From the tops of such ridges, they could see the blue line of distant pines, that marked the journey's end.

Shadows were long when they came out upon a level tableland, and after a sharp climb, entered the scented shade of the pines. Presently a spark of fire showed. A dog barked. A hobbled pony snorted away from the trail.

The girl halted and called. A chorus of barks and yells came in answer.

The scout put a quick hand on Ben's shoulder. "I'm going to hide out," he stated. "Always better to have a card in the hole. You go in with the girl. I'll be watching."

Scarcely had the scout melted silently away on the pine needle strewn path, when Navajo braves seemed to spring from the ground. They surrounded the girl and Ben, barking quick questions at her. And if scowls were evidence, none too pleased with what she told.

A chill of fear ran coldly up Ben's back. His hands went to his guns; but before he could act he was pulled roughly from his horse and disarmed.

Trusting to the scout and the girl, he made no resistance when his hands were tied behind him, and he was pushed roughly ahead.

The girl made a useless protest. Squaws came running. The girl spoke to them with gestures, and in a pleading voice.

A wrinkled old woman faced the man who was evidently Spotted Pony. Almost spitting her words, she jerked claw-like hands to accompany the vehemence of her speech.

The Indians hesitated; spoke assurance to the squaw, and without further roughness, Ben was led into camp.

Some fifteen lodges stood in a natural clearing. A few horses, a flock of sheep, and a pair of goats, fed in the distance. A peaceful scene.

Ben, his heart beating high with hope, looked from lodge to lodge for a sign of the Mormon girl and her companion. He had only time for a sweeping glance. He was thrust into a lodge, the curtains jerked together, and when he twisted to peer beneath the skin that did not quite reach the ground, he saw the moccasined feet of a guard. He relaxed for a moment, working at the bonds on his wrists. A question darted into his mind. What had the girl made the scout promise, that he did not want Ben to know?

He was to have his answer.

He lay there debating the matter of calling out. Even if the Indians understood any English, the name, Vega Spears, would mean nothing. He crawled close to the opening, and called. He thought he heard an answer just as the guard strode in, and catching up a dirty bit of cloth from a smelling heap, stuffed it into his mouth, and tied it up tightly with a thong.

Waiting until the scowling guard had gone out, Ben tried working the gag loose by rubbing it on the ground. He made no progress. He lay quiet looking under the lodge bottom. His arms ached. He wondered why he had followed the Mormon girl. Something stronger than reason held him to the chase.

He became interested in what went on outside. A fire was built. Men gathered close about it. They spoke low for a time, the earnest, but dour, expression on all the faces, making Ben's heart drop.

SPOTTED PONY made a long oration. He pointed to the lodge in which Ben lay, and to another. The faces in the firelight began to reflect the feelings that he wanted to arouse. He had his audience sitting stiffly forward, intent on his words, and grunting their approval, when a shrill voice from one of the lodges cut into the argument.

Ben strained his eyes to see what this meant. It was the same old woman who had defended the girl and himself when they reached the camp. She shouted short pungent sentences that were not compliments to Spotted Pony, judging by his face, and the sly grins that broke out in the circle.

Spotted Pony, his face black with rage, hurled a stone at her.

She spat an answer that brought a roar from the circle, and high cackles from the watching women, but she went inside.

Two men left the council. They went to a lodge and came back with the Mormon who had led the second train. Thrust into the circle of warriors, he faced them without fear.

Spotted Pony spoke to him in Spanish. "We have decided," he announced, "that you are our brother. We will let you go, if you will take the Navajo girl with you. We will keep the woman who came with you until we are sure that you do not intend to harm us."

"The Mormons have never harmed the Indians," said the prisoner. "Instead, they have given them good horses, sheep that make long wool, and cattle that are easy to fat. I cannot go back to my people unless I take the girl with me. Then your people and my people will be at peace."

Seeing that the words were having some effect on his followers, Spotted Pony stopped him roughly. "I do not speak as a child," he snarled, "but as a man after much thought. These are my words: You may go, but the woman stays."

"Then I stay also," said Gabe Laton, all the stubbornness of a Mormon in his face.

Spotted Pony leaped to his feet mouthing his rage. He bounded high in the air, and with a wild yell, launched his hatchet at the Mormon's head.

Laton, the stubborn expression still on

his face, sagged to the ground, as a dozen braves jumped to hold their chief.

A chorus of wails went up from the watching squaws. The old woman came flying out to look, and turned on the chief with a flood of words.

But nothing could undo the harm done. This murder had brought on a crisis. It would be impossible to let any prisoners go now. They would carry a tale. Resolution was evident in the black looks of the warriors. Spotted Pony had won his argument.

So intent was Ben on the swift scene, that he almost forgot the scout. No doubt he had lain quiet with his cheek close to his sturdy gun, while this happened.

Two braves dragged the fallen Mormon to a little distance, and the council began again.

Staunchly, Spotted Pony faced the black looks of his men, and began to talk again. He gestured to the lodge where Ben lay watching, and to the one where the Navajo girl had been taken by the squaws.

The braves stiffened, protested, and finally, with sullen faces moved to their separate lodges.

Ben heard shrill voices in almost every one of them. The decision of the council did not suit the women. He grinned, although he knew that his fate had probably been decided.

The silence of the night whispered in the pines. An owl hooted mornfully. Hooted again. Ben tensed at the signal, and began to work at his bonds with renewed hope.

But nothing happened. He fell into the tortured dozing that is only half asleep. He was beset by dreams, half-real. The hours wore away. The moon slowly waned as the sun came to send gold arrows slanting down the corridor of the pines.

MORNING found Ben dry-mouthed, and feverish. He would have given a year of life for a cup of the scout's bitter coffee.

Almost at once, it became doubtful if he had any life to give.

The Indians were about early. They gathered around the breakfast fires, wolfing food, and belching loudly. They seemed agreed on a course of action.

Ben had little doubt what that was.

There was no way out. Now that they had killed the Mormon, their only safe move was to get rid of the rest of the prisoners. His only hope lay in the presence of the scout. But he realized that Jide was practically helpless against numbers unless he could surprise them, and in some way cause a change of heart in the braves who had protested at the words of Spotted Pony.

Spotted Pony wanted the Mormon girl. Perhaps he ought to do everything to help her. Prisoners were often well treated. Life offered a chance for a change. Death was final.

His troubled thoughts were cut short by the approach of three men. They came into the lodge, tore the gag from his mouth, and jerking him to his feet, shoved him toward the knot of braves.

Spotted Pony eyed him sourly, and spoke in bad Spanish, "The girl, Isk-ka-da, has told us that you speak with a straight tongue. We do not wish to harm you. Give me your promise that you will take her away, and tell nothing of what happened. We will not harm you, if you will do this. Unless you do, both must die."

Ben, cramped and weak from a day and a night without food, his arms burning with aching torture, looked out into the sunshine. Through the fringe of pines, he could see a great spread of country rugged and beautiful in tints of brown and yellow gold. There was life. There was freedom. He had only to speak a word.

Only a word, and he would lose forever his chance of looking into the eyes of the woman he loved.

He made his decision.

A great raven in a low pine jerked his glistening body in a sarcastic caw, and launched into flight over the valley, as if to lead Ben there.

Quick thoughts burned in his brain. What of the Navajo girl? She had told the Indians nothing of the scout. Did she, too, depend on him? Had she a plan?

But no matter what his brain counseled, he saw the eyes of the Mormon girl. To have her, to see the clear laughter that glimmered always in her eyes, was like camping beside a sparkling brook. He could not leave.

"You have another prisoner," he temporized. "What of her?"

"She is mine," stated Spotted Pony, looking quickly around his circle of braves.

Ben saw little approval in their glances.

"Let me speak with her," said Ben. "I wish to know if she wants to stay. If she does, then I will go gladly."

Spotted Pony gave a grunting denial. "She has nothing to do with this matter," he countered. "I give you a chance to live. Choose now!"

Ben felt himself trembling with a rush of emotion that was really not fear, but a realization that the moment had come. And he could not choose life, not even if the Navajo girl must go through the dark doors with him. He stared straight at Spotted Pony. "I have made a promise that I must keep," he said.

A tiny hope was in his heart. Jide Benette still watched.

It was evident at once that the words angered Spotted Pony, and displeased the rest of the muttering men. The women set up a shrill protest from the lodges.

With harsh words, the chief silenced them. He stalked past Ben, giving his stalwart form an appraised look, and reached out a dirty hand to jerk a lock of yellow hair, as if thinking of a scalp lock. He ordered Ben bound to a tree.

AS Ben was being bound securely two men brought out the Navajo girl. They tied her to a slim pine a few feet distant.

Her black eyes met Ben's with tender sadness. But she honored Spotted Pony with a dart of bitter hate, and spat on the ground at his feet.

The evil-faced chief sneered at them both and with a meaning look hinted, "You may change your mind."

For an instant Ben's knees went weak. Death was one thing, torture another. He had seen men who had escaped after an ordeal with the Indian—shaken, furtive men, with a fear greater than the fear of death in their shifting eyes.

The braves, urged by Spotted Pony, began a slow, circling dance about their victims.

An old man beat out a crazy rhythm that sent the dancers into a frenzy. Shrill whoops split the air. They were working themselves up to the work of killing. Death was in the sunshine like the stink of carrion.

Ben watched them, wishing that he might have one more sight of the Mormon girl.

Spotted Pony came to dance wildly before Ben. Bright knives flashed close to the throats of the prisoners. Hatchets slashed close to their heads.

The Navajo girl stood calm, breathing easily, the lift and fall of her pointed breasts outlined by the crossed ropes, her eyes disdainful.

Spotted Pony, his face twisting in a frenzy, the foam of madness on his lips, was a devil incarnate.

Ben knew stark terror for a moment. He lunged at his bonds, as the chief drew back a sinewy arm with the hatchet held lightly in the fingers; the position for a throw.

Spotted Pony measured the distance to his prisoner's head, tensing for a throw.

His arm swept up.

As it did, a shot blasted from the woods.

The chief leaped high with a yell that died on a rising note.

Ben's heart leaped with him. He gave a great cry of joy. His eyes sought the girl's.

She hung limply against her bindings. A growing spot of red showed above one of the outlined breasts.

A black sickness that robbed him of strength, and turned his bones to water, swept over Ben. Dimly he saw the old scout running toward him, menacing the Indians with his great gun as he ran.

The touch of cold steel on his wrists as the scout slashed his binding brought him back to alertness.

The scout thrust his knife into one of Ben's stiff hands and swung on the Indians. "First one moves, dies," he snarled, crouching at ready. "Drop yore knives and hatchets. I only want the Mormon girl and this man. Let the women bring her out!"

The sullen braves made a move to scatter, thought better of it, and tightened into a group under the blazing eyes of the scout.

Ben, eager to get sight of his girl, and to know if she were safe, ran to the lodge from which he thought he had heard the answer to his first call, and threw the skin flap wide.

The girl came trembling into his arms. She tried to speak, but only her eyes gave her thanks.

Ben put a quick arm about her, leading her to the scout.

The old man was speaking earnestly, not in Navajo, but in Spanish. "My brothers," he said, "I have lived with you. I know your hearts. I blame but one of you for this. That man is now dead. He was not a chief worthy to lead such as you."

Affirmative nods and grunts punctuated the statement.

"Let us smoke the pipe, then," he suggested. "And let this be as something that has never happened."

The reaction of the Indians showed plainly that they wished it to be so.

Jide strode to Ben. "Let's get out," he prompted. "This place stinks."

With these words, he walked defiantly by the braves, and cut the body of the girl from her bonds. He took her tenderly into his arms, and backed away into the shelter of the pines.

Ben and Vega followed, her hand tight in his.

They found the horses on the edge of the mesa that was pungent with sage in the noon sun.

The scout, his dirty buckskin shirt stained with the bright blood of the Navajo, loaded her carefully, and, wordless, led the way back down the trail until they reached a point that gave a wide view of the desert, and would be lighted softly with early morning sun. There he made a shallow grave, and laid the body gently into it.

The Mormon girl picked a cluster of the red Indian Paint Brush, and put it into the bronzed hands of the girl.

They stood looking down on her face, calm and beautiful in death, as if that was what she wished.

There was a deep, sad tenderness in the sharp eyes of Jide Benette when he raised them to say simple words. "She made me promise to kill her if it looked like you'd be killed. I lined her up with that devil Spotted Pony. I think she would have liked to know that the same bullet killed both. Mebby she does. Sometimes death is better. . . ." He began gathering rocks to cover the grave.

With the instinctive knowledge of a woman, the Mormon girl led Ben to a little distance. They stood close with their arms about each other while the old scout finished his task, and stood for a long moment with bowed head.

But he was apparently his wordy self when he joined them. "Dang!" he blustered. "Dang you, Ben. What you aim to do now? Go to Santa Fe and get married, or take a trip to Salt Lake to see if it's all right?"

Ben's eyes questioned the girl.

"Santa Fe," she said, as with her eyes laughing at the old scout she clasped Ben's hand tightly.

Belle Starr— Bandit Queen

M. LINCOLN LEE

A True-Life Story of the Old West's Most Fascinating Outlaw

By CLIFFORD L. SWEET

IT was a winter night and the dance at the Surratt place was in full swing. A big log fire blazed in the yard. Suddenly the door opened. A man and a woman came out, followed by the whine of fiddles and the throb of shuffling feet.

Seated on a log by the fire was a United States marshal, half-dozing in the glow of the log-embers. He was a member of the posse that a few nights before had en- gaged in a running fight with a slippery horse thief, Sam Starr. The thief had escaped.

And now the man and woman who had just left the dance sauntered across the yard, the woman in front. Suddenly, the man spoke.

"Frank West, you killed my horse, damn you!" The tense but repressed tones were those of a man looking for trouble.

The marshal, buttoned up in an over-coat, stirred on the log and looked up. There was no trace of fear in the drawling voice that carried his denial. He did not recognize his challenger; thought perhaps that he was a drunk.

As if the marshal's denial was a pre-arranged signal, the raven-haired woman moved quickly aside, revealing the man back of her with pistol drawn. It was Sam Starr. The report of his gun flat-tened on the frosty air and West slumped forward on the log, a bullet through his jugular vein. In falling, however, he managed to drag his own weapon free of his overcoat pocket and fire four times. Both men pitched to the frosty ground and died with less than the length of a six-gun between them.

Belle Starr was a widow again.

BORN of wealthy and influential par-ents at Carthage, Mo., on February 3, 1846, Myra Belle Shirley reached an im-pressionable age in the midst of the fever-ish days preceding the war. Judge Shir-ley, her father, was a staunch supporter of the Confederacy. It pleased him when Ed-ward, Belle's twin brother, rode away to join the Missouri bushwhackers under Quantrell. It is little wonder that the spirited and romantically inclined girl be-came a fiery partisan of these dashing horsemen.

The times and Belle's natural inclina-tions schooled her well for the role she was later to play. At fifteen she was as much at home on the back of a half-wild horse as she was in Judge Shirley's parlor. And she could handle the heavy pistols of the '60's with the smooth and efficient ease of a veteran gun-toter.

Early in the war she spent her time spy-ing on a Federal troop stationed at New-tonia, Mo., under Major Enos, and riding in the company of such notables as the James boys, Cole Younger and Jim Reed, the latter the son of a wealthy Rich Hill farmer.

When news came that Edward had been killed in action, something changed in Belle's nature. From that time on she hated Yankees bitterly and wholeheartedly. Even after Appomattox she was still a rebel and she continued to ride with the horsemen of her brother's command.

Soon after the war, Judge Shirley moved to Texas and bought land at Scyene, ten miles east of Dallas. He took Belle with him. In 1866 Jim Reed, former com-panion of her brother, and accompanied by several members of Quantrell's old gang, showed up at the Reed home and Jim decided then and there he wanted Belle for his bride. Belle fell just as hard for the ex-bushwhacker, but not so Judge Shirley. To escape the latter's stern and profane objections they eloped, Bill An-derson, a noted guerrilla, acting as best man.

They showed up next in Rich Hill. In 1869 Belle gave birth to a girl baby whom she christened Pearl. Jim Reed, having killed a man who had slain his brother—which the times but not the laws of Mis-souri condoned—cleared out with his wife, baby and a price on his head.

He acquired some land near Dallas and made an honest effort to settle down, but his last killing cost him his last chance of ever becoming a law-abiding citizen. Re-ward hunters kept him on the dodge, and one day in 1875 he rode north, heading for the Indian Territory. He traveled with a man named Morris, in whom he reposed great trust. They stopped at McKinney, the county-seat of Collin County, for lunch. In accordance with Western eti-quette, they left their Winchesters in their saddle scabbards.

During the meal Morris left the room on some pretext or another and returned armed. Reed saw him at the door and as Morris raised his rifle he threw himself backwards, carrying the table over with him and holding it up as a shield. Heavy bullets tore through the pine top. Reed had drawn his pistol, but a man at an ad-jacent table knocked up his pistol at Mor-ris' shout, "It's Jim Reed, the murderer!" Jim aimed again and died before he could squeeze the trigger.

Belle received the news dry-eyed and stoical.

She swore the Judas would never collect the reward for her husband. She rode to McKinney, and masking her grief from curious eyes, gazed down at her murdered husband.

"That's not Jim Reed," she swore. " 'Pears to me you've shot the wrong man. Sorry, Morris, but you'll have to shoot

Jim Reed if you want the reward Jim's worth."

With a disappointed howl, Morris watched her ride away. The widow had denied the identity of her husband. The frontier code of the day canceled any offer of reward in the face of such contingency.

AFTER Jim's death, Belle invaded Dallas with her thorough-bred racers and became a sensation. Her horses were the best in Texas and won race after race. Men coveted her winning stable. Women envied her her smart carriage, and her frocks, which were always the newest and most fashionable.

Belle was not unlike a lot of other women; it pleased her to dress up in men's clothing and pose as a man. One night in a small Texas hotel, two strangers occupied the same bed. One of them, a young man fresh from the East, asked questions —many questions—about Belle Starr. Next morning he waxed confidential to his roommate of the night before; he was in Texas for the express purpose of arresting the bandit queen to collect the reward. He cautiously displayed a tin star of the correspondence school type. After breakfast, the officer, with his new saddle and his .32 pistol in its shiny holster, stood by the door preparing to leave. He reached out his hand to say good-bye and was caught by the collar and given a swift kick where he would never have received it had he been sitting down. His companion of the night tossed his .32 into the brush and said, "You better run home to your mamma, Willie. Tell her you talked too much about Belle Starr. And don't come back here any more—some of my boys might see you and get rough."

Arrested for horse stealing, a grave offense in the seventies, Belle eloped with her jailer. She returned him next day. The man's family found a card sewed into his coat bearing the inscription, "Found to be unsatisfactory after using."

Belle was not pretty, but she was a fine-looking woman, tall and well-made. Five feet seven inches tall, she weighed 145 pounds. She could vault easily from the ground to her horse when the latter was equipped with a man's saddle. She danced well, sang "Jesus, Lover of my Soul," to little children and shot better than most

men. Spectacular, fond of the melodramatic at times, she attracted men of similar traits. There was Jim French, Jack Spaniard and "Blue Duck," all eventually dying to do whatever she commanded them.

Blue Duck borrowed $2,000 from Belle once and left her band in the Territory and went to Ft. Dodge to try his luck in the gambling dens. The squalid little cow town at the end of the Santa Fe railroad was also the end of a notorious cattle trail. Longhorns driven by even wilder men from Texas spewed in off the trail. The town was wide open.

Misfortune frowned upon Blue Duck. He returned to his mistress with empty pockets and a slug in his pistol arm. The bandit queen was ever a staunch believer in her fitness to fill a man's shoes. After listening to Blue Duck's tale of woe, she rode to Ft. Dodge and invaded the gambling den that had fleeced her friend. At the first hand she beat the dealer and the players to the draw. Deviltry backed by iron nerve was what the astonished players saw in the attractive eyes regarding them across the sights of a .44.

Belle raked in the stakes, $7,000 in gold, thanked the players in a voice that froze them to their seats and backed toward the door.

"Come down to the Territory if you want your change," she invited. With all the dignity of a queen, she faded from sight untouched by the fusillade of lead that splintered the door as soon as it closed.

SUCH elemental methods of banditry palled on the outlaw queen's sense of fitness. In 1878 she answered the urge to cash in on her comeliness, and in a short time she was flitting in and out of the best suite in the best hotel in a thriving Texas town made prosperous by cotton and cattle. She soon became a popular and much sought after figure. She trained the battery of her charm, however, on the cashier of the town's best bank.

Results were soon forthcoming. The harsh, cold man of money thawed beneath her smiles like tallow against a candle flame. After the acquaintance had ripened, Belle strolled into the bank one day at lunch time and found the smitten swain alone. Under the spell of her charm, some of the daring of his lost youth awakened to glow in the banker's eyes. Emboldened by the sudden discovery of this unguessed power over a member of the other sex, he bent to steal a kiss and found something round and hard pressing his chin.

"Don't yell, honey," Belle's soft voice purred. "Just dump those bills from the safe into this bag or I'll shoot your damn' head off. Hurry—hurry."

Shaking in his boots, the crushed gallant obeyed.

In 1880 Belle married Sam Starr, a citizen of the Cherokee Nation, and thereby became a citizen herself. Sam was a handsome man with flashing white teeth, coal-black hair and ambitious to steal as many horses as his outlaw spouse.

Shortly after the shooting died down in the Surratt yard the night of the dance, Belle married a full-blooded Cherokee Indian named Bill July. Instead of changing her name to July, Belle changed his name to Jim Starr. Jim in memory of her first husband; Starr for number two. Jim had none of Sam Starr's qualities save a fixed habit of stealing horses. He fell in with a man named Watson, who was wanted in Florida for murder, a secret which Watson guarded well. It was Belle's practice, however, to learn the secrets of those who might help or hinder her and she soon had Watson's secret from his wife.

In a quarrel over the division of loot, Belle threatened to expose Watson's past to the Federal officers. Watson said nothing at the time, but fear made him a dangerous man.

ON her forty-third birthday, which was February 3, 1889, Belle accompanied her husband twenty-nine miles on his way to Ft. Smith to attend court. She turned back at San Bois Creek in the Choctaw Nation. Two miles from Younger Bend, her isolated home, she halted a few minutes at the Barnes home to get some sour dough, for which Mrs. Barnes was noted. She either failed to see, or ignored, Watson, who was loafing in the yard at the time. She rode on at about three o'clock.

It was remembered afterward that soon after her arrival Watson left for his cabin 150 yards away. As she rode on a couple hundred yards beyond the Watson cabin Belle might have caught a glimpse of her enemy where he stood in a fenced field beneath a big tree had she been less engrossed with her thoughts, which were moody that day. So it was that he shot her in the back with a double-barrel shotgun loaded with turkey shot at a distance of twenty feet.

In a rough coffin, without benefit of preacher or prayer, the bandit queen was buried near the door of her old cedar house at Younger Bend. Above her is a headstone badly defaced now by curiosity hunters. At the top is the image of her favorite horse, branded B-S on the shoulder.

In tribute it might be said that Belle Starr lived to justify her belief in her fitness to fill a man's shoes: and died with her boots on to prove it.

The Powderhorn Trap

By TED FOX

The luck of the damned rode with red-handed Tarrant. But even as the Indian-hater dismounted within the safe stockade, the just Fates were feeling for his scalp-lock.

SERGEANT JEFF McLEAN rode slowly through the half dozen tepees pitched on the river-bank. He was standing up straight in the stirrups and his wiry, saddle-hardened body was tense with anger and disgust. His horse snorted suddenly and shied away from the body of an Indian sprawled out in the dry buffalo grass at its feet. Further on in front of the central lodge was another Indian, dead, along the ground, five braves, two squaws and a child.

With an oath Jeff slid his carbine back into the scabbard under his saddle-boot. The barrel was cold and unused. He'd no part in this massacre. All blame lay on Guy Tarrant's shoulders. The young lieutenant had lost his head.

Jeff drew rein and swung stiffly out of his saddle beside the blanketed body of an Indian lying face down on the frozen earth. He squatted on his heels and rolling the Indian over, peered intently at the savage, pain-contorted face upturned to his. This was the half-breed Sioux they'd been ordered by Colonel Bristley to bring in, dead or alive. They'd trailed him forty miles to this little encampment on the Bear Paw River. He'd tried desperately to escape, fired a shot.

That one shot had killed a trooper. Without hesitating Guy Tarrant had given the order to charge. They'd killed the breed with the first volley. They should have stopped then. But they hadn't. Something had snapped in Tarrant's brain and he'd given the order to charge the Indians, the men and the women and the children running out of their tepees.

For a split second the troopers, twenty-four men toughened by war and life on the frontier, had hesitated. But Guy Tarrant had cursed them until they were forced to obey his order. Tarrant had gone crazy with the lust to kill. These Indians belonged to a tribe that had always been friendly to the whites. It wasn't their fault that the breed had stopped at their camp in his flight across the prairie.

JEFF McCLEAN hadn't fired a shot and there were others amongst the troopers whose gun-barrels were cold now like his. Guy Tarrant had led the charge with pistol blazing. He'd snatched a rifle from one of his men, emptied it and then drawn his saber and driven it deep into a redskin's chest. Jeff had seen men that way before. They were bullies usually, cold-hearted, brutal, just as savage as the savages themselves.

Jeff squatted on his heels beside the breed and watched the troopers hunting through the tepees. A cold wind was blowing out of the north and the sky was growing gray and bleak. Jeff could feel the cold creeping into his bones. Tiny icicles clung to his drooping mustache and he wiped them away with the back of his mittened hand. Guy Tarrant cantered up and looked down at the breed.

"That him?"

Jeff nodded. There was a fierce light in Tarrant's eyes that made the young sergeant scowl. Tarrant was, fresh out of military school, young, raw, inexperienced. He was big anyhow, but in a sheepskin coat and sheepskin cap he looked over-sized. Only his mouth and his nose and his burning eyes were exposed to the weather.

"We'll take him back to the Post and show him to old Bristley," Tarrant said and his breath smoked in the wintry air. "Catch up an Indian pony and tie him on."

Tarrant wheeled and rode off shouting orders at his troopers. Jeff stared after him grimly.

"His father is the commander at Fort Webster," Colonel Bristly had told Jeff before they'd left the Post at Laughing Springs. "The general wants his boy to have some experience in the field. He's got a bad reputation and he hates Indians, so I don't know what you can expect. This is his first command."

And it would be his last, Jeff swore under his breath. A court-martial would see to that, though it couldn't repair the damage that had already been done. All along the frontier the Indians would go on the war-path. It was serious business, Jeff knew, but if Bristly had put him in charge it would never have happened.

Jeff rose slowly to his feet and walked to the nearest tepee and peered inside. A fire smoldered in the middle of the earth floor and it was warm in there and he stepped inside and looked around curiously. A piece of venison was cooking on a spit over the fire. Jeff picked up a doll made out of deerskin and stuffed with grass. He held it in his hand for a long second, then put it back carefully where he had found it. For forty years he'd fought the Indians—but never this way. He'd never preyed on women and children before. It wasn't his way of fighting.

Jeff pulled his sheepskin coat up tight

around his neck and pulled his cap lower over his eyes and then stamped from the tepee into the cold February air. It didn't pay to warm up too much this weather. He glanced at the leaden sky overhead and frowned. He mounted his horse and rode after Tarrant.

"Snow," he said, pointing up to the heavens. "Smell it? Looks like we're in for a northeaster."

Tarrant glanced up casually and shrugged. Jeff persisted.

"I think it would be wise, sir, if we started back as soon as possible."

"Nobody asked for your opinion, McClean." Tarrant's voice was harsh, his eyes brittle. "What if it does snow a little?"

"If it snows, sir, it'll be a blizzard, not just a little," Jeff answered quietly. "When it grays up like this it usually means business."

"I'm in charge here, McClean, and we'll leave when I give the order, not a minute before."

Jeff flushed and swore silently under his breath. He turned his horse away and swung his arms across his chest to keep the blood circulating. The wind was rising steadily, moaning down the valley now with an eerie sound. A trooper drew rein beside him.

"POOR devils," he said, looking down at the bodies of the Indians strewn at their feet. "Bad business, Jeff. These Indians trusted us. They weren't even armed."

"Same with those out yonder," Jeff said, pointing to a huddle of tiny specks far out on the flat prairie. "They didn't have any choice but to run."

"I killed one of those Indians there. I wish now I hadn't."

Something white flew past Jeff's face. It was a snowflake. Another clung to his mitten. This was the way it started, slowly and easily.

Ten minutes later Jeff would hardly see his hand before his face. He fired his rifle into the air at regular intervals and one by one the troopers loomed up out of the blinding snowstorm, their horses whinnying nervously as they backed around and put their rumps to the storm.

Over his regulation army uniform each trooper wore a heavy sheepskin coat and on his head a cap with ear muffs and snow visor. Knee-length boots protected feet and legs. Cartridge-belts were strapped about their waists over their coats. Some wore spares slung to their shoulders. They were carrying their rifles, butt against hip, muzzles to the sky and fingers on the triggers, ready for instant use. Tarrant counted twenty-three men.

"Where's the guide that brought us here?" he barked when they were all assembled.

A blanketed figure kneed his horse out of the gloom and said something in Indian.

"What's he talking about?" Tarrant asked.

"He says he's not going back with us," Jeff translated. "These people were our friends and we betrayed them. These people are his friends, too, and he says he's going now to help them."

"The hell he is. Tell that redskin he's guiding us back to the Post or I'll—"

The Indian turned his horse away even while Tarrant was speaking.

"Come back here, damn you, come back!"

A pistol flared and roared and the guide pitched forward onto his pony's neck, fell heavily to the ground. The trooper's horses stamped their feet nervously and tossed their heads into the air with a jingle of bit rings. Jeff stared down at the dead Indian and he suddenly felt sick inside.

"That's the punishment for desertion in this man's army," Tarrant snarled.

"You're wrong, Tarrant," Jeff answered quietly. "Our guides are not enlisted men. They're hired by the job and they can quit whenever they want without being called deserters."

For a moment Jeff thought the young lieutenant was going to shoot him, too, and his hand dropped to the pistol at his belt.

But Tarrant lowered his gun and slid it back into the holster at his waist.

"We don't need a guide," he snapped. "I can find the way back. Close up there, men. Stick together."

For a moment Tarrant looked about him hesitantly. There was nothing to be seen now except snow. It was in the air and covering the ground at their feet with a white blanket. It was in their eyes and noses and mouths. It settled on their shoulders and frosted the ears and manes of their horses. Saddle leather creaked as the men stood in the stirrups and moved about in their saddles to keep from freezing. Ice formed on Jeff's mustache and he left it there because it only froze up as fast as he could wipe it away.

They crossed the river on the ice and mounted the farther bank. Behind him Jeff heard the troopers muttering in low tones. He glanced back and saw the two immediately to the rear. He could hear the others but he couldn't see them in the swirling snow clouds. Snowflakes stung his leathery face and he pulled the flaps of his cap closer about his cheeks with clumsy mittened hands. Snowflakes blew into his eyes, melted, and ran down his cheeks only to freeze again.

TARRANT struck off at right angles to the storm and he hunched his left shoulder against the driving fury of the wind that howled down across the prairie from the hills. It was forty miles to the post at Laughing Springs. They'd been traveling all day yesterday and all last night. Both men and horses were dead with fatigue, cold and hungry.

Yet they dared not stop. The pass through the hills would be blocked if this snow kept up for long. And their food would last for only a day or two longer. They'd traveled light, sacrificing safety for speed. An hour they rode.

Then abruptly a piercing scream rang out above the moaning of the wind. Startled, Jeff flung back on the reins. Wheeling, he raced back down the line of men.

"What's up?" he shouted. "What's wrong?"

Then he saw the body of a trooper lying prone in the trail made by the horses' hoofs. He was lying face down in the snow with an arrow sticking up out of the middle of his back. Jeff knelt beside his body and rolled him over gently as Tarrant sprang to the ground beside them. The trooper was dead.

Tarrant shook his gloved fist at the white wall of snow hemming them in. "Damn murderers," he swore. "All right, McClean, you don't have to look at me that way. I know what you're thinking."

"It's revenge they're after," Jeff said quietly. "They'll camp on our trail like buzzards, pick us off one by one. And they can get close enough to do it in this storm, too."

"We should have wiped them all out and burned their tepees," Tarrant growled. "The best Indian's a dead Indian, McClean. You ought to know that by now."

They slung the dead trooper onto the pony bearing the guide's body and continued on across the prairie. Twice, when the snow lifted momentarily, Jeff glanced back and thought he caught a glimpse of blanketed horsemen following close behind them. A trooper's gun roared and another man cursed as they rode on grimly. The wind was rising steadily and seemed to be blowing from every direction at once. And the snow was piling up. It was above the horses' fetlocks already, growing steadily deeper. Jeff worked his arms back and forth across his chest. The cold was eating right through his sheepskin coat and the regulation army tunic he wore underneath and the heavy woolen underwear beneath that. He clenched his fists inside his mittens to warm his numbing fingers. The cold air hurt his lungs when he breathed.

Then a second scream sounded faintly above the rush of wind. Jeff flung his horse around and yanked his rifle from its scabbard. The whole line was turning, racing back. Angry shouts and curses burst out, then a volley of shots flung at random into the white wall of snow blinding them.

A second trooper lay face down in the snow with a feather-tufted arrow jutting up out of the middle of his back.

"They'll get us all like that," a trooper snarled.

"Shut up," Tarrant shouted. "We'll lay a trap for them. Get back on your horses, men, and see that your rifles are loaded."

They left the dead trooper lying where he had fallen, unloading the dead guide and the other trooper, and turning the pony free. The dead men's bodies were frozen stiff in the shape of Ls and their faces were beginning to grow black.

For another mile they rode, then Tarrant called a halt and split his force, placing a half on either side of the trail. A soldier on Jeff's right cursed and sucked a bleeding finger. He'd touched it to the trigger of his rifle and the skin had peeled off as though it had been pared with a knife.

IN grim silence the men waited, their rifles at the ready. The horses were restless with the cold, but their stamping feet made little sound in the soft snow. Saddle leather creaked and groaned, the sound borne away on the furious rush of the wind. Jeff stroked his animal's neck and the big piebald shook the bridle reins and pawed restlessly at the white earth. It was hungry and cold but rest was what it needed most of all. They'd come a long way in the last thirty-six hours.

Jeff strained his eyes to pierce the white clouds of snow and all at once a lone horseman loomed out of the mist. A gun boomed in the same split second. Then a whole fusillade and a scream and then another scream.

With an angry shout Jeff spurred his horse into the trail. A rider loomed up out of the mist. It was the blanketed figure of an Indian. A bow twanged and an arrow whined past Jeff's head.

Then the sergeant's rifle roared. But his aim was bad. The bullet sped high and slamming the gun back into its scabbard he whipped out his knife. Two jumps and his horse was alongside the Indian's. The redskin raised a tomahawk into the air. His savage face was twisted with rage and hatred. The hatchet slashed down.

But Jeff was a split second too fast for him. The young sergeant lunged in and plunged his knife deep into the redskin's chest. Without a sound the Indian flung up his arms and fell heavily to the ground.

Stepping out of his saddle quickly, Jeff pulled his knife from the Indian's chest. He wiped the blade in the snow, swung back into the saddle as Guy Tarrant raced up.

"They had one Injun riding the trail and the rest on the flanks," he was shouting furiously. "They knew we'd try and ambush them. They got two of our men."

"They're slick," Jeff growled and peered grimly at the dead Indian lying in the snow at his feet. "There couldn't have been more than half a dozen of them at the most."

"How the hell can they see to follow us?" a trooper asked. "The snow's filling up our tracks as fast as we make them."

"They don't have to see," Jeff growled. "They're like wolves, they can smell us. Don't forget, those Injuns 're mad. They won't drop the trail until us or them is dead, or we get back to Laughing Springs."

"We ought to be halfway by now."

Jeff shook his head vigorously. "Ain't quarter way yet, maybe not even that."

"You're crazy," Tarrant snapped. "We've come over ten miles."

"We've come fifteen," Jeff said, "but I don't think we've been makin' it in a straight line."

The troopers exchanged uneasy glances. They all knew what it meant to be lost in a blizzard. Their horses already were beginning to stumble in the deepening snow.

"When I want your opinion, Sergeant, I'll ask for it," Tarrant snarled. "I know where I'm going. Fall in, men, and make it fast if you don't want your horses to freeze under you."

Jeff closed his mouth up tight. Maybe Tarrant was right; only they should have reached the hills by now, reached the pass through the hills before the storm grew any worse and they couldn't get through at all. The snow was a foot in the open, over a man's head where it had drifted, and growing deeper by the minute.

At a slow, plodding walk they pushed forward again. They rode bunched up instead of strung out in a line, and many were the nervous glances cast over their shoulders. At the end of an hour, when they hadn't reached the hills, Jeff fell in beside Tarrant.

"WE'RE not headed in the right direction," he said grimly. "We should have reached the hills long ago."

Tarrant whirled in the saddle and his eyes blazed angrily. But the words never passed his lips. With a savage oath he reined his horse to a halt. Jeff stopped beside him. The troopers pulled up behind them and stared in consternation at the ice-covered river blocking their way. No one spoke for thirty seconds. Then a trooper found his voice.

"That's the same damn' river we crossed three hours ago," he whined. "It must be. There ain't another one within fifty miles of here. We been riding in a circle."

Tarrant wheeled his horse around. His

eyes were hard as flint. "We'll try again," he said harshly. "And we won't miss it this time."

"You'd better let me take the lead," Jeff urged. "I know the country better than most of us. I can sort of feel my way to the pass."

A shrill, blood-curdling yell punctuated Jeff's words. Then came the swish and thud of arrows striking sheepskin coats, the startled cries of the troopers. Jeff wrenched his rifle from its scabbard, fired at a vague shape outlined in the swirling snowflakes.

Then as suddenly and as swiftly as they had come the savages melted away into the storm. The shouts and cries died out. Only the wind and the loud cursings of the troopers were to be heard.

Jeff reloaded his rifle quickly and stared down at the two troopers lying in the snow. Arrows stuck up out of the middle of their backs. They were dead, dead like the other four, dead like they all would be before long.

Tarrant pulled his horse around. "Fall in," he shouted.

He took the lead once again and Jeff swore silently under his breath. Tarrant wouldn't admit he was lost. He'd flounder blindly through the snow in circles until one by one they were picked off by the Indians or died from cold and exhaustion. The snow was halfway up to their horses' bellies now. There was no sign of the storm abating. And it would be dark in another few hours.

With his rifle slung in the crook of his left arm and his mittened finger touching the trigger, Jeff spurred up beside Tarrant.

"You're not headed for the pass," he said quietly. "It's over there further."

"Are you looking for trouble, Mc-Clean?"

"No, sir, I am not. It's just that I've had a little more experience than you have and I think I can find the pass."

Jeff didn't see or hear a thing until that swish and thud and then Tarrant's choked-off cry as he fell forward onto his horse's neck. With a shout to the men behind him, Jeff sprang to the ground and caught Tarrant's body as it toppled from the saddle. He laid the young lieutenant out in the snow and knelt beside him. The troopers were running up and forming a circle about them.

"He's alive," Jeff said. "They got him in the shoulder."

"Too bad they didn't kill him," a grizzled trooper said.

"One hell of a mess he's gotten us into."

"He ain't fit to be an officer," another growled.

"That'll do," Jeff snapped. "No more of that talk, you men."

Tarrant was unconscious. Jeff opened his sheepskin coat and tunic, put a hand inside and felt where the arrow had bitten deep into the soft flesh. Tarrant was bleeding only slightly. For a moment Jeff hesitated. Then he snapped the arrow off close to the heavy sheepskin coat and rose to his feet.

"Take him up in front of you," he said to one of the troopers, "and don't let him fall off. He's bad hurt but he'll live if he doesn't freeze before we reach the Post."

JEFF took the lead then and bore slightly to the left of their former course. Instinct and the way the ground sloped were the only aids he had in judging direction. He'd never seen the air so filled with snow before. He'd never felt the air so cold before. It was hard going for the horses now. They were stumbling often now.

An hour passed. The Indians didn't bother them again and Jeff wondered if their thirst for revenge hadn't been satisfied. Perhaps they'd gone home to their lodges. Tarrant didn't regain consciousness. He was mumbling deliriously and the trooper riding double behind had difficulty holding him in the saddle.

Then abruptly the ground began to rise sharply. They'd reached the hills. A sheer wall rose on their left and when the snow underfoot suddenly grew deeper, Jeff knew they were in the pass. The snow was belly-deep where it had drifted and suddenly his horse whinnied and came to a stop.

Jeff spurred him on. It was killing work for the lead horse and they took turns breaking trail. It was slow going, too, but Jeff kept them moving as fast as they were physically able. The light was beginning to fail. Night was almost on them.

Then the savage cry of the Indians rang through the pass, followed by the dreaded swish and thud of arrows. Jeff fired at a gray shape in the mist, saw it whirl around and drop. With an angry shout he spurred forward. But he couldn't see any more of the savages. They were there—somewhere—invisible.

"Keep moving," Jeff shouted to the line of troopers behind him. "We're almost through and it'll be dark in a minute now."

Darkness fell swiftly and the savage yells died away. Once more the air was still but for the moaning of the wind and the grunts of men and beasts as they toiled slowly through the snowdrifts. Behind them, already covered with a shroud of white, lay the body of another trooper.

Then all at once they reached the summit of the pass and the trail sloped down to the open prairie. The snow wasn't as deep on the lee side of the hills nor the wind so cold. They made better time and the spirits of the troopers revived. Even the horses put up their ears and stepped out more eagerly. They were halfway to Laughing Springs now and the storm was letting up.

Then the Indians swooped down and left a dead trooper lying in the trail. Three more were wounded. The troopers struck back in blind fury, but the savages were elusive shadows.

Then Jeff called a halt and in a thicket of young cottonwoods the troopers dismounted stiffly and sank to the ground.

"No sense keeping on until we're all picked off," Jeff told them. "We're safe now that we're through the pass. We'll wait until daylight and hope the storm blows over so we can see those devils."

THE night passed slowly and without any sign of the Indians. Nor were they in sight the next morning when daylight came. It was still snowing, but only lightly now; and after eating the last of their smoked venison and journey-cakes the troopers mounted their horses and rode away from the hills in the direction of Laughing Springs. The snow was only a foot or so deep out on the prairie and they made better time than they had the night before.

It was twenty miles to the post at Laughing Springs and they reached it shortly after noon, riding into the stockade under the astonished eyes of the garrison. Tarrant was carried away on a stretcher and after tending to their horses the men disappeared into their quarters. Jeff thawed out a little over a fire, then went to report to Colonel Bristley.

"Tarrant's out of his head," the colonel said. "He's been talking like a crazy man about Indians and—" Bristley paused—"What have you to report, Sergeant?"

"We trailed and caught up with the breed at an Indian camp on the Bear Paw, sir," Jeff answered stiffly. "He resisted and we opened fire. In the fight several Indians, including the breed, were killed. It snowed on the way back, sir, and the Indians troubled us a bit. We lost eight men."

Bristley's eyebrows shot up. "Is that all that happened?"

"Yes, sir. Lieutenant Tarrant may have more to add to it, but that is all for me to report. It was one of the worst blizzards I've ever seen in this country. We were lucky to get back at all."

"Mr. Tarrant said quite a lot in his delirium, Sergeant, and I have a pretty clear picture of what happened. I also overheard two of your troopers talking on my way back here."

Bristley rose and went to the window and looked out across the Post. "You've been soldiering under me for five years, Jeff," he said, "and I know you pretty well. But don't forget one thing—Tarrant's father is General Tarrant, commander of Fort Webster as well as this entire district. Any accusations made against his son wouldn't get very far, I'm afraid."

"Yes, sir, I know."

Bristley nodded. He strode to his desk and picked up a letter. "We won't have Tarrant with us much longer," he said. "This came through yesterday. He's being transferred, Jeff. By his father's order. He's going with one of our ablest soldiers, who will train him well and also see that no harm comes to him."

Jeff shrugged. A court-martial was what Tarrant deserved. "I suppose his father wants to give him a safe job," he growled, "especially after his just being wounded."

"He'll be safe enough," Bristley said. "No Indian will ever get him . . . now that he's going to be with General Custer."

HAWK OF THE PLAINS

A Novelet of Calico and Buckskin

By

BILL COOK

The blue-eyed mountain man was wedded to that fierce carnival of beaver-plewing and Indian fighting, and the blood-flowing rendezvous at Bent's Fort and Santa Fe. Yet the desperate gaze of the emigrant-train girl gripped and drew wild-hearted Gil Carney.

ELEVEN bronzed weatherbeaten men rode down out of the Rockies above the headwaters of the Snake in the early spring of the year 1844. They were headed for Santa Fe with a stop at Bent's Fort on the Arkansas. With the men rode three moon-faced silent Indian squaws muffled in blankets, their sloe-black eyes watchfully searching the precipitous trail. For with the coming of spring the red warriors of the valley and plains tribes would be emerging, too, from their winter hibernation.

Among the eleven men were leather-skinned pioneers from Missouri, from New England, the South and even from Canada. With bristling beards and their uncut hair rubbing their shoulders these mountain men of the trapper clan sat their creaking saddles, their eyes turned southward and eastward. The snow-capped heights down which they pushed their heavily laden pack train watched in grim stark silence, the melting blue-white blanket sparkling like diamond drifts, the warm breezes whispering through the bare branches of the trees softly. The air was clear and the sun was bright, and the vast solitude spread out before the riders like a dawn on some new unpeopled world.

At the head of the train rode Old Jim Lewis, a grizzled giant of a man who dwarfed the mule he rode. Hair covered his face almost to his eyes, and these, black and snapping, peered ahead alertly from between the beard and an enormous engulfing wolfskin hat, fur out and bushy tail dangling behind. A huge thick gray blanket was wrapped about his body. From the rear he might have been an Indian.

Behind him, astride a chunky rust-black horse, rode Gar LaFlamme, mostly called Frenchy by those who knew the half-breed in the frontier towns and trading posts to the south. LaFlamme's blue-black eyes glittered sharply in the sunlight. The scraggly beard did not hide the rippling muscles of his wide square jaw, clamped like a bear trap on a worn pipe stem. Like most of the men who strung out behind him, LaFlamme hunched in a warm buffalo robe.

A S the trail they followed dipped lower and lower the air grew warmer. One by one the riders let their robes slip from their shoulders, exposing their fringed deerskin blouses or heavy woolen home-spun coats. In the crooks of their elbows could now be seen the long brass-bound rifles. Across their shoulders were fixed straps of buffalo hide and about their narrow middles were belts of the same

material. From these hung powder horn, bullet pouch and mold, long and sheathed knives or gleaming hatchets, according to the preference of the hunter.

The horses and mules plodded warily downward, sure-footed, nostrils flared to the scent of the new green in the valleys and plains below them. All winter they had gnawed the bark of the cottonwoods and aspens; grass beckoned them now, the breezes brought the freshness up from the lower lands. Like their riders the animals were long haired and shaggy, and the only sound of the pack train was the brittle clatter of the animals unshod hoofs. For a half dozen miles no man had spoken except to his horse or the pack-laden beast nearest him. Each was busy with his own thoughts. And their thoughts, mostly, were concerned with two men of this very mountain band. One man was Frenchy LaFlamme. The other was young Gil Carney.

Carney was the last man. He rode the rear guard, alert to every whispering breeze, each tumbling pebble. Mounted on a hammer-headed red horse whose winter coat gave him the look of a fat-bellied, blaze-faced goat, Carney sat his saddle like a Comanche brave, his fair skin hardened by the winds and suns of many wilderness years. On his upper lip clung a sparse sandy mustache and his lean square jaw was golden in the glint of the sun. A short, stubby nose gave his face the appearance of being broader than it really was, but the outstanding feature of his face were the steel-blue eyes that caused most strangers to give him a quick, second glance.

Carney's yellowish, sandy hair hung low on his neck, too, and he wore a shiny black bearskin hat cocked over his right eyebrow, its thick fur matching the worn black velvet collar that adorned his soft tanned buckskin jacket.

Far ahead of him as they wound their way down the long mountain trail, Carney caught sight of Frenchy LaFlamme's familiar back. The voyageur's thick neck was as stiff as a ramrod and Carney grinned as he recalled the breaking of camp back on Crooked Creek. He and Frenchy had finally tangled. Carefully avoiding the breed all winter the clash had come with the packing of the train.

"He's a genuine bad feller, Gil," Bill Wallace had warned Carney after the two had been separated by their companions that morning. "Yuh mind what I tell yer an' don't let him git behinst yuh."

Gil Carney had laughed away the whole thing just as he chuckled to himself now. Certainly he was not going to let a tricky lobo like Frenchy sneak up on him, but no animal that walked on two, or even four, legs could frighten old man Carney's kid. Matter of fact, and the whole party knew it well, Carney would have settled right then and there with LaFlamme, knives, pistols or tomahawk, if the others had not forced a tentative peace on the pair.

"He'll bear watchin'," admitted Carney thoughtfully as the train snaked its way down the trail.

BECAUSE he was conceded to be one of the best packers in the mountains, Frenchy LaFlamme had won no little reputation among the trappers and hunters. Frenchy could throw ties and hitches in the pitch black of a midnight storm. He could also throw vile words and a knife with a razor-keen edge. His temper was as hot and swift as a prairie fire and men who knew the breed all agreed that when Frenchy was not chanting in his own quaint half-musical fashion, whether afoot or astride, it was wise to keep an eye on him. When Frenchy did not sing he was troubled or angry.

Their route lay through territory that, with the opening of spring, would be the hunting grounds of such warlike tribes as the Crows, Cheyennes, Teton-Dakotas, then the Arapahos and finally the Cheyenne plains Indians. Every man of the party would be on the alert to danger day and night. And Gil Carney, when they made their first night camp on Big Stone Creek, shrugged off the idea that La-Flamme's brooding portended harm to himself.

"He's all right, Jim," said Carney to his older partner, Jim Lewis, that night as they hunched around the blazing fire. "Like a lobo wolf. Only kills with his pack. He'll wait till we get to the Fort or down Santa Fe. But I'll be waitin' for him."

Old Jim Lewis stroked his beard, staring off into the deep dark of the wilderness night. He had not wanted to take Frenchy in the first place. The hombre was a hairtrigger, touchy breed; but he was a good man on the line and the best packer between Fort Leavenworth and Hangtown.

As they rolled in their blankets, Lewis nodded grimly, knocking out his pipe and smothering the hot sparks. "I never did like the way he treats that squaw o' his'n, Gil. He's ornery mean as a carcajou. Better you keep yore eye skinned till we get shet o' him at Bent's."

Frenchy LaFlamme, however, fooled them all. As the fur-laden pack train pushed south day after day he appeared to be carefully avoiding the young sandy mustached Carney. In fact, he held little conversation with anyone except Jim Lewis and a trapper known as Nongat Pete. There was tension, however, among the party; most of whom began to wish by the time they had crossed the Sweetwater and come within a day's journey of the newly rutted overland trail running through to California and Oregon that Carney and LaFlamme would grab the ends of a bandanna and begin cuttin' for "best man."

Two days south of the ruts, Wallace's shout of "Injuns!" snapped every man to action. The petty family troubles were forgotten in a flash. Old Jim Lewis cried out angrily to push the pack animals toward a clump of trees a quarter mile away. But in that instant the air was filled with the shrill war whoops of redskins that seemed to pop up all about them from holes in the ground. Arrows and bullets whipped and tore the air about the trappers.

Gil Carney yelled to throw the pack animals and fired at a painted buck, then flung himself from his saddle. There was a rush of men whirling the stampeding brutes into a circle. The three squaws with the white men dashed into the safety of the crude breastworks.

"Save yore lead!" barked old Jim Lewis, realizing the trap into which they had walked. He swore savagely as he saw a couple of the pack animals shot down. A hunter's mount fell with an arrow through its gullet. The redskins seemed to be everywhere.

"Every man down!"

In a cloud of dust, sod clods and gun

smoke the trappers flattened out behind their squealing animals. The packs would serve as bulwarks against arrows, even the Injun bullets. The long rifles thundered and were passed back to the squaws for reloading while the men aimed their heavy cap-and-ball revolvers. Carney squatted with Lewis and Bill Wallace facing south, and close by was Frenchy LaFlamme, his teeth bared and snarling each time he fired.

"Hold 'em off till dark," Gil Carney called over his shoulder to his companions, then to Lewis: "Can you make out who they are?"

"Sioux," growled Old Jim, "an' they tricked us like a pack o' tenderfoots, damn 'em. Half o' our pack ponies are finished."

THEIR situation was quickly evident to all of the men. Fortunately none had suffered worse than minor scratches, thanks to the bulky packs and their taking cover. But they were practically helpless to save a small fortune in furs. Even if they could escape themselves, it would mean abandoning the valuable pelts. A whole winter's catch!

The redskins charged again and again. Each time they dragged a dead or wounded warrior out of range, and as the battle raged the smoke thickened to a choking fog that hung like a leaden gray cloud over the ground. The swiftly setting sun changed the smoke hue to a dense mauve, and the darkening sky gave the scene a ghastly unreal glow that was only alive with the crack and rattle of the rifles and the thunder rush of the charging Indian ponies.

Carney noticed the sudden lull and rose cautiously to probe the strange new silence. "They're drawin' off," he declared, searching the shadowy fringe of tree-studded low hill. "Mebbe they got enough, an' mebbe they're holdin' council. Now listen, everybody! Here's a plan."

He kept his eyes on the ground around them as he told the others of his idea. His companions, smoke-grimed and thirsty, nodded in agreement. Here was the young trapper's plan: With their pack animals either crippled or dead they must leave their furs; must dig a pit after dark —if they could hang on that long—and bury the furs. Then, if the wind was right they could drag some dead animals over the spot, touch off the old last year's grass and make tracks.

"Damn good idee, Gil," said Old Jim. "Worth tryin'."

"Gar damn!" ejaculated Frenchy with a glance around in the gloom at all but Carney. "Is one bon treek. LaFlamme say yes."

Both Lewis and Carney were to recall Frenchy's enthusiastic approval of the plan at another time, but that night under cover of the dark as they worked cautiously to cache their hard-won wealth, none gave Frenchy more than a glance. The common enemy had drawn them all together again; the feud between the breed and the sandy-haired Gil was forgotten.

A check-up showed horses and mules had suffered all the casualties. There were barely enough able to travel to mount the party, but it was agreed that if they got far enough on their way without a renewed attack or chase by the Sioux, they would turn the three squaws off eastward near the south fork of the Platte; sending them to their native Arapaho village. From there the white men could take turns riding and walking—or running.

Carney strewed a trail of black powder carefully as the others drove their worn mounts away in the dark. A mile or more away on the hill he could see the campfire of the angry Sioux. If the wind did not change the grass would burn straight toward their camp. Listening a moment for a sound of his own party creeping slowly away from him, he struck a sulphur match to the powder.

Then he leaped to his feet and ran swiftly, his lithe buckskin-clad legs carrying him like a young bull elk over the ground, his moccasins making no sound. Behind him he could already hear the crackling of the dead grass and he grinned. This was the sort of stuff he liked: matching wits with the wily redskins. It was times like this that added zest to life in the open, the life that he loved.

"It's a ten to one gamble," he chuckled, running easily. "Mebbe they'll see the trick an' mebbe they won't." The cool night wind felt good on his sweat-streaked, powder-blackened face as he ran. Soon he saw the vague shapes of his friends, they were riding slowly with heads cocked over shoulders.

"That you, Gil?" called Old Jim cautiously.

"Sure 'nough," replied Carney, breaking through the dark and leaping to his saddle. The party was already moving off swiftly now, pushing the horses fast over the uneven land, determined to cover ground before the moon rose.

Carney shot a glance behind them, laughing. He saw the rising trail of flame and its light in the billows of smoke. And far westward he could make out the sudden commotion about the Sioux fire.

"If we lose them furs," he called to Wallace, riding close, "we'll be eatin' grass ourselves, Bill."

"I ain't got the teeth fer it," chuckled Wallace.

II

DAYLIGHT broke on a ragged, worn little band, but there was no sign of pursuit by the Sioux. With what they had salvaged from the battle they made breakfast of dried buffalo and bull elk and at once pushed on toward the fork of the Platte. Here, finally, they bade the Arapaho squaws *adios* and headed them for their home village.

Carney, riding beside Old Jim, raised the question of their route to Bent's. Their horses were none too strong.

"Follow the old Cherokee Trail down?" he mused, " 'r should we stay in closer under the shoulder of the hills?"

"I'm fer huggin' them hills," said Old Jim, " 'count o' the streams. Spring 'n all, we'll meet bank-full fords, Gil."

They struck westward gradually as they rode, in order to cross the streams while they were small and less hazardous in the foothills of the Rockies. The new green grass was springing up as they traveled south, and they saw many signs of spring in the fluttering of prairie hens, the yipping of prairie dogs and occasional small bands of deer darting like shadows through the brush. Once, past midday, as they crept cautiously through Boulder Canyon, they came upon the fire of two men who snatched up rifles on their approach. One proved to be a white hunter, his companion a tall, bronze Delaware buck.

From these men Carney and his party learned that there were already rumors of trouble on the plains; that the Indians of a dozen tribes had sent word to the army officers at Fort Kearney and Fort Leavenworth warning the white men to stop sending settlers across the red man's buffalo range.

"There'll be a heap o' scalpin', gents," said their informant, an old fellow who said his name was Williams. "I been huntin' an' trappin' an' wallowin' 'round this kentry nigh onto fifteen year. Too many damn' furriners movin' out here. Don't blame the Injuns." He glanced sidewise at his partner, the big Delaware, who puffed a pipe made from an antelope's horn and nodded.

"Injun no savvy," he growled with a bit of a twinkle in his red-tinged eye. "White man no savvy. Nobody no savvy!"

"They're out a'ready," warned Williams as the visitors made ready to depart. "We seen two parties 'atween here an' the Seven Trees."

"We seen a few ourselves," laughed Gil Carney, relating in quick sentences their fight with the Sioux. "Where you travelin'?"

"Crossin' the range fer Salt Lake," advised Williams. "Me an' Charlie Two Wolves here have got a hankerin' to git away from trouble."

"Well, so long, then," waved Carney and his friends. "If trouble gets in our track we'll tangle with it if we have to."

Leaving the pair at the fire the trappers rode on. Neither Carney nor his staunchest friends observed the glance that Frenchy shot toward Nongat Pete, nor did they catch a word of the hurried whispers passing between the two. Following the clash with the Indians, Frenchy had fallen back into his sullen silence, his only talk being monosyllables, at camp halts. Now he rode knee to knee with Pete, the half Mexican, half Navajo.

Talk of Indian menace was an annual subject and the trappers as a band gave it no more thought than called for their usual vigilance. Injuns were Injuns. The mountain men as a class had had but little trouble with the redman. Why, didn't Frenchy and Pete and the rangy Fred Mosby marry into the Arapahos? Weren't their squaws even now homeward bound for their usual summer visit with their people?

CARNEY and Lewis, leading the strung-out trappers, noted the familiar landmarks as they began swinging eastward. Another hundred and fifty miles and they would reach Bent's Fort.

"We can pick up a dozen or so fellers," said Old Jim, "an' buy us some fresh hosses an' mebbe some pack mules."

"And go back for them furs, eh?" added Carney readily. The thought of those rich furs and the hard work that went into their getting put all else behind.

"Yeah," nodded Old Jim, "less'n this dust cloud turns out to be a passel o' scalp snappers."

Gil Carney glanced toward his right quickly where his companion pointed. All the others turned in their saddles and looked, too. Looked like a large party of horsemen—and it was Indians.

"Break for that draw!" barked Carney at once, sending his horse forward at a fast gallop.

Old Jim hesitated, then cut after the younger man and there was a rush for the draw. Once there they would have shelter for the horses, good cover among the rocks and trees.

Swinging down from his horse, Old Jim shouted, "They want t' parley, Gil. A bunch o' Cheyennes. The leader give us the sign."

"Everybody down," called Carney, who because of his instinctive keenness in his dealings with the red men, had been acknowledged as captain. "Every man with rifle cocked. I'll see what they're after."

Cautiously Carney rose up from behind his rock, watching the Indians coming slowly but steadily forward. He held his rifle in the crook of his arm and had loosened his old cap-and-ball pistol in his belt. He held up his right hand, palm to the fore, and called out loudly: "How, my Cheyenne brothers!" He lowered his hand and drew it meaningly across his lower left arm, making the Indian sign of the "Cut Arms" to show them that he knew them for Cheyennes.

Like most men who have spent years on the plains and in the mountains, Gil Carney knew the tribes by their dress. He was surprised, therefore, to see these savages advancing slowly now toward him with right hands upraised, rifles ready, but still no word, no reply to his greeting. For an instant there was a volley of whispers from Carney's companions. Something was wrong. These fellows meant to ride right up on their stronghold.

"Hold!" shouted Carney, stepping forward daringly. "What brings you, brothers of the coyote? Why do you not make talk?"

Then the big bare-chested, three-feathered chieftain lifted a spear and the band halted. In a voice like jagged lightning he cried out: "White brother is blind. Injun Pawnee." He raised his two hands and placed them one at either side of his head above his ears, like the ears of a wolf. It was the red man's Pawnee talk.

Carney knew it for a lie and he frowned, letting his rifle slip down into his hand. He heard Old Jim call up to him. "He's a lousy liar, Gil. Lookit his leggin's. They're up to somethin'."

"Cheyenne lies," said Carney coolly to the chief.

Angered by the sharp eyes and cool courage of the white man, the Indian let out a whoop, shouted a shrill signal and booted his pony straight for Carney. With him came the yelling, blood-thirsty riders. Gil Carney stood his ground a moment, leveled his long weapon carefully and drove a ball through the leader's breastbone. Without waiting to see the redskin topple from his mount, Carney leaped backward to the rocky bulwarks, amid a thunderous volley of rifle fire and the whir and shriek of arrows. *"Yeowwwww!"* The war cry rose like a calliope from the throats of the trappers as they saw the slaughter of their first fire.

There was a fierce yelling among the savages and the swift turning of ponies, their drumming hoofs shaking the earth. The deadly shooting of the white men threw the baffled Indians into a panic. A half dozen of their braves were either dead or wounded badly; riderless ponies ran right and left, snorting, shocked by every volley.

Wallace crept close to Carney's rock. His beaver slouch hat was minus the brim at one side and blood trickled down from his scalp. "Want me to try to make it to Bent's Fort, Gil?" he asked calmly. "These redskins mean business."

Carney shook his head and grinned, patting his friend on the shoulder. "They'd chop yuh in forty hunks, Bill," he said grimly. "No. We'll fight it out together. It's a big hundred and fifty miles."

BILL crept back to his position, the smoke stinging his eyes and the dust from the racing ponies choking all of them. But no man whimpered or complained. For nine hours they held the savages off. Occasionally a trapper would dash from his cover, knife in one hand, gun in the other, to snatch the scalp from a fallen Cheyenne before his friends could race in and drag him away. Slowly the white men cut and lead-whittled the attackers, shooting with fine accuracy, their weapons hot in their hard fists.

As the redskins drew off again, Old Jim Lewis began creeping about their position, calling to the scattered trappers, checking each man. Of the eleven it was quickly learned that Mosby and Joe Reynolds were dead. Old Jim searched around for Frenchy LaFlamme and Nongat Pete. They did not answer to his call.

"What the hell!" cried Gil Carney as the word was passed along.

"Mebbe they wuz taken prisoners," guessed Wallace.

Two dead and two missing! The seven looked at each other, a bloody, wearied band. Finally Carney stood up and searched around the edge of their natural fortress. The Cheyennes, like beaten curs, were dragging themselves off to the west, carrying their dead and wounded. Carney was thoughtful. The last time he had seen Frenchy, the breed was behind that clump of rocks.

"He ain't there," cut in Old Jim. "I looked. Neither is Pete."

"Keep an eye on those Injuns," ordered Carney, wiping sweat from his eyes as he walked away in the dusk toward the pocket where they had hobbled their mounts.

When he returned his jaw was set and his fists clenched. Fire glowed in his hardened blue eyes as he halted before what was left of his party. His voice was filled with repressed emotion as he spoke: "Frenchy an' Pete loped," he said icily. "Four hosses gone, three more were hit an' they're down in their hobbles, stiff."

"The fur cache!" snarled Old Jim without a doubt in the world. "The dirty, sneakin' snakes!"

The others stared at him a moment wonderingly.

"Else why the four hosses?" demanded Old Jim. "They're goin' fer the choice stuff shore as I got hair on my chest." He started running recklessly for the remaining horses, the others chasing after him.

In the grove near the frightened animals Carney managed to calm the others and called a council. He showed the men where the trail of the four running horses had knifed through the slash in a northeasterly direction, and quickly closed up, running swiftly. There, too, were the unmistakable footprints of Frenchy and Pete, leading the animals before they mounted.

How much start the pair had, they could only guess. They might have sneaked away during the shooting a couple of hours ago, unseen by the redskins. If they had ridden south, they would have had to come out into the open, but northward they were masked by the trees and the ridge.

With the quick decision of their kind they faced their situation. No time or words were wasted. Carney selected Wallace to accompany him in the chase. They took two of the best of the jaded horses, some of the dried bull meat and rode off rapidly into the lowering night amid a low chorus of bitter oaths.

Behind them five men faced the burial of their two dead friends and the problem of keeping their scalps until they could reach Bent's Fort on the Arkansas.

FRENCHY LAFLAMME was a superstitious man. All day, thus far, Nongat Pete had noticed, Frenchy had uttered no gloating taunts along their back trail. Nongat watched Frenchy with crafty eye. Every day since they had dug the choicest bales of fur from the cache Frenchy had chuckled and laughed along the way, heaping curses on the head of the yellow-headed Carney and all the rest. They were fools; dumb tenderfoot hunters. But today it was different. The reason struck Pete with a suddenness that dropped his mouth open like the end gate of a settler's wagon.

It was the thirteenth day.

"Today," Frenchy had declared over their meager breakfast, "we keep on move, Pete."

Pete pondered this as they plodded

along afoot, urging the four laden horses with their quirts. It took a long time for the reason to germinate. Pete forgot it a dozen times during the day. Then, suddenly, he swung about toward Frenchy. "Thirteen days, huh, Frenchy?" he said. "We been runnin' thirteen days."

"Six days it is," snarled Frenchy, his eyes blazing, "six days since we take our furs f'om de cache."

But Pete knew they had been seven days reaching the cache. Today was ominous. He saw Frenchy turning his head frequently looking back over their trail. And he saw the quick look of concern in the black eyes that changed to one of downright fright. Pete shaded his eyes and looked. Far, far back on the horizon, creeping like infinitesimal specks over the last ridge, were two mere dots.

With a curse on his parched lips Frenchy lashed at the animals to make them hurry. He began running again himself now and Pete fell in behind him. Not far ahead they could make out the narrow walled entrance to a purpled, shadowy canyon.

"Queek!" yelled Frenchy. "Once we get in de canyon we be safe."

"Mebbe they'll turn off," hoped Pete, panting alongside the wearily trotting horses. "Mebbe they ain't after us."

"Mebbe they are," retorted LaFlamme hotly. "We find out soon."

With eyes accustomed to vast distances, the two renegade trappers turned in the mouth of the canyon and recognized the growing dots.

"*Sacre!*" hissed LaFlamme through his clamped teeth. "This is a bad luck day, I tol' you. It is that son Carney and he has with him Wallace."

Swallowed up in the cavernous walls, the two disappeared with their plunder laden horses. But Carney and Wallace were too close to shake off, and Gil knew they were the fleeing fur thieves. He let out a tired yell. The strain of the chase was over. Their quarry was in sight.

"Spread out, Bill," he said with a motion of his rifle hand. "You come up to the mouth from that side and I'll approach this side. Keep 'em busy watchin' two ways in case they're fixin' to ambush us."

Wallace swore hearty agreement and swung his horse away from Carney's. Gil scanned the rocky, boulder-strewn defile

as they arrived by the canyon entrance. No one was in sight. At a sign from Carney the pair dismounted, began stalking cautiously into the high-walled narrow trail, leading their horses with reins looped over crooked elbows, rifles at ready in their grips.

At first the place was as still as a great cathedral, then came the brittle sounds of the horses ahead as their hoofs struck the rocks. The canyon twisted and turned.

"Steady now, Bill," warned Carney, grim faced, an eager light in his blue eyes. "May be a blind canyon."

Wallace nodded, grinned. "Yeah. We'll catch 'em like rats in a trap."

The words barely left his lips as the two rounded a bulging jut in the wall. The defile rocked with the thunder of two rifles. Carney felt the shriek of the slug and flung himself down and forward. With half an eye he caught a picture of Nongat Pete's head and shoulders, a smoking rifle. And he heard Bill Wallace grunt something that sounded like "Huh?" He squirmed around from behind his rock, saw Wallace face down, his body twisted strangely.

"B ILL!" Carney called softly. "Bill—?" but Wallace's body remained motionless. Somehow Carney was calm. He'd looked at death often during his years of wilderness wandering. But this was different. He felt more like a little boy again, back East, a little boy who had lost his father, even as he had. Bill Wallace gone—in a breath. No tears welled in Carney's eyes, but he swallowed bitterly and his strong fingers clamped like an eagle's talons on his long rifle.

Crouched back of a boulder, he heard the soft slip of a moccasin on a rock face. Suddenly a hurried scramble. Peering around, he saw Nongat Pete creeping toward him, and beyond, Pete, scaling the canyon wall, was Frenchy. Carney lifted his rifle, pushed its muzzle past the stone. Pete came again into view, his ferret eyes glittering evilly.

"A life for a life," whispered Carney, as he pulled the trigger.

Nongat flung his arms up and his rifle dropped. He hung for an instant like a man balancing himself on a precipice edge, mouth open but soundless. Then he pitched over and slid down along a slanting ledge. Drilled plumb center. A screeching rifle ball tore down from the wall, but Carney was covered, pouring powder and slug into his own weapon. When he rammed down the patch, he eased out warily, caught a fleet glimpse of Frenchy high on the wall, body half hiddent in a crevice. As he raised the gun, Frenchy shouted a taunting curse and faded from view.

Corney looked long at the canyon wall, and his bronzed face wore a worried frown. With Frenchy above him, he dared not emerge from his rocky fort. But there beside him was poor Bill that needed burying, and there were the four jaded pack horses with their fur cargo.

While the sun sank lower and lower and the canyon depths grew somber in darkening purple shadows, Gil Carney squatted warily behind his rocks, rifle cocked, listening, watching the wall above him. He knew Frenchy, knew the animal patience of the breed.

"Unless I pinked him," Carney mused thoughtfully, "he's lurkin' up there some place with an eye on my first move. I've gotta draw his fire some way."

The only sound, other than the occasional move of the tired ponies, was the incessant buzzing of the sand flies and fleas. The sound made Carney drowsy and every muscle in his lithe body cried out with utter fatigue. Perhaps that was what Frenchy was waiting for; for Gil to doze off. The danger of this caused him to decided quickly. "He's gotta shoot down," Carney figured. "He'll overshoot, like as not. And if he misses I've got the bulge on him. I'll take my chance."

He braced his feet firmly, peered out carefully. Then he sprang straight across an intervening space for the shelter of rock like a giant arrow head. Once there he drew a deep breath. Frenchy had not fired, nor had he made a sound to indicate his exact position. But from his new fortress, Carney could examine the wall above at another angle. There were splashes of orange light from the setting sun up there, wedged between the rock faces. And one of these outlined a sharp, clean shadow of Frenchy's head and shoulders. Carney raised his long rifle. If he could bounce a slug off the face of the rock he might,

with some luck, score a hit; at least drive the fur thief out of his ambush.

The boom of the weapon shook the shadows, and through the thundering echoes there was lifted a shrill shout of pain and rage. Carney crouched back, quickly reloaded, listening, watching for the breed to appear. He stood up, exposing himself, alert, ready to snap a shot upward. Shook his head slowly, his blue eyes sweeping the wall.

But no Frenchy appeared. Gil Carney kept his eyes on the wall and began backing cautiously away, groping for the laden horses, dragging them with him down the canyon floor out of range. Then, deliberately, he returned to recover the body of his friend, Bill Wallace. In a hastily dug grave he buried the old mountain man, covering the spot with slabs of loose rock. With another stone he scratched a rough epitaph:

W. WALLACE
MAY 1844
A MOUNTAIN MAN
AND TRUE FRIEND

Something out of his past moved Carney to raise his face as he stood there at the end of Bill Wallace's trail. Gil's eyes lifted beyond the deep indigo of the walls, to the strip of sky above. His lips moved in soundless communion. Whether it be the God of the whites or the Great Spirit of the red man, Bill Wallace had gone to count his coup in the big council house. Happy hunting, Bill. . . .

III

TWO days' march from the canyon and the fight with the fur thieves, Gil Carney reached a groove in the hills known to the mountain men as Boulder Notch. Here, after a day of back-breaking labor, he managed to cache the packs once more, carefully obliterating all traces of his toil. From here he started, driving his spare ponies at a faster pace. Relieved of their burdens, the animals raced before him willingly while Carney kept a ceaseless vigil against surprises by roving bands of Indians. Twice in as many days he narrowly escaped meeting small parties of redskins after which he rode for days without sight or sign of either red man or white.

It was late in the afternoon of a bright day as he headed his animals down the eastern slope of the Great Divide that his keen eyes made out the wagon train. Like tiny toy wagons and miniature animals, he saw them far away and below him, the wagons bumping across the plain at a break-wheel pace, drivers lashing the beasts and a half dozen mounted outriders shooting desperately at a swarm of whooping redskins that swept around and around the train, striving to halt it in the open.

"By the jumpin' jingo!" shouted Carney, his eyes ablaze and his neck hair erect in an instant. "Those greenhorns ain't got savvy 'nough to fort up. They'll all get skinned alive!"

Carney's mind was made up without hesitation. Quick as a flash he saw the nearby stream and the fringe of trees. The Indians were closing in fast, picking off the team leaders. The brittle cracking of the guns reached Carney's ears and he saw the puff balls of powder smoke. With a boot of his heels he sent his mount plunging down the slope and as he rode, the cries of the emigrants came to his ears, mingled with the war yells of the blood-thirsty savages.

Along with him raced his ponies, unguided now, but following without question as the lone white rider skirted the stream and dashed for the cover of the trees, keeping them between him and the fight on the prairie. Directly opposite the wagon train Carney drove his mount into the wood. It was a crazy plan but—well, Carney reflected, he was a white man, and white men and women needed help desperately.

"Yeeooooowwwww!" yelled Carney, while still hidden by the trees. "Yeee-oooowwww!" Shouting at the top of his voice, he bellowed the battle cry of the mountain men, rapidly, turning his head, to fling his voice as if from different directions. The crash of his horses in the brush added to the rattle and din, and Carney fired his long rifle at the nearest of the redskins, their attention by now drawn, temporarily, from the beleaguered train. Then the lone trapper played his aces. Riding swiftly through the trees, but keeping fairly hidden, he fired his heavy cap-and-ball pistol, and with but one shot left

in the chamber, he swung his mount straight out for the open, yelling like an Indian himself. Straight for the battle point he rode, whooping, swinging his arms in a wide motion, suggesting that he was calling on his slower friends to catch up with him.

A wild yell rose from the white settlers and their women. In the bat of an eye, Gil Carney's panting horse had raced through the swarm of redskins to the shambles that had but recently been an orderly wagon train. He flung himself from his mount, shouting orders to the battered emigrants.

"Close up! Git together!" he cried, diving in with his long knife to cut down a brawny buck whose scalping knife was poised for the slash.

In a welter of dead and wounded men, women and animals, Carney fought like a cornered panther, aware that the main band of redskins, thinking that he was but the leader of a trapper party, had turned tail and were riding madly toward the hills to the north.

Amid the rattle and bark of pistols and long rifles and the grunting oaths of stubbornly fighting white men were mingled the shrill yells of the Sioux as the hand-to-hand fight raged between the wagons.

WHEN it was over, when the few survivors of the train, blood-smeared and panting, were gathered close about the charred wagon where Gil Carney had torn a half-fainting young woman from the arms of a feathered warrior, those men who faced him wearily saw their train a wreck. They knew, even before Gil Carney told them, that their hopes for crossing the vast wilderness to the Oregon settlements had been blasted in one fell swoop of the Indians.

"They been harassin' us ever sence mornin'," growled a gray-haired oldster who stepped nearer to Carney, his smoke-watered eyes bleary and tired. "We thought they wuz jus' bluffin'."

Carney nodded grimly, looking at the faces around him. The catastrophe had left its stamp in their eyes. Some of these people would never get over it. "How come," inquired Gil gently, "that you been trackin' this country at all? This is an ol' Injun path we calls the Cherokee Trail."

"We met a party o' huntin' men near a place they called Courthouse Rock," explained the oldster. "They tol' us to swing over there an' pick up this trail runnin' south o' Pumpkin Seed Creek. Said it was shorter an' straighter."

Carney nodded again. "True," he agreed, "but the Oregon trail is two hundred miles north o' here. An' them settlers that crossed overland last year followed that. They got through, too, I heard.

"Well, I guess we're licked;" cut in another haggard settler. "Less'n you-all could join up with us an' guide us to Oregon. Could you, pardner?"

"Not with this outfit, mister," replied Carney. "You ain't in no fit shape to go on."

At this point, the young woman whom he had just rescued came within arm's reach and faced the young mountain man. "Please," she pleaded. "Please help us, sir." Her tear-stained, frightened dark eyes begged Gil Carney earnestly, and she raised one slim arm from beneath the crimson shawl which a neighbor woman had placed about her, to brush her blue-black hair from her face. "You've saved us— what shall we do now without your help?" She buried her face in her shawl and burst into fresh tears. One of the older women took her in her arms.

A man's voice said, "That air's Frances Hilton. Her daddy an' ma wuz both killed by them hellions."

Carney threw up his hands. He wanted to go on—to travel light. But these pilgrims were completely helpless without leadership.

"I'll do what I can," he declared. "But you'll have to agree to follow my orders."

"We will," shouted the man with the drawl, at which there was a general chorus of assent. "What y'all plan to do?"

"Count heads," said Carney solemnly. "Then post a guard and get to work buryin' yore dead. Then, cut out yore dead stock and see how many teams an' wagons yuh can move. I'm leadin' yuh back to Bent's Fort where yuh can reorganize."

"Bent's Fort?" growled one of the emigrants. "Why, thet's on the Arkansaw, ain't it? Yuh drivin' us back south!"

"Shut up, Dinsmore," snarled the southerner. "We do like this gentleman says."

Before nightfall they were on their way back. With Carney at their head, the mournful but brave little band of settlers were plodding eastward and southward, their weary, tear-filled eyes frequently glancing over their shoulders at the crude mounds they had left on the prairie; monuments of stone piles heaped by heavy hearts to mark the graves of loved ones in the grim, flaming glory of the setting sun.

GIL CARNEY'S knowledge of the wilderness trails, his constant vigilance and cool courage when the lowered morale of the men might have made them easy prey to the redskins, finally led the little wagon train to within sight of the thick-walled 'dobe safety of Bent's Fort. The Indians were rising up against the white invaders all over the broad frontier. Almost every valley through which they drove their jaded teams gave sign of the red man's tracks or hunting camp-fires.

When the walls of the fort loomed gray in the distance a glad cry broke from the lips of the men and women. The drivers lashed at their animals to hurry them on. Carney warned them.

"Now, when you get nearer," he explained calmly, "yo're goin' to see Injun tepees an' wickiups around there. Mebbe a whole lot o' them. Can't make 'em out from here. But don't go gettin' warlike. The Injuns come in there to trade with the Bents. Sometimes they stay around for a month 'r two. So don't pay no 'tention to 'em. You savvy?"

The Southerner, who was called Blue Grass Shelby, answered for the party. Since the death of their first trail captain, Strayne, Shelby spoke for the settlers.

"We owe you more than we'll ever be able to repay, Carney," said Shelby as they rolled nearer and nearer the now easily distinguishable Indian camps about the fort. "We'd all like for you to reconsider yore decision; to help us reorganize an' captain our party to Oregon. What do you say, Mountain Man?"

Carney smiled tightly, lounging easily in his saddle. A score of times during this drive to Bent's these men had tried to persuade him to join their overland group. But Gil shook his head.

"I don't cotton to the idea, Shelby," he replied, his casual eye flickering over to where Frances Hilton sat on the seat of the nearest wagon. "I been livin' like an Injun too long, I guess," he added. "I'm plenty satisfied with life in the mountains. I can go where I have a mind to an' stay as long as I like. Settlin' down is something I haven't thought about yet."

"They say its beautiful country in Oregon," urged Shelby. "Most fertile land discovered yet."

Gil nodded, smiling half to himself. "Yes," he admitted. "I heard that, too. Was a party went through last year; a Doctor Whitman. They got across. Some trappers come back along the trail just before winter set in. They come through their settlement up on the Walla Walla.'

"Look," cut in one of the drivers close to Carney and Shelby. "Look at them Injuns. They're comin' toward us!" He clutched at his rifle as he spoke, nervously.

"Don't pay any 'tention to 'em," advised Gil Carney. "Let me do all the talking. You men just keep the train moving. There! Look beyond to the fort gate. See them white men comin' out?"

The gate was swinging open. A score or more of hairy faced, roughly clad frontiersmen were sauntering out, ignoring the silent Indians, their squinted eyes fixed on the approaching train. Among them Carney quickly made out the tall figure of Old Jim Lewis. Old Jim had a brown leathery hand canted above his eyes to shade them from the glare of the sun. Carney raised an arm and waved salute to him and those with him. Then he turned to his settler friends.

" 'Member," he said calmly. "Don't get excited. Just keep yore wagons movin' for the gate. One o' the Bent's 'll show you where you can unhitch. Steady now. Follow me an' just say 'How' to these damn redskins, like you see me do."

IN a few moments they were completely surrounded by the savages, wrapped in gaudy blankets and robes made of skins. Carney picked out the more important of the Indians, showing them his palm and grunting "How" or ignoring them as his instinct bade him. In no time they were at the gate of the fort, being received by George Bent himself.

Old Jim Lewis burst through the crowd and grabbed Gil Carney's hard hand. "Gil, you ol' he wild-cat," he roared heartily. "I'd rather shake yore paw than President Tyler's, dammit. Boy, you wuz beginnin' to fidget me some. You find Frenchy?"

"Found him an' lost him," grinned Gil, dismounted now and leading his horse as he walked through the gate with Old Jim, grasping the outstretched hands of several traders he recognized. "But I got the furs. Tell you 'bout it soon as I can get me a scrub. I'm fair itchin', Jim. Where's the boys?"

"They're out buffler huntin' with Kit Carson an' some hombres from Santa Fe. Meat's gittin' scarce."

Carney glanced sidewise at Lewis with a grin on his lips, his hard even teeth bared. His blue eyes twinkled, as if the humor of the other's words were a good joke. "Scarce?" he said. "How come?"

"Yeah," nodded Old Jim, scratching through his beard at his throat, "Injuns kickin' like cantankerous mules, too. Say us white men is drivin' all the buffler offa the plains."

"So that's what's got 'em stirred up, eh?" mused Carney. "If the buffalo are being slaughtered this territory will be hotter than the Devil's pet hole. Injuns depend on the buffalo for nearly everything they need, Jim. Nobody knows that better'n you. Say, where's the old squaw that gave me a bath last time we were here?"

"What fer you lookin' for her, Gil?" demanded Lewis craftily, his keen old eyes lighting as they fell upon one of the wagons. "Ain't you got no eyes fer beauty?"

Carney followed Lewis' gaze, saw Frances Hilton, sitting alone on the wagon-seat. Her great, dark eyes were turned in his direction. The young plainsman waved a jaunty greeting

"Make yourself at home, Miss Hilton," he said. "This is Bent's Fort. You'll be safe here."

"Thank you, sir," replied the girl, lowly. "You are very kind and we all wish you'd change your mind about Oregon."

Gil grinned, broadly this time, waved his hand and set off with Old Jim Lewis for the Bent's private quarters. On the way across the hard-packed court, littered now with bales and boxes, Gil told Lewis about his adventures since last they had parted; about the death of Wallace, the recovery of the furs and Frenchy's disappearance. Lastly he told of the embattled wagon train and what the girl meant by "changing his mind about Oregon."

"You ain't goin' to throw in with them?" snapped Old Jim, "an' go fer Oregon, Gil?"

"No," replied Carney, readily, but the word carried but small conviction. In his own heart he was not yet sure. The look in Frances Hilton's eyes had troubled him for many a mile.

For that matter, Oregon held out great promise to emigrants. Once Carney had journeyed to Fort Hall up on the Snake River. It was grand country. A man might make a fortune as a trapper. Gil, however, kept his confused thoughts to himself. Better not clutter up Old Jim's mind with stuff about a girl. Besides they both had work to do. There were the furs to get and to sell, and Carney had a hunch that, if Frenchy LaFlamme was not already dead he might run into him around Santa Fe.

OF the eleven men who started down from the mountain fastness with their ponies loaded with the winter's fur catch almost two months before, seven rode out of Bent's Fort in June of the same year, 1844. This time they drove a fresh herd of mixed horses and Missouri mules. And this time their destination was the cache in Boulder Notch.

Gil Carney, with more meat on his bones after a few weeks' rest at the trading post on the Arkansas, led the way. Old Jim Lewis rode silently beside him, while the remaining five members of the party, all armed to the teeth and ready for redskins or varmints, flanked and trailed the pack animals. They were a gay band, each man busy with his thoughts and the thoughts of each the same. They had started with eleven men; eleven had pooled their interests. Now there were but seven.

"Frenchy was a double damn fool," chuckled Old Jim on their third day northwest of the Fork. "He's got a share an' share alike split on the ketch an' he tries to steal the best stuff we got. He loses that an' now he don't even get what he was entitled to."

"If he's livin'," rejoined Carney, "he's kickin' himself hard where his pants rub the saddle. Our split will make a nice stake for a man."

"Huh?" Old Jim edged his horse closer to Carney's mount. "What yuh talkin' about, Gil?" he queried earnestly. "What kind of a stake? You aimin' to quit the mountings an' jine them Oregoners?"

"Did I say that?" countered Carney, sharply.

"Well," argued Lewis, "What else would a feller want a stake for? Is it that Hilton gal that's gnawin' yore vitals, boy?"

"She's a pretty fine lady, Jim," said Gil, and Lewis noted the peculiar far-away look that crept into Gil Carney's eyes, the rippling of the younger man's jaw muscles. A sure sign that Carney was thinking over something.

"Men like us—uh—mounting men, Gil," he made his voice as pleading as he could—"ain't got no right to have notions 'bout white women; I mean, good gals like this Frances Hilton, fresh out from the East. You—I mean, we—got too many vices, been livin' like a ol' he-bear too long. Bears b'longs in the mountings where the goin's rough. Iffen I wuz a young lad—say like yourse'f—I'd git me a nice warm squaw. A squaw savvies a mounting man; she kin build him a skin hut, kin make his moccasins an' cook his bull meat. You take my advice, Gil, my boy."

He nodded sagely.

"When I want it, Jim," answered Gil, stiffly, "I'll ask for it. Right now you an' me are trackin' furs. Let's do one thing at a time."

Old Jim Lewis closed his mouth like a snapping bear trap and said no more on the subject. But he looked at Gil Carney many times during that journey while they were retrieving the furs from the Carney cache in the Natch and from the original cache, dug that night after the slaughter of their pack animals by the redskins. Days and weeks went by during which the mountain men returned safely to Bent's Fort and disposed of their catch, taking credit and gold and dividing their shares, man and man. Nothing further was mentioned by Old Jim but he was often puzzled by the absorbed expression on Gil Carney's face.

ON their return to the fort on the Fork, Carney found himself strangely happy to see that the wagon-train of pilgrims was still there. Blue Grass Shelby told him that his Oregon party had been unable to recruit any members. He and Frances Hilton held confab with Carney beside one of the wagons.

"They all shake their heads," stated the Kentuckian to Carney. "Lot o' ninnies, I calls 'em. Tell me the Injuns'll take our hair 'afore we git across the Rockies. Now, Carney," he placed a hand on Gil's shoulder and his fingers bit into the young trapper's muscles, "if we could git you to captain this train, I'll wager a Conestoga wagon wheel thet a lot o' these fellers would join up right off."

Frances Hilton's dark eyes searched the young trapper's face. "These people can't stay on here forever, Mister Carney. What is to become of them if you don't take them through?"

"But you could take up with one o' the trader's outfits trailin' back East, couldn't you?" countered Gil thoughtfully. "Go back among your—well, your own people —where you come from."

"I have no—people, Mountain Man," she said, her voice faltering suddenly. "My father and mother were all I had. My only blood kin is in Oregon. They're expecting me."

Shelby made a great to-do of filling and lighting his pipe, grunting. "That's right, Carney. An' besides, what's left of our party has every confidence in the world in you."

"Mebbe, grinned Gil, unwilling to commit himself definitely, "I haven't got confidence in myself. Mebbe I ain't cut out for a settler. Trappin' and huntin' is my life. I come out here when I was a kid of fourteen, an' I've been wandering these mountains for ten years."

"Then you, too—" murmured Frances Hilton, "you have no real home?"

Gil looked at the girl's upturned face. There was a strange echo of the word "home" repeating itself in his brain as he looked into her dark eyes. She had no home. Neither had he. He was a nomad, a roamer of the far places; the sky was

his roof and a drift of pine needles his bed. A mountain man.

"Yes," he managed to say, fumbling for words, for something inside of him to come out and tell this girl what was in his heart. "I have no real home—any more, I guess. I'm just like the buffalo or the panther or the timber wolf."

"They can all be tamed, Carney," cut in Shelby, moving away with a wave of his hand. "Wish you'd reconsider yore decision." He chuckled suddenly. "Mebbe, if I leave yuh with Frances, she kin induce yuh to come along."

It was the first time he was absolutely alone with the girl, Gil had no idea of what to say to her, and racked his brain for an excuse to rush away. Fortunately for him, at that very moment, one of the lookouts posted above the gate cried out the news that a trader's party was approaching over the Taos route. The excitement caused by the news stirred the occupants of the fort to action. Everyone, not busy, rushed toward the gate. The arrival of travelers was always an occasion, especially this season when news of the Indian uprising was expected any day.

Gil Carney fumbled with his long rifle, his tongue suddenly dumb. Frances Hilton moved closer to him as the crowd rushed past. "I have heard, Mister Timber Wolf," she said half lightly, "that you and your friends are planning a trip to Taos, or Santa Fe." Gil nodded, a shame-faced grin on his face, still avoiding her eyes, and she went on, "I wish, when you get back here, you'd let me know what you are going to do. Whether it will be Oregon—with us—or your mountains!"

Relieved at the postponement, Gil was himself again. "We're goin' for our annual cut-loose," he laughed eagerly. "Sort of a man's frolic. It'll be just us—a lot of rough, good-natured men. No harm done to anybody. But I'll make up my mind before we get back. And I'll tell you first thing."

She was gone with his last word, a smile on her lips, her nimble feet carrying her swiftly across the smooth dirt court to her wagon. In her heart she was confident of his answer; knew she had won. The Mountain Man would ride beside her into a broad green Oregon valley, his rocky, bronzed face and his steel blue eyes, her champion in the face of all skulking red foes.

IV

IT was in Taos that Gil Carney and his trapper friends picked up news of Frenchy LaFlamme. And it was this word that guided their moccasined feet southward from the quaint 'dobe town in search of the traitorous Frenchy. LaFlamme, so they heard from one of Kit Carson's recent overland party, had appeared in Taos with part of his lip and famed mustachios shot off.

"He's tarnation mad at you, Carney," said their informant. "Claims yuh ambushed him in the mountings. Says he had no ammunition."

"The damn' mud turtle," growled Gil, turning to Old Jim Lewis, whose black eyes were twinkling. "Yuh hear that, Jim? The scoundrel was tryin' to scatter my brains."

"Well," cut in the overland veteran, "I hear tell that he's gone to Santa Fe to try growin' a new mustache an' when thet's done he's plannin' to make a corpse o' yuh, Gil."

"Then I go to Santa Fe," declared Carney emphatically, his anger warm and his eyes blazing fire. "I want a chance to prove he's as yellow as a buffalo calf's hide."

"We'll all go to Santa Fe," roared Old Jim. "We got dinero to spend and Frenchy to catch up on. Come on!"

SO it was that ten days later Gil Carney and his companions rode into Santa Fe and pulled their horses to a walk as they reached the public square. The sun glared down on the sprawling little city and the walls of the low, flat 'dobe buildings flung heat in their faces like the blaze of a log camp-fire.

"Hey, Jim! Hey, Gil!" They all heard the shout and turned in their saddles to see a red-bearded, brawny fellow in a checkered blue shirt hailing them from the porch of the American saloon. "Hey! Climb down, you hombres, afore yuh rides right into a hornet's nest!"

"What d'yuh mean, Morrison?" demanded Carney, booting his mount up to the porch until the horse had two fore feet upon the rough planking. "What hornet's nest, mister?"

"Feller used t' trap with yuh," replied the husky Morrison. "Name o' Frenchy LaFlamme. Him an' some o' Miranda's chinky-faced bad men are all primed to take you gents where yore collar button sets."

"Thanks," nodded Gil with a savage grin, his eyes sweeping over his listening friends. "Well, we came to the right place, compadres. All down and wet the dust. We'll fool Frenchy yet."

Santa Fe buzzed and hummed with the mingling of tongues that July day in 1844. Caravans of traders' wagons and overland packers threaded their way through the dusty, rutted streets where Americans and Mexicans laughed and bickered and emigrants speaking a dozen dialects inquired directions to the Spanish Trail, to the Palacio or to the nearest and wettest saloon.

Inside, lined up at the bar of the American, Gil Carney, with his friends, greeted numerous acquaintances of the trail and the trapper clan. None observed the slinking exit of a scar-faced, swarthy Mexican, who, at sight of Carney's readily recognized features with their blue eyes and mustache of corn-silk hue, shuffled to the door and disappeared. He had news for Frenchy LaFlamme and his cousin, Pedro Miranda.

Carney, always a temperate young man, took one drink of the tarantula blood that the dispenser called whiskey, and screwed his face into a knot. "I'd rather chew a Kiowa moccasin," he said. "Let's get goin' and locate Frenchy. We can do our celebrating after, if we have luck."

"How we goin' to know Frenchy?" demanded Birkland, as the seven pushed through the crowded door and out into the equally populous street. "With his face all changed like we heard, he mebbe—"

Old Jim broke in, chuckling: "Didn't yuh never see a big cat with his whiskers singed offa one side?" he laughed. "Don't worry none; we'll find him."

But although they hunted high and low through the dives of Santa Fe, no Frenchy was to be seen. Nor was Pedro Miranda. At Miranda's 'dobe corral it was learned that the bandit chieftain, with his gang, was on a foray in the vicinity of Apache

Pass, where more than one wagon train, feeling safe and within sight of the capitol, was plundered in broad daylight. It was gossipped in Santa Fe that Miranda, one of the first and worst of the robber kings of the early Southwest, was a crony of Frenchy's.

Carney swung about to Old Jim as they completed a search of the town. "Jim," he said, as the others gathered around him, "I've got a hunch that Frenchy is here and that he's seen us. You notice how funny all these Mex and those Injun breeds been watchin' us. Something is in the wind, and we're not goin' to meet up with the Canuck until he gets ready."

"Looks like," agreed Lewis, stroking his beard.

"Mebbe they're figurin' on gettin' Gil alone," put in Hopkins, one of the trappers.

"Mebbe is all right," said Gil. "But I'm for gettin' washed up and takin' a fling at that fandango they saw is comin' off over there at the Don's tonight. What do you fellers say?"

"A fandango suits me," chorused the others. So it was to the fandango the mountain men marched as dusk settled down over Santa Fe, and the surrounding mountains faded away into a purple mist.

THE fight that night at the Don's was to go down into New Mexican history along with the killing of the Ute chief by Governor Martinez. The governor gained his fame with nothing more than a chair with which he brained the demanding redskin, but the Mountain Men with Gil Carney resorted to their cap-and-ball Dragoons and the hunters' natural weapon, the skinning knife.

For two hours or more the fiddle and guitars set the pace for the dancing and rough frontiersmen of a dozen nations, slicked with bear's grease and the local barber-shop lotions, danced with the gay and flashing-eyed señoritas, clad in brightly colored shawls and sashes. It was a gala affair and the night echoed with the singing and shouting of laughing men and women. About the walls, their watchful eyes alert to everything, sat the older women, the duennas, like mother hens guarding their chicks against the hawks.

A sudden lull in the music turned all eyes toward the low platform where sat the native string quartet. Gil Carney, his face flushed and lips parted in a smile, caught the frightened look in the eyes of the musicians. Slowly, stiffly, he turned his head to follow the line of their startled gaze. One look told the story.

Every man of the seven mountain clan stepped considerably clear of those nearest him. Gil Carney's smile changed to a tight, dangerous grin. Coming slowly, menacingly, through the main 'dobe doorway into the long, low-ceiled dancing-room was a nasty-looking Mexican whom he recognized immediately as the bandit king, Pedro Miranda. And at the killer's shoulder was Frenchy LaFlamme, looking very strange and furtive.

"Everybody weel stand so," commanded Miranda. "I am hunteeng some gringo by name Carney. My friend, here," he flipped a heavy pistol muzzle toward Frenchy, "has a leetle business to settle with heem."

Nobody moved in the room. A low, sibilant whisper seemed to rise. Then the señoritas began cautiously to sift through the crowd toward the walls. Miranda watched like a sleek wolf. "Wheech is heem, Frenchy?" he purred softly. "Point thees fellow out to Pedro Miranda."

Gil Carney, with a swift glance about, noted the positions of Old Jim Lewis, Birkland, Hopkins and the others. He lifted his head, tilt'ng his chin belligerently. "Who do you think you are, Mex?" he called with a deliberate taunt in his tone, his steely eyes fixed directly on Miranda. "I'm Carney, an' you damn' well know it. Get yore yellow carcass out of the way an' give Frenchy room to run!" He paused, staring coldly at Miranda, then at Frenchy. "Or is that really Frenchy?" he demanded with a grin, noting the purpling scar across the breed's upper lip where the left side of the mustache had been. "Looks like his razor slipped bad."

Frenchy's own voice answered suddenly. "What about my share of the catch?" he snarled. "You sell my fur but nobody spleet me my share. Before I settle with you, Mister Carney, I weel talk weeth Ol' Jeem Lewis 'bout my share of the pay for the fur. Eh, Jeem?"

Carney's hand crept slowly toward his waistband where his pistol was half exposed. He heard the shuffling of many feet as natives began to edge out of the way. And he heard Old Jim's voice behind him like a mighty roar, but he kept his eyes on Frenchy and Miranda.

"Fer a lousy thief," said Lewis, "yuh got plenty gall, Frenchy. If this was a law-abidin' settlement an' we had a mind to, we could throw yuh into the calabozo. Yore share just ain't, Frenchy. Yo're a outlaw's far as our company's concerned. Ferget it."

"*Sacre!*" yelled Frenchy in a rage. "You hear heem, Pedro?" Then, like a lightning streak the long-feared knife of Frenchy LaFlamme split the smoke-blued air. No one had seen the move, so quick it was, but the glittering blade sped like a steel arrow, its dagger point ripping the buckskin shirt and flesh under Carney's left arm as the American leaped and fired his big pistol. There was a scream, and another. A girl in a yellow scarf flung herself through an open window and half a hundred voices were lifted in turmoil. Pistols roared and flamed and powder smoke quickly filled the room with a stinging haze. Carney, fighting as a mountain man would· fight a grizzly bear, shot and leaped, this way and that, his own teeth bared and his blue eyes flaming. The shriek and thud of heavy bullets made a bedlam of the hall-like room and the musicians, with a score of cowering Mexicans, had, from the first shot, buried themselves behind the platform and a pile of heavy benches.

FROM behind a strong oaken post Gil Carney punched a slug into the crouched body of Miranda, who screamed in mortal terror and fell in a heap. Frenchy was nowhere in sight. The mountain men, scattered like Indians, yelled like redskins and drove the bandit gang, man for man, backward, cursing to the outside. Carney stepped across the inert body of the famed robber chief, probed a dim corner for Frenchy.

Someone cried out from behind a half door made of planks: "He is killed! He has run away. Go away, Americanos!"

Carney shouted instantly: "Hey, Jim Lewis! Hey, you fur-bearin' animals, anybody seen Frenchy?"

Hopkins appeared through the smoke, his face smeared gray. "Didn't you see him. Somebody cut his ear off with a bullet. Think it was you, Gil. He run through that window with it hangin' off and bleedin' like a ham-strung buck."

In two jumps Carney was out of the building crouched in a black night shadow, searching the darkness for sign of Frenchy LaFlamme. Far down the dim street toward the center of the city, he could make out hurrying figures; men and women fleeing the scene of the fight. But no Frenchy.

Birkland came out blowing smoke from his pistol, saw Carney. "You shoulda give him that first shot, Gil," he opined, "'stead o' Miranda. Though I reckon the wagon trains'll thank yuh a heap. Now what?"

Old Jim Lewis had joined them and his sharp eyes saw the soldiers approaching at a trot. "Come on, quick," he whispered. "I jus' picked up a gent inside with a hole in his leg an' he says Frenchy ducked like a jack-rabbit when the shootin' started. Gil almost got him though 'fore he ran. Look comin'—Mex soldiers from the barracks. This way, pronto, fellers, or they'll hang us up by the thumbs!"

With minor wounds and bruises, the mountain men, still seven, sped through the protecting darkness. By devious paths they fled, after an hour or more reaching the corral where they had left their horses.

"Next year," said Old Jim as they hurriedly saddled and booted their mounts for the trail northward, "we kin come back an' they'll fergit all about it. What's ailin' yuh, Gil, old son?" He saw Carney wince even in the dark.

"Nothing much," growled Carney, trying a deep breath. "Got me a bit of scratch under my arm, I guess. Damn Frenchy anyway! He nearly ruined my best buckskin shirt."

V

THE journey to Santa Fe set Gil Carney's mind straight on his decision, on the answer he would give Frances Hilton and Blue-Grass Shelby. He was now fortified with a double-cinched reason for telling the Oregoners that he would not accompany them overland. Almost the first thing he did when he and his companions arrived at Bent's Fort was to seek out Frances Hilton.

She saw him as he approached, saw his

erect, straight figure and the ruddy bronze of his fair skin, and her dark eyes showed frankly the pleasure of the meeting after Carney's absence of more than a month.

"Gil Carney!" she cried out happily.

The sight of her made Gil regret deeply the thing he was about to tell her. But he knew in his heart, as strongly as this girl drew him to her, that he belonged to the mountains and the plains, that the free, foot-loose life of the trapper was his destiny. To live in a log cabin in some Oregon valley, even if this beautiful girl would marry him, and to till the soil—that was for a man who had never tasted the haunch of a doe elk roasted over a mountain campfire, a man who had never spent his years like an eagle, watching down from the heights at the dots that were the buffalo, the antelope and the black bears playing in the sun of a summer evening. It was not for Gilbert Carney.

"Hello, Frances," he called to her as he came up and shook her small warm hand. "You look fine, but I'm surprised to find you here, honestly. I thought you'd have started overland by this time."

"We've waited for you," she countered with a smile. "You'll come with us now that you've had your fling . . . as you call it? Mister Shelby says we must go, no matter what, if we hope to reach Oregon this year."

"He's right, Frances," agreed Gil, throwing himself on the grass at the girl's feet. "Winter comes early in this country, and the snow might catch you in the mountains."

"Mister Shelby has managed to enlist a couple of families who got here since you left," she continued. "He's bought some animals from the Bents, too. We'll need supplies and he said he would leave them to you—for you would know more about what we could take with us."

Gil looked relieved. He could at least be of some service at the parting. "Good," he said. "I'll see Shelby and talk it over with him." The young trapper stopped. Then he said sharply, anxious to get the thing over: "But I won't be able to make the Oregon trip."

The girl's face fell and a dark shadow seemed to deepen her eyes. She was visibly and frankly affected, and Gil was wretched.

"I can't go, Frances," declared Gil, moved by her eyes to tell her the real reason. "This is the life I like. I'm a Mountain Man, an' I know now I'd never make a settler. I must stay here and I'm sorry, for I had decided to see you at least as far north as Fort Hall. But you'll make it, don't worry."

"I'm sure we'll be perfectly all right, Mister Carney," replied Frances with sudden coolness. Carney sighed, and got to his feet. The girl sobbed once, "Oh, Gil. . . ." Then she was running toward her wagon.

IT was the last talk that Gil had with Frances. In fact, in the rush of preparation for the trail, he saw but little of her during the next few days. The Mountain Men were to leave Bent's Fort at the same time as the Shelby train, and like the emigrants, were in the throes of departure. Both outfits were busy mending rigs and harness; the trappers making ready their traps and supplies; the Oregon party loading wagons, buying blankets and things from the fort's stores and the Indians.

Neither Gil Carney, Old Jim nor any of the seven mountain men had noted the presence in the fort one day of a swarthy Mexican who managed in his own characteristic fashion to learn all he wanted about the plans of the two parties. The swarthy fellow, as Carney found out almost a year later, was one of the late Miranda's lesser cutthroats and the information he sought he carried on a swift horse due north to a certain camp of the Arapahos. Here he told the smoldering Frenchy, sharing a wigwam with his lumbering squaw, what he had learned about Carney's plans and—about the girl in the wagon train. A girl in whom Gil Carney was especially interested.

Frenchy was pleased. Here was his chance for revenge. He could fix two birds with one stone. He'd stir up the Indians to attack the train and he, with a couple of his Santa Fe ruffians, would dash in and plunder the wagons. And steal the girl, to boot. It was Frenchy's idea of a suitable punishment against Carney, whom he hated now with a crimson fury. The girl would pay for many things.

The day the two outfits marched out of the gates of Bent's Fort was a bright one. The sky was a clear, unclouded azure blue and the rolling expanse of the prairie was an endless wave of green in the fresh breeze of the Western summer. White men and Indians waved them adios, and a few guns were fired. There were shouts of "Good luck!" and "Ho for Oregon!"

Carney rode in the lead with Old Jim Lewis and Blue Grass Shelby. Behind them plodded the trappers' pack animals, then came the wagons of the Oregoners, brave and bright in paint and white canvas hoods, and in the rear rode the mounted men of the overland party. The trappers would accompany them northward as far as the Laramie River. Here, in accordance with the plan worked out by Carney, George Bent and Shelby, the wagon train would proceed straight north, following the river to the fort of the same name, while the mountain men turned westward on the Cherokee Trail, traveling lighter and consequently faster.

For days the combined train plodded north, its strength and the fact that the trappers were recognized by several meandering Indian bands, giving it safe passage unmolested.

At last they came within sight of the Laramie River. The train halted to camp for the night. The trappers mingled with the men and women of the wagon train, making their farewells in the silvery glow of a high, bright moon. Cook fires crackled and the guards, with their heavy rifles, watched the luminous eyes of hungry wolves drawn by the scent of the tethered horses and cattle.

Gil said his good-bye to Frances Hilton that night and it was a sober occasion. "From here on," he told her, "you'll be quite safe. At Fort Laramie, Mister Shelby can arrange to combine with some big train coming overland."

"It sounds very simple," she replied. "And we're not to see you in the morning?"

"We'll be movin' on by daybreak," Gil said. "And I want you to know that it's been a pleasure for me to know a girl like you. If I should ever get out as far as Oregon I'll look you up, Frances."

She extended her hand and it looked as smooth as satin in the moonlight. Gil took it and held it a moment, feeling strangely sad and lonely. She spoke: "It's good-bye then, Mountain Man. Lots of luck with your winter's trapping."

Gil remembered it afterward and how awkward he had felt when he turned away from her instead of taking her in his arms as he desired.

At dawn the mountain men rode westward, around the source of the Laramie River. The bridling influence of the settlers' women-folk was behind them and as they rode they broke forth into song, often ribald, chanting verses, the singer adding his own ideas to the words. The blue sky was overhead and good grass underfoot.

"We'll climb the next ridge," said Old Jim Lewis, "and take a look-see. Mebbe can git us a saddle o' deermeat if we go quiet."

They had ridden only a mile or two when they swung toward the foothills, and Old Jim led the way upward on a long slanting course that the horses could crawl without effort. As they neared the crest of the ridge, they halted their mounts, and several began to dismount for the purpose of stalking any game on the other side. Gil Carney flung out a hand suddenly and clutched Hopkins' arm.

"Listen!" he warned. "I hear shootin'!"

Old Jim turned about, frowning. He, too, heard the rumble of gun fire, muffled by the rolling hills and the forests. "Damn' right, too," he growled. "Injuns, mebbe."

"The train!" snapped Gil Carney, excitedly. "It's the train. Shootin' is right across there," he pointed a brown finger. "Injuns attackin' our train!"

Hopkins snatched a long rope and shouted eagerly: "We'll tie all these hosses here. Can't take 'em with us."

The shooting of guns was now plainly heard, carried on the wind. The mountain men moved swiftly, making their pack animals fast in a clump of willows and alders, then, grimly, they mounted and rode like men with the very devil after them. They rode silently, each one armed with rifle, pistol and knife, each one an experienced Injun killer. Gil Carney, far away in the lead, rode recklessly, a tight hand on his mount's lines, his jaw squared and his heart thumping with every leap of the animal between his knees. His thoughts were self-accusing. Frances Hilton was in that train.

OVER the hill came the panting, lathered horses and in the saddles swayed the mountain men. Before them lay the Laramie Valley and there in the belly-deep grass where the teams struggled with the heavy wagons they saw the Shelby wagon train with a swarm of yelling savages closing in on the rear of the party. Rifles barked and pistols snapped. The smoke whipped and tore in the breeze.

Carney shouted as he set his horse to the dangerous run down the steep slope. "White men, Jim! White men with 'em, the dirty scavengers!"

As the fighting yell of the mountain men rose like thunder against the slope, the settlers caught sight of them and a cheer went up amid the rattling fire of the battle.

"It's Frenchy!" cried Old Jim, whose keen eyes had picked out the squat, thick-necked voyageur. "Frenchy and his greaser pals. We'll cut their hearts out."

For a moment confusion reigned. The redskins, urged on by Frenchy LaFlamme and his half breeds, tried to circle the wagons and get out of the path of the snarling trapper clan. A wild yell showed Carney that the emigrants had taken heart. They were rushing forward now, afoot and mounted. He saw a settler stagger with an arrow in his chest, but another smashed the skull of a redskin with a clubbed rifle. Carney's eyes searched the mêlée for Frenchy.

One of the lighter wagons far up in the front of the train suddenly started away with a man lashing at the spent horses. From its covered depths Carney heard the frightened cry of a woman—a girl. Lifting his horse into a dead run, he swung away after it and the horse put its belly to the grass, foam flying backward onto Carney's shirt. For a half mile he pounded the prairie, closing the distance, with the yelling, shooting bedlam behind him. Four jumps, three, two—Gil hurled himself from his saddle and grabbed the rear bow of the wagon, fairly kicking his way through the canvas.

On the wagon seat, cursing the heavens, horses and deep holding grass, crouched Frenchy, driving with one hand, his other fastened around Frances Hilton in a vise-like grip. A turn of his head showed Frenchy the last man he hoped to see.

Carney did not speak, did not pause for breath. In one leap he bashed Frenchy over the skull with the barrel of his Dragoon pistol. The blow loosed the voyageur's grip on the girl and Gil snatched her backward as she began to slip over the dashboard of the wagon. Frenchy, he permitted to fall over sidewise, so that the breed was kicked by the off-wheeler before he sprawled in the grass.

He placed the girl on some of the grain bags and reached for the reins. When he had turned the team about and arrived where Frenchy lay groaning, Carney halted, shot a swift glance downward, then toward the rest of the train. The mountain men were making short work of Frenchy's half-hearted killers. The only Injuns not riding for safety were either dead or wounded.

"Get up, Frenchy," ordered Gil, dropping from the wagon, "an' take yore medicine, you low-down, dirty woman stealer." He approached Frenchy cautiously, and as he did the breed snapped alive, lashing out with a concealed knife. "Damn you, Carney!" he screeched insanely. "I feex you now!"

It was trail's end. Carney fired the pistol he held in his hand. Frenchy stared at him for a moment, horrified. Then, with a choking rattle, he fell over on the ground. Frenchy LaFlamme was dead.

GIL drove the team carefully back to where Old Jim was making a check of the casualties. Shelby had been killed, as had three men of the rear guard. Birkland was dead with an Indian bullet in his heart. It was a gloomy gathering and Old Jim suggested that the trappers take the settlers as far as Fort Laramie, leaving them there.

Frances Hilton was badly shaken by her experience. She sat on the wagon-seat silently for the rest of the journey, staring at the ground rolling by. When they reached Fort Laramie, Gil hastened to find her a place to stay with a trader's wife. Frances looked up with dispirited eyes when he came back to the wagon.

"I'm getting to be a burden to you, Gil," she said dully. "I'll try to get someone to let me go back to St. Joseph, some traders, I hope. But I'll always be grateful to you, Gil, and remember you in my prayers. You are very brave."

"I came to tell you, Frances, that we're goin' on from here," he said, weighing his words, "Old Jim and us. We'll be gone till next spring, but—well, I've already made arrangements to have you stay on here with the trader's wife—if you'll do it."

"Stay here," she repeated, confused, not daring to say what she made of his words. "But why stay here—until next spring, you say?"

Gil hunched his shoulders awkwardly and gravely stroked his corn-silk mustache. "Well, you see, Frances," he explained carefully, "I can't take you into the mountains with me and it'll be spring before we can get out again. Then I'll have my furs—my stake. Would you mind waiting?"

To the young trapper's horrified amazement, the girl burst into tears. But as he moved forward, awkwardly, to console her, Frances Hilton threw her arms around his neck. "Oh, Gil!" she whispered happily. "I'll be waiting here for the spring—and for you!"

The Earp-Clanton Feud

A KILLER COMES TO TOMBSTONE

By BUCK RINGOE

Wild Dodge City and bleeding Kansas lay behind justice-toting Wyatt Earp. Ahead, under gouged and hungry hills, lay Tombstone, the gun-hellions' paradise.

THE stagecoach, loaded with the mails and three passengers, two men and one woman, stood in the rutted street of Dodge City. It was the Dodge of many years ago, the Dodge of "Bleeding Kansas," a roaring, thundering frontier Hell Hole where buffalo hunters, army scouts, early railroad engineers, ranchmen and cowboys, gamblers and border renegades swarmed in and out, lagged for a while, then rode away or were dragged with clanking spurs to the bleak, bald cemetery on the edge of the town. Boot Hill!

As was the custom in those turbulent days of the frontier, an official of the stage company came out of his office to halt be-

The four men, spreading out across the rambling sidewalk, began the now famous march in the direction of the O.K. Corral.

A long blacksnake whip uncurled, there was a wild, concerted movement that included the quick kicking off of the brake by the driver, the loud, vicious, pistol-like report of the whip lash, the four-in-hand jumping into collars, the kicking of four yards of mud skyward. A dozen men in the roadway, three mounted, leaped from the path and the stagecoach fairly shot along the main thoroughfare of Dodge City on its run to Caldwell. On either side of the narrow lane cowboys waved and shouted, firing wildly into the air with their six-shooters, watching the swaying, creaking coach skin the hocks of snapping ponies, while a score of mongrels yapped shrilly in its wake.

Bull-team drivers and hunters of the plains bulged in and out of the saloons. Men in moccasins, men in high-heeled Spanish boots, in rough suits of homespun butternut, fringed buckskin, in overalls and cowhide shotgun chaps crowded the streets, wound their various ways between crudely built wagons loaded with buffalo hides, and merchandise bound outward along the trail to Santa Fe lounged before the boisterous saloons and gaming places.

Two drunken cowboys staggered from one of the many palaces of chance, eyes blazing with the strong fires of raw whiskey. Whipping out his revolver, one of these fired wildly into the window of the store across the street. A fierce yell broke from his lips and he flung himself about, glaring, seeking a challenge from one of a dozen men who stepped gingerly from the range of his wavering gun muzzle.

"I'm a wild he-wolf," the cowboy bellowed, "and—"

Face to face he came that very moment with one of the coolest gunfighters the early West has ever known. Tall and straight, this man's face was long and thin. A light, sandy-hued mustache half hid his youthful mouth, the lips of which were wide and thin and firm. Eyes of steely blue-gray bored into the crazed cowboy's bleary orbs. There was a glinting flash of sunlight on a marshal's badge which did not come within the scope of the puzzled cowpuncher's vision.

"Behave yourself," commanded Wyatt Earp in a cold, calm manner as with one swift snatch he jerked the six-gun from the other's grip. "Go away and get your-

side the waiting coach. High up on the seat perched a grim-faced, bewhiskered fellow with the long lines of his half-wild four-in-hand wrapped around his wrists. Beside him, sprawled lazily against the baggage lashed atop the vehicle, sat the guard—the shotgun messenger.

To the pair atop the stagecoach seat this was an everyday occurrence. They gave no ear to the voice below them. The driver held his team. The shotgun gentleman was thinking of the high time he'd have in Caldwell—when they got there.

self some sleep before you kill somebody."

For a bewildered moment the angry, surprised disturber of the peace balanced himself on rocking bootheels. Somebody laughed softly on the fringe of the gathering crowd. The cowboy spat a curse in the marshal's face and leaped to recover his gun. Wyatt Earp never moved an inch. Only his hand came up; the same hand that had snatched and still held the offender's six-shooter.

Thud! The barrel came down across the plunging man's head and down he went, face first, in the mud. And from behind one of the wagons nearby appeared the cowboy's pardner, galvanized suddenly into action at sight of his companion at Earp's feet.

Here was the chance to gain a reputation and avenge the insult against his friend—perhaps his death. Thus thought the second rider of the cattle trail. And without warning—no cry or curse came from his snarling lips—he dragged out his revolver.

Straight between Wyatt Earp's shoulders he leveled the weapon of death. And Earp, standing for an instant on the brink of death, was looking down at the man by his feet.

"Look out, Wyatt!" a shrill shout broke the tense silence of that scene in Dodge City, as John D. "Doc" Holliday cried his warning. "Behind you!" But no move, however swift, would have jerked Wyatt Earp from the path of the blood-mad cowboy's bullet. The "Doc" could save him.

As he shouted his warning, Doc Holliday fired. The sawed-off shotgun, which was his special pet and which he carried slung from a strap to his shoulder beneath his coat, boomed thunderously. A short fraction of a second before the cowboy's gun exploded, Holliday's volley smashed the would-be killer down, spoiling his aim and ending his days on the spot.

That quick action by Doc Holliday saved Wyatt Earp's life and Earp knew it. There began a friendship between two of the most famous figures the West remembers. To the end of Wyatt's career as frontier lawman Holliday was like his shadow. Occasionally, Earp deputized Holliday as a member of a posse, but whether he did or not, the Doc was always there, relishing a fight and ready to stand at Earp's back against any army of outlaws the West could muster.

WYATT EARP, so historians tell us, was a native of Illinois, having been born in Monmouth, in that state, March 18 or 19, in the year 1849. He spent some few years of his youth, upon leaving his home, as a buffalo hunter and freighter.

When he was twenty-five years old he landed in Wichita, Kansas, and took up the duties of policeman. In less than six months he won for himself a place among frontier lawmen for, at that time, Wichita was second to none in the wildness of its desperados.

From Wichita to Dodge was but a natural move for the tall, yellow-haired fighting man. He was keeping pace with railend. Dodge became the center of the cattle shipping, the end of the Texas trail and the shipping pens. The lawless element swarmed into Dodge City. So did Bat Masterson, Wyatt Earp, Luke Short, Lin McLean, Charley Bassett, Neal Brown, W. H. Harris, Clay Allison, Bill Tilghman and a half score other purveyors of law and order.

None of these was more feared than Wyatt Earp. He became known far and wide as a man without nerves, a crack shot with the twin six-guns he wore at his belt, absolutely fearless and possessed of a keen, natural shrewdness in the judgment of men; a valuable faculty in his dealings with the toughs and bullies of the border towns. As a peace officer, his name has gone down in history, and as a gunfighter he had few masters, for he outlived the fiercest period of the famed Tombstone's blood-spattered silver stampede.

Tombstone, Arizona, the city of silver and six-shooters, was in the early Eighties the battle and playground of the outlaw clan. Under the wily leadership of a ruthless hellion known as "Curly" Bill, a gang of outlaws comprising the worst of the murderers, cattle rustlers and highwaymen between Utah and the Rio Grande, disported themselves high, wide and handsome in the newly born metropolis.

This was early in 1879, to be exact. April saw the first word of the silver strike spread over the land, and the month of May found a mining town sprawled and seething with life, in the very heart of the cattle range. The horde pored in. Miners, engineers, speculators, drifters, cowboys thrilled with the promise of quick riches, teamsters to haul the wealth-laden ore to mills. Carpenters to build the mills, the homes, the saloons, dancehalls and theater.

In December of that year came Wyatt Earp, armed with a badge that announced him a United States deputy marshal. Also, snug in the holsters slung from his belt, he carried his twin six-shooters. And at his heels, the shadow that Tombstone was to learn much about—Doc Holliday, the sawed-off shotgun under his neat coat giving never even a hint of its presence.

Shortly thereafter came other men with the name of Earp. There were Morgan, Virgil, Warren and James. These were Wyatt Earp's four brothers. Five of them were there when, to the accompaniment of the gunman's orchestra Tombstone staged its Dance of Death.

Through the booming thunder of gunpowder and the scream of leaden slugs these five—and the ever-present Holliday—marched with charmed lives, like men of steel, daring the human wolf pack that hung in the shadows around them—a Six-shooter Sextet and the closest corporation of gunfighters the West has ever known.

II

THERE was no blare of trumpets needed for the entrance of Wyatt Earp into Tombstone. He was readily recognized as the terror of the Dodge City lawmen. But Wyatt Earp, in his own quiet way, went about his deputy marshaling business and promptly discovered where he could make himself useful.

Almost once a week for the previous six months the Wells-Fargo stages out of Tombstone had been held up on the road to Benson. This was then known as the Benson stage. Wyatt Earp took over the duties of shotgun messenger for the Benson route. Word quickly spread around the land.

"That Dodge City hombre," whispered the lawless bunch, "is ridin' the Benson road for Wells Fargo. They say he can blow yore head off with that sawed-off —an' with a Colt he's plain poison."

Almost miraculously the robberies ceased. The Benson stage rumbled through, trip after trip. Not a road agent showed his face, let alone a gun. They wanted no part of this man who shot at a man as he would the pip on a playing card. So, for more than six months Earp rode the stage line until one of the owners of the Oriental, a saloon and gambling palace, decided it would be a good business move to take Earp into the Oriental as a partner.

David Rickabaugh, the Oriental owner, approached Earp with his proposition. Wyatt Earp, looking down from his six-feet-two, heard the other's offer and decided to consider it. After all, he had left Dodge City because he wanted to retire from the profession of hired gunfighter. He had only been induced after much persuasion by C. P. Dade, Marshal of Arizona, to accept the appointment as deputy, and here was a chance to get onto a thriving business.

"I'll think it over, Dave," said Wyatt Earp, little knowing how soon he was to make up his mind or what would be the cause.

According to Tombstone newspapers of the time, it seems that the Oriental was having difficulties with the tougher members of the wild bunch. Rickabaugh had been threatened. No little damage had been done by reckless shooting in the place. And Dave Rickabaugh had hired Luke Short as faro dealer, knowing full well that Luke was a gunman of the first water—a fine shot.

Short, it will be recalled, was one of Wyatt Earp's side-kicks on the law force of Dodge City. He and Bat Masterson had followed the Earps to Tombstone, but Masterson, after a couple of months, was drawn back to Dodge. Now Luke Short dealt faro for the Oriental and things were getting warm.

One day, very soon after Rickabaugh had propositioned Wyatt Earp, a hard-boiled hombre by the name of Charlie Storms, who had brought a reputation with him from the ill-faced Deadwood, and who believed himself not only an ace gambler but a killer with a six-gun, picked on Short to start some real trouble in the Oriental.

"You're a cheap so-an'-so of a tinhorn!" Storms declared loudly to Short, at which most of the drinkers at the bar shuffled uneasily out of range.

But Luke Short, who was only a human splinter and weighed probably no more than one hundred and ten pounds, merely bit his lip and continued dealing.

Storms cursed and heaped slanderous accusations against Short's ears, getting madder with every moment, wetting his raspy throat with drink after drink of raw whiskey. Still Luke Short said nothing, made no move. He was anything but the killer Dodge City said he was as he sat there silently, ignoring Storms. Finally, some of the Deadwood bully's companions, knowing Short for what he really was, succeeded in jockeying Storms out of the Oriental.

"That hombre's got a nasty tongue," said Luke Short as he went out to eat. That was all. Short never wasted a word, or a bullet.

When he returned to his dealer's chair, to his surprise he found Charlie Storms already there.

"Say, you mangy, cheatin' dude," roared Storms, snatching out his revolver and waving it boastfully in the air, "I'll give you first shot!"

Luke Short glanced up now, casually. Did his ears deceive him or was it right that he heard this damn' fool offering him first shot? Well, there was a gun in the blustering idiot's fist anyway. Short whipped out his own weapon and fired three times. Three .45-caliber slugs plowed into Charlie Storms, killing him instantly.

Whereupon Luke Short stacked his deck, straightened his neat bow tie, put on his trim, stiff-brimmed Stetson, and, with a nod to Rickabaugh, walked coolly out of the Oriental and disappeared as quickly as possible from Cochise County. When Short shot at a man he killed him.

"Somebody'll be gettin' the undertaker, huh?" grunted Rickabaugh and immediately went in search of Wyatt Earp.

Earp heard the news without a change of expression. Too bad that Luke had to leave that way. A nice little fellow. A bit quick on the trigger, but he seldom missed. Now if that was the sort of trouble that threatened the Oriental it added some zest to the ownership of the place.

Earp stuck out his hand and shook with Rickabaugh. It was a deal. And from his first day as a partner in the place the menace faded from the doors of the Oriental. Open hostilities became a thing of the past. The presence of Wyatt Earp, his big, panther-like stalking gait, the cold, inscrutable face, the deadly promise of the handsome six-shooters in his belt holsters. Not forgetting that he was a United States deputy marshal.

"One of these days, Wyatt," warned Doc Holliday playfully, "one of these gents will get you from behind. Keep your eyes open."

WHEN Wyatt Earp resigned from the Wells-Fargo messenger detail it was taken over at once by Morgan Earp. As far as courage was concerned, the younger brother was the elder's equal the worst day that Tombstone ever knew. But he lacked the cold reserve, the stature of Wyatt. However, he filled Wyatt's boots like a double and kept the bandit bunch from the express box until Wyatt took him into the Oriental.

All of the wild bunch now had its eyes on the Earps, and when Virgil Earp, who had also once been a peacemaker in Dodge City, was appointed city marshal of Tombstone, the fat was in the fire.

Keeping the town in order was the simplest of the tasks that confronted the "Earp faction"—as it soon became known. Wild cowboys, rustlers and miners were all in a day's work with the Earps. When things got toughest and the town boiled over on pay nights, or the wild bunch rode in en masse to liquor up and play with Lady Luck, Doc Holliday would gird on his sawed-off and side the Earps as, Wyatt in the lead, they handed out traveling orders without a shot.

Then came the robbery of the stage, just outside of Tombstone, and the beginning of what has been handed down in history as the Earp-Clanton Feud.

Wyatt Earp and his brothers, with Doc Holliday, made up a posse without a moment's delay and rode for the scene of the hold-up where they picked up a trail that led them on a seventeen-day hunt.

Virgil Earp, it must be known, was an experienced trailer, having served with the Union Army during the war. When, at the end of almost three weeks of hard riding, short rations and utter fatigue, he halted the others, shaking his head wearily, his brothers and companions knew they had reached the end of the trail.

"It's no use, Wyatt," he conceded. "I can't see anything to follow. If any of you can find tracks I'll stay with it, but I give it up."

The outlaw trail had petered out like tracks in melting snow. Vanished in thin air. Wyatt Earp and his riders turned their badly worn mounts toward Tombstone, and upon reaching town Wyatt promptly got word to "Ike" Clanton that he wanted to see him.

III

OLD MAN CLANTON, as he was always known, had a ranch in the San Pedro Valley, scarcely more than a dozen miles from Tombstone. He and his sons, Ike, Phinn and Billy, were important members of the outlaw band known for miles around as "the Cowboy Gang." Curly Bill was known to be the head of this gang and had for his right bower the picturesque killer, John Ringo.

Posing as cattle buyers and ranchmen, the Clantons' isolated place became a rendezvous for wanted men and the gathering point for thousands of stolen cows. Working hand in glove with the ill-famed McLowry boys, Frank and Tom, this ruthless gang of renegades made regular raids on nearby herds, attacked buyers en route on the trail and ambushed the Mexican pack trains who in that day used the ghostly passage through Skeleton Canyon as an out-of-the-way route for their nefarious profession of smuggling.

At the time, Old Man Clanton had turned his San Pedro ranch over to his boys and himself moved to new headquarters in the Animas Valley of New Mexico. Here, at last, he played with the game of murder and plunder once too often. The Mexicans, upon whom he had preyed for years like the gray bewhiskered mountain cat that he was, finally caught up with him one night and shot him to pieces in his blankets.

But the boys, Ike, Phinn and Billy, remained. With Tom and Frank McLowry, they rode the loot trail roughshod. Ike, the eldest of the trio, was Curly Bill Graham's special robber chieftain, a surly, slinking thief who bore a reputation as a bad man with his guns. He was backed, of course, by his cohorts.

It was Ike whom Wyatt Earp sought. Together this pair, deputy marshal and captain of the cowboy gang, held a secret conference.

"There's a thirty-six-hundred-dollar reward," admitted Wyatt Earp to Ike Clanton, "for the capture of the gents who robbed the stage."

"Yeah," said Ike Clanton, warily, his hard eyes agleam.

"We know who did it," continued the determined Earp, "and I want my hands on them. You get me Jim Crane, Harry Head and Bill Leonard and I'll see that the reward money is turned over to you."

The three men mentioned were positively identified as the highwaymen. Everyone in the Tombstone district knew this. Ike Clanton knew it, naturally, before Wyatt Earp told him. Ike knew, too, and Earp was certain of it, just where the three wanted men could be found.

"Does it mean I get the money—dead or alive?" demanded Ike. "They'll be hard to deliver alive."

This was a point Wyatt Earp had not yet determined. He must consult with the Wells-Fargo people. So the matter rested.

A very simple thing this was. Just a small matter of payment for the bodies of three murdering express bandits. They'd killed Bud Philpot, a well-known and popular mule-skinner for the express company. To land this trio in the county calaboose would have been a feather in the Stetson of Wyatt Earp, who cared nothing for the reward if he could make the arrest.

This affair, however, proved unfortunately to be the actual starting point of the fierce Earp-Clanton feud.

Ike Clanton waited for further word from Wyatt Earp. The deputy marshal himself made inquiry of Marshal Williams, of the Wells-Fargo. Could the reward be paid if Head, Crane and Leonard were killed? Williams telegraphed for advice from his superiors and promptly went and got himself drunk.

In the midst of his carouse he met up with Ike Clanton, and though Earp denied on oath that he had ever mentioned Clanton's name to the express company representative—Williams himself put two and two together. Hadn't Earp and

Ike Clanton been seen that day walking back in the valley behind the Oriental! Sure, it was Ike who would deliver the hunted men—dead!

Therefore the express company official unconsciously touched off the fuse. He as much as told Ike Clanton that as soon as they got word from San Francisco the ball would be opened. Ike Clanton flared in fury, denying flatly that he had anything to do with the traitorous scheme.

"You're a crazy damn' fool!" he swore hotly at Williams. "I never even heard from Wyatt Earp. Do you think I'd play a crooked game like that?"

But straightway he went to Wyatt Earp and confronted him with Williams' statement. Earp, of course, denied ever bringing Ike Clanton's name into the matter. But the seed was planted. The leader of the cowboy gang was faced with a dangerous situation, or so he felt. If the word got around that he was plotting with Wyatt Earp to betray three of his own friends, members of his own profession, his life would not be worth a peso.

Clanton did not believe Earp, nor did he trust Marshal Williams. Ike, so it seems, had taken Frank McLowry and Joe Hill, another member of the gang, into his confidence. The three of them were going to pull the trick on the wanted men and split the reward. Now Clanton was in tight. If the story got around these two would believe he had drawn them into the net, the law trap.

IT was a situation loaded with dynamite. And Ike Clanton, unscrupulous coward which he proved himself, was desperate. Cunningly he started the story circulating that Wyatt Earp's best friend, Doc Holliday, was really one of the wild bunch who had stuck up the stage and killed Philpot and one of the passengers, Peter Roerig, of Tombstone.

The silver metropolis seethed with excitement. Ike Clanton realized that he and his gang must either hit their saddles and high-tail it out of the district or—get rid of the Earps. This was a big order. There was Wyatt Earp, Morgan Earp and Virgil Earp, not forgetting Doc Holliday. Two more Earps were also in the background, Warren and Jim. These, so far, had taken no active part in the gun mastery of Tombstone, for Wyatt and Virgil led the way and considered the youngsters, Warren and Jim, too inexperienced in years for the grim business of outlaw taming. They could not, however, be overlooked.

Curly Bill, too, was heartily in accord with Ike Clanton's plan. Gun the Earps down, kill them all! Hadn't Curly Bill met up with the Earps himself?

Wyatt Earp, only a short time before, had had occasion to put Curly Bill under arrest and the process included the thorough battering of Bill's skull with a six-shooter barrel. This left the king of the outlaw bunch with a wounded scalp, a badly hurt pride and an itch for revenge. He would have liked to see the Clantons and McLowrys shoot the very hell out of the Earp faction. In this, too, they could pretty well count on the aid of Sheriff Johnny Behan of Tombstone who, by the way, was no friend of Wyatt Earp or his brothers.

Like the skulking wolf that he was, Ike Clanton did not organize and ride into Tombstone with guns blasting. Instead he played the waiting game, while the town held its breath and watched. Several times the Clantons and McLowrys, inseparable companions, cantered into the city of silver and six-guns, walked about their business, bent the elbow in the numerous saloons and glowered with unmasked hatred whenever they passed any of the Earps.

Doc Holliday, true friend of the Earps, is the man whom Western historians designate as the individual who eventually precipitated the showdown. It was in a Tombstone restaurant. Ike Clanton, for some strange reason unarmed, but well liquored and alone, entered. It was midnight. Seated at a table he looked up to see Doc Holliday before him.

"What the hell are you up to?" demanded the Doc. "I hear you've been lying about me around town again." Holliday, always loyal to the Earps, was in a cold rage. A killer himself at heart, and a strange man even in this land of outcasts and adventurers from the ends of the earth, he appeared unable to hold himself in check. Ike Clanton was a menace to the Earps and Doc was their friend. With a burst of profanity he hurled damnation in the face of Ike Clanton. "Let's settle this now, once and for all. Just the two of us." Doc seemed suddenly to be almost pleading. He glared at Clanton. "Drag your gun, you miserable son—!" he shouted. "We'll shoot it out right here!"

As he spoke he snaked out his own six-shooter and took deadly aim at Ike Clanton's heart.

"Don't!" cried Ike, eyes wide as he stared at the yawning muzzle. "Don't, Doc—I—"

"Get your gun in your hand, damn you!" ordered Holliday, his finger tight on his trigger.

"I haven't got one," pleaded Clanton. "I ain't armed."

"You're a liar," roared Holliday, unbelieving. "No dog like you would take a chance in this town at night without a gun. Be a man for once in your life. Pull it out and let's open the ball."

Ike Clanton cautiously spread out his coat and showed Holliday that he had no weapon. The Doc was disgusted, disappointed. He fairly spat in Clanton's face.

"Go and get one!" he said bitterly. "I'll wait for you. It's time all this killing talk was ended."

Clanton walked out, his eyes smoldering red fire. His hand had been called. Straight before him he saw Morgan Earp, whom he ignored as he plodded home after his revolvers.

That night later, so the records state, Ike Clanton, armed and nasty tempered, met Wyatt Earp in the Oriental. He told Earp that he had had words with Doc Holliday and that the two of them were going to settle things. Wyatt Earp ordered Clanton to go to bed and sleep off his drunk.

Then, next day, the war was declared.

IV

WYATT EARP was in bed when word was brought him that Ike Clanton was armed to the teeth and on the rampage. The news spread swiftly. Wyatt Earp shrugged his huge shoulders and belted on his twin sixes. Morgan Earp and his brother Virgil were roused, too.

Tombstone was still half awake. Doc Holliday was primping himself in the mirror behind the bar at the Alhambra. Someone rushed in and caught Holliday by the arm.

"Be on your guard, Doc," was the warning. "Ike Clanton's looking for you to kill you."

Holliday smiled calmly. He was an immaculate dresser, something of a dandy, thin as a rail, and for years had known he was destined to cash in from the ravages of tuberculosis. So thin was he, in fact, that he often laughingly said it was his narrowness that made him a difficult target for a bullet.

"Is that so?" remarked Holliday, casually assuring himself with a touch of the hand, here and there, that he wore his six-shooter and the sawed-off shotgun which nearly always hung in a trick rigging under his coat from the shoulder. "Well, we'll see about Ike."

Clanton, at this moment, stood on a street corner near the Oriental. He was searching the streets for a sign of either the Earps or Holliday. Suddenly from behind him he heard a voice. It was that of Virgil Earp. Virgil, be it remembered, was city marshal of Tombstone.

"Hello, Ike," greeted Virgil Earp. "They tell me you're looking for someone."

It was a complete surprise to Ike Clanton. He jerked his rifle about and in a flash Virgil Earp had ripped it from his grip, at the same time bending a six-gun over Clanton's head. Ike staggered a moment and toppled to the ground. At this juncture arrived Wyatt and Morgan Earp, who promptly relieved Clanton of his six-gun, placing him under arrest.

In court, a few moments later, Ike Clanton swore luridly and warned Wyatt Earp that he would even the score as soon as he was released. Morgan Earp, they say, was for handing Clanton his six-shooter and blazing it out right there. But Deputy Sheriff Campbell interfered.

"You thieving coward," snarled Wyatt facing Clanton, "if you hanker for a fight you can get it right out in the street. I'm sick and tired of this gang of yours and the sooner we shoot it out the better. You come smokin' next time we meet. Savvy that?"

Clanton raved and swore. "Wait till I get out o' here! You'll get all the gun-fightin' you want."

Wyatt Earp growled and walked out. As he stepped into the open air he realized on the instant that there was a stilly tense-ness hanging over the town. His quick, sure eyes caught signs of men lurking in places of safety. A few bolder citizens were lounging across the street. And turning on his heel to walk down the street, he met, face to face, with Tom McLowry.

"So you're lookin' for fight, eh?" challenged McLowry viciously. "How about me? I'll give you plenty of it whenever you say the word."

Wyatt Earp wasted not a split second His voice and hands were heard together. There was a glad eagerneses in his roar.

"Good!" he shouted at Tom McLowry. "Let's get at it—now!"

One hand, even as he called the turn, lashed out and struck McLowry full in the face. An open-handed slap that resounded in the street like a whip lash. And with his right hand he grabbed the butt of his six-shooter.

McLowry stiffened, his face stinging, crimson. But he made no move to reach for his gun. He was completely baffled, and Earp, keyed up to the fighting edge now and set on finishing the nasty business, stepped up close. A swift, sure move.

"Come on," snapped Earp. "Draw your gun and quit bluffing." With his own six-shooter he smashed McLowry over the head. The blow sent McLowry, bleeding and dazed, into the gutter, and Earp walked calmly off.

The Earps had called the Clanton-Mc-Lowry hand. Blood had been drawn, and the O.K. Corral, a mere alley on Fremont Street, waited quietly in the sunshine for fame.

WYATT, Virgil and Morgan Earp, with Doc Holliday, stood on Allen Street, near the corner of Fourth. They had been holding a council of war. The time had come to wipe the slate clean. It was one side or the other, and no Earp had ever been known to sidestep a frontier showdown. Wichita knew this. So did Dodge City.

Doc Holliday smoothed his coat over the slight bulge of the sawed-off shotgun.

"I just heard," he told the Earps, "that Johnny Behan tried to stop the Clantons and McLowrys from parading around town wearing their guns. And they refused. They want the fight, Wyatt. They told Behan as much."

Such was the story that flew like wildfire around Tombstone. Four of the outlaw clan had come to town determined on a fight with four men who, in the main, were representatives of the law. Wyatt Earp, United States deputy marshal; Virgil Earp, city marshal of the very town in which they stood; Morgan Earp, then a special police officer on the payroll of the city, and Doc Holliday, inseparable sidekick of Wyatt Earp.

Wyatt Earp looked grimly from Doc Holliday to his brothers. There was understanding in their eyes, determination and courage. The time had come. Whispers were breezing along Tombstone's street, up the shabby alleys.

Ike Clanton and his brother Billy, a young, headstrong, wild youth little more than a boy; Frank and Tom McLowry; Billy Claiborne, a reckless, wild cowboy who rode now and again with the Clanton-McLowry gang on its depredations. Five of them were quietly waiting in the O.K. Corral.

There was no word passed. Wyatt Earp flashed a signal with his eyes. The men with him nodded calmly. Each man felt to his weapons. And the four, spreading out across the rambling sidewalk, began the now famous march in the direction of the O.K. Corral.

Citizens drew back into doorways, dodged behind anything that promised even partial protection. It was written in the bright Arizona sky that here gunpowder would burn, lead would scream its deadly message, men would fall in bloody welter.

Virgil Earp, the city marshal, was on the end of the line as the quartet swung across the street straight for the entrance to the corral. Twenty feet from them, their backs against the 'dobe wall that formed one side of the enclosure, stood the two Clantons, two McLowrys, and Billy Claiborne.

"Say, Earp!" It was Sheriff Johnny Behan calling as the lawman hurried upon the scene. "This can't go on. There must be no fight."

The Earps ignored Behan as if he were some pesky cur yapping at their heels. And the sheriff, knowing it was now too late, backed off for safety.

"We've come to arrest you," began Virgil Earp coolly. "Hand over your weapons."

At once Claiborne, hands raised, declared he was no part of the fight. In haste he rushed from the scene, unmolested.

"Put up your hands!" commanded Virgil Earp of the others.

Tom McLowry threw wide his coat, shouting, "I'm not armed."

But within arm's reach of him stood his brother's horse and from its saddle hung rifle and six-shooter. Ike Clanton, he of the violent death threats, shrank like a terror-stricken rat. Hunched low, he scurried, as the first shot blasted the battle open. Lunging at Wyatt Earp, he clutched at the lawman's arm and tried to jerk him off balance, and, as Wyatt Earp flung him off, he ran for his life.

"It's fighting time," roared Wyatt Earp. "Shoot or get out of the way." Ike Clanton fled for the security of Fly's photograph gallery.

IT was man to man now. Billy Clanton's six-gun thundered the first shot. Wildly reckless, the young Billy stood, feet spread wide, taking deliberate, careful aim. Virgil Earp raised his weapon and the rattling explosions of six-shooters filled the narrow defile of the O.K. Corral.

Wyatt Earp yanked a pistol from his coat pocket and shot soberly at Frank McLowry, who cried with sudden agony, a .45-caliber slug through his belly. Staggering gamely in a sort of drunken, aimless circle, Frank McLowry tried to shoot back, but his vision was bad now. Tom McLowry leaped for the gun on his brother's horse. The animal bolted and Tom, hanging close on the far side, hauled the weapon free and joined in from behind the plunging pony.

Billy Clanton, meanwhile, was desperately trying to kill Wyatt Earp. He ignored Morgan Earp, who, seeing his brother's danger, drew a bead on young Clanton and knocked him off his feet. Billy Clanton fell backward against the 'dobe wall, slid down, flat, then rolled and raised himself, gun smoking, still in his fist.

It was here that Tom McLowry managed to shivvy the frightened horse to where he figured he could get a good clear shot at Wyatt Earp.

Doc Holliday saw Tom McLowry, saw the rifle that bore down on his dearest friend. So the Doc flipped back his long coat and yanked that sawed-off hellish death spreader of his. There was the new note of booming thunder added to the din and rattle of revolvers. Smoke billowed up in a cloud, and Tom McLowry keeled over like a tree in a gale . . . dead as he hit the ground behind the wounded horse which raced in a mad panic from the scene.

"You would, eh?" growled Doc Holliday with keen satisfaction as he let the shotgun fall back under his coat, to swing about and rush to where Virgil Earp was down with a bullet in his leg.

Tom McLowry's bullet, however, fired the same moment he was killed by Holliday, had gone wild, missed Wyatt Earp and instead crashed through Morgan Earp's side.

"I'm finished, Wyatt," yelled Morgan. "They've got me!"

Wyatt Earp, calm as a stone image, called over his shoulder to his brother.

"Then stay behind me, Morg," he said. "Keep out of it."

But Morgan Earp did nothing of the kind. There was still Billy Clanton, now propped up against the 'dobe wall, and Frank McLowry, staggering around near the entrance, jockeying for a killing shot.

Gunshots were cracking from all angles. Lead flew like hail. It was only seconds, swift, fleeting atoms of time. Bloody, wounded gunfighters facing showdown. Wyatt Earp was unscratched yet. Frank McLowry tottered and fell, rising a moment later to try again with his six-shooter. Doc Holliday, who was once more armed with a six-gun, sauntered about picking his shots. Suddenly, there was a cry.

"O.K., Doc," shouted Frank McLowry. "Here you go!"

McLowry had a fine bead on the cool gambler, as Holliday swung sideways and shot from the hip. Both bullets screamed together. McLowry's slug cut the Doc through the hip, and Holliday's bullet crashed into McLowry's brain. Morgan Earp, too, had caught a flash of Holliday's danger. His gun thundered and Morgan flung himself around at the scream of Billy Clanton, while McLowry fell dead.

"Damn you all!" called out the youthful desperado. "I'll get one o' you before I cash."

Wyatt and Morgan Earp both saw the thing in an instant. Virgil Earp, still on his knees, was shooting it out with Billy Clanton. The kid, gun wavering, teeth clenched, eyes ablaze with fury, propped by the wall. Two guns dedicated to death! Virgil, Wyatt and Morgan Earp paused one single infinitesimal glimmering breath. Then Virgil's weapon barked and Billy Clanton's revolver slid from his spasmodic fingers. With a strangling cough Clanton slumped over.

V

AS a gunfighter Wyatt Earp was one of the real aces of the Old West. As a politician he was too honest, too direct in his actions; too thoroughly intolerant of the buck-passers, the hand-shakers and the underground borers. True enough, he had settled the gun feud between his brothers and the leaders of the Cowboy Gang. But the outlaw element was strong. Even while the better element of Tombstone, by far the minority at the time, congratulated the Earps on their victory, the lawless side was tearing down the pedestal upon which Wyatt Earp and his little group of followers basked for the brief while.

Had not the Earps in cold blood shot and killed Tom McLowry, who was unarmed and peaceable? This was the damning point that the outlaw legion drove.

Wyatt Earp saw the writing on the wall. His friends, staunch as they were, numbered but few. He was not a friendmaker. He was a lone wolf, a cold-eyed, courageous man of steel nerve and a natural expert with the six-shooter. But the link between the reigning local political leaders and the outlaw legion was too firmly welded to be broken by even Wyatt Earp.

Then the shots from ambush. There were none who dared to risk the deadly shooting of the Earps, face to face. So warnings were sent. Wyatt and his brothers, several men who were known to admire him, were warned, threatened.

At last the bad bunch struck from the dark. Virgil Earp was shot by hidden enemies. He walked easily through the street in Tombstone; two, three months after the celebrated gunfight at the Corral.

Alone, unsuspecting, he was fired on from three angles at once. The rumbling thunder of shotguns filled the air. Smoke clouds puffed from hastily deserted hiding places. The shooters fled.

Virgil Earp fell with buckshot wounds in his left arm and body. Citizens shouted. Men rushed for Wyatt.

"They've got Virgil," they cried. "Down the street in front of his hotel."

Wyatt Earp rushed to the spot, swore softly to himself, and with grave face saw that Virgil was made comfortable. Immediately he set out to run down the men who had shot him. His hunt, however, proved fruitless. Aided by their friends, the would-be assassins made a clean getaway.

Then came the murder of Morgan Earp.

Playing a game of pool with some friends in the back room of Campbell & Hatch's saloon, Morgan chalked his cue, shuffled around the table until his back was squarely facing a glass-paneled door that opened onto an alley beside the building.

He was about to bend over the table. Came the quick crash of glass. The quiet calm of the game room rocked with the belching thunder of a gun. Morgan Earp, shocked by the bullet, half spun around, and, like an echo of the first shot, a second roared its entry through the shattered door. Earp tried to call, threw up his hands, and sprawled, dying, on the floor.

As he fell one of the onlookers, George Berry, struck by one of the bullets which had passed clear through Earp, toppled over, dying instantly.

Wyatt Earp was at his brother's side before he died. Grim and silent, he came rushing into the saloon on hearing the shots. Leaning down, he heard Morgan whisper something. Wyatt pressed his ear close to his brother's lips.

"Guess I'm—dying, Wyatt," gasped Morgan, as the two hands were clasped.

Wyatt Earp's face grew dark, and he shook his head. But there was nothing he could do. Only a moment later, "Morg" was dead.

It was the end of the trail for Wyatt Earp, gunfighting star. They were bent on wiping the Earps out. Not that Wyatt Earp feared death. He feared nothing, man or beast—or guns.

But there was nothing left in Tombstone for Wyatt Earp. Virgil was a cripple now. Morgan was dead. It was time to ride on. They would take Virgil with them, a somber, silent party accompanying Morgan on the train on his way home, to his last resting place; Colton, California, where the elder Earps lived.

Tombstone was draped with mourning the day that the Earp brothers and Doc Holliday entrained for California. No man knew what thoughts stirred in the mind of Wyatt Earp. But one man guessed.

Doc Holliday was the man. Side by side he sat with Wyatt Earp, hard-eyed frontier fighting man, staring blankly out of the train window. There were names on the soundless lips of the pair, and first came the name of Frank Stillwell, one of the Clanton Gang.

"We'll take a little walk," mumbled Wyatt Earp, "when we reach Tucson. Stretch our legs, Doc."

Holliday nodded knowingly. Word traveled fast, even in those early days of seeming distances, vast areas of rolling range. Yes, it would be a splendid idea to stretch the legs at Tucson.

When the train rolled into Tucson it was dusk. Two silent men stepped from the car and walked swiftly away. The train halted there but a few minutes. The night came down blacker, deep shadows spread over Tucson.

A man was killed close by the railroad tracks that very night, shot literally to pieces, his body when it was found next morning filled with wounds made by .45-caliber slugs and almost torn in two by a shotgun charge fired close up. So close that powder burns were plain on the man's clothing.

Yes, it was Frank Stillwell, one of the murderers of Morgan Earp. A tricky, sly fellow, but he too talked more than was good for him.

THE other one of the killer pair, a breed known as Indian Charlie, but who was said to be really Florentino Cruz, paid for his part in the dastardly crime with his life. Who shot him to death has never been definitely stated. But the grim, walrus-mustached Wyatt Earp was there when it happened. That much is true.

So passed the Earps from Tombstone's seething brawl. Not like cowards running apace with fear, but like the conquerors, they marched out of the City of Silver, defiant, unbeaten—a little sadly.

They say that Wyatt Earp with Doc Holliday at his side, stirrup to stirrup, followed by, four-abreast, Warren Earp, Texas Jack Vermillion, Jack Johnson and Sherman McMasters, rode calmly along Allen Street on the morning of March 25, in the year 1882, through two man-packed lanes filled with the outlaw adherents of Curly Bill, the Clanton-McLowry Gang and the friends of Sheriff Johnny Behan —all personal enemies of Wyatt Earp, and his little following.

Hatred gleamed in the eyes of the watchers. Keen alertness danced in the eyes of Wyatt Earp, Doc Holliday and the others. Their guns were in their hands. And so they rode, unchallenged, out into the rolling mountains northward, and westward.

"*Adios*, Tombstone," rumbled Wyatt Earp deep in his throat as he glanced backward over his sholder once. "*Adios.*"

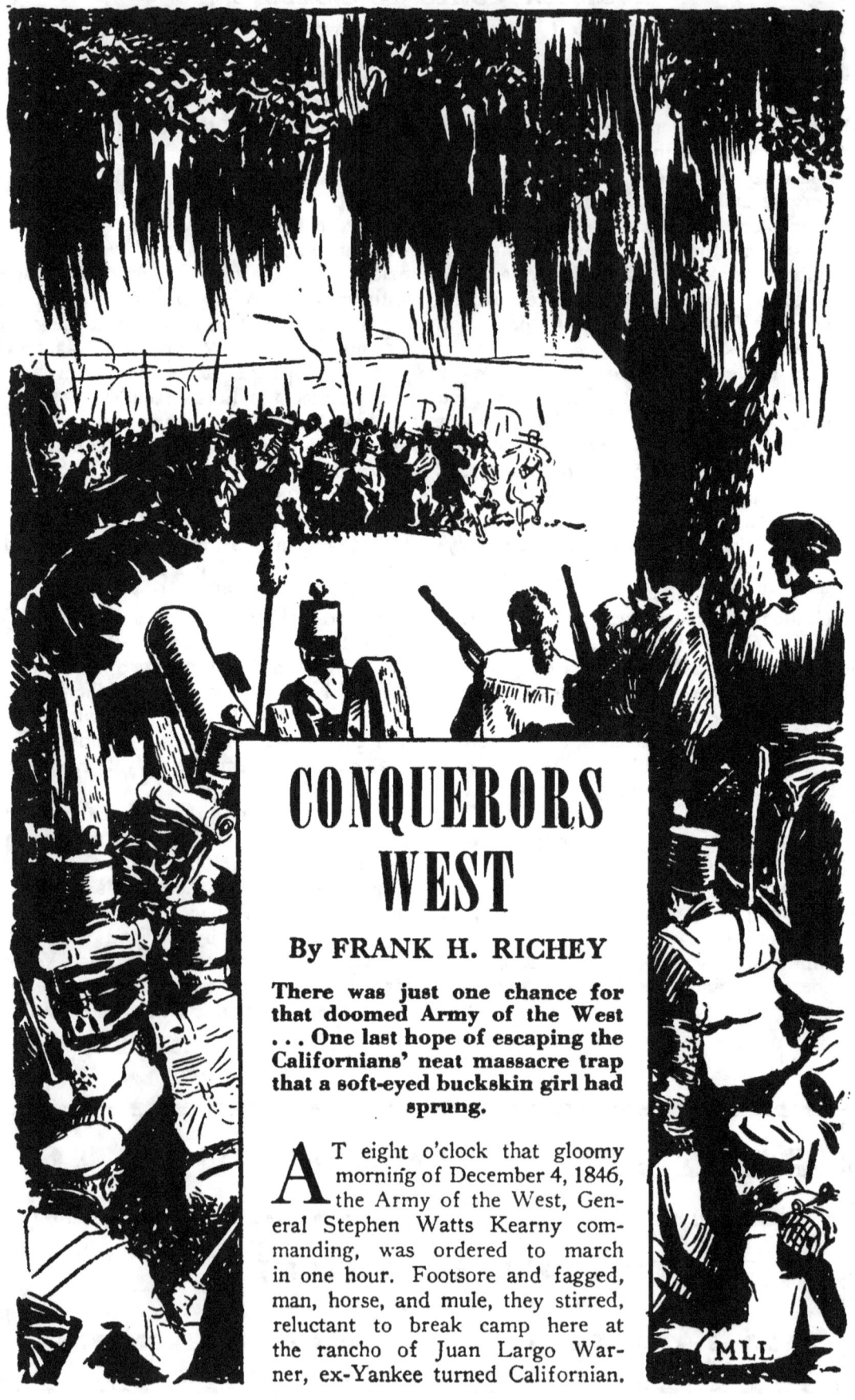

CONQUERORS WEST

By FRANK H. RICHEY

There was just one chance for that doomed Army of the West . . . One last hope of escaping the Californians' neat massacre trap that a soft-eyed buckskin girl had sprung.

AT eight o'clock that gloomy morning of December 4, 1846, the Army of the West, General Stephen Watts Kearny commanding, was ordered to march in one hour. Footsore and fagged, man, horse, and mule, they stirred, reluctant to break camp here at the rancho of Juan Largo Warner, ex-Yankee turned Californian.

Behind them lay the desert and death—the Gila and Hell.

Now once more. Rise and shine! Boots and saddles!

San Diego, sixty miles to the southwest, was rumored still held by Commodore Stockton's tars and marines. But between Warner's and the town rebelling Californians in strength unknown rode and ravaged and flung defiance to the Stars and Stripes.

Sergeant Bucky Connor, Company K, First Dragoons, worked silently and steadily with Kit Carson, rolling up the beds and striking the tent.

Carson paused, glanced around. He said: "If'n Kearny had the sense of a goose he'd wait fer Stockton to march out 'n' jine us."

"Do you figure Pico's strong enough to give us a fight?" asked Bucky Connor, his long frame straightening from his bed roll.

"Dunno. But a hun'erd an' ten dragoons an' thirty of us civilians ain't a-gonna 'mount to much if'n she's a real hell-bendin' scrap. An' if'n you think these here Californians won't fit fer blue blazes yo're plum crazy!"

Sergeant Bucky Connor lifted his blue-black eyes to the sky. There would be no sun today. A dark rack of clouds lay close by the western hills and even with the activity of the camp a chill, damp silence lay on the tawny world. He left Kit Carson and walked rapidly along the street, now and then clipping out a command to some laggard.

In the foothills above camp the adobe house of Juan Largo Warner invited with a column of blue smoke from its chimney. Connor went that way, his steady glance fixed on a covered wagon in the yard. Juan Largo Warner was a prisoner to the Americans in San Diego, although his *major-domo*, a Yankee, remained in charge of the rancho.

Coming up to the house, he saw the girl again. She was in the covered wagon and Bill Marshall, ex-sailor and *major-domo* for the imprisoned Warner, was talking to her. Connor resented this, just as he had the day before. Bill Marshall had the gift of gab and he was plenty smooth with women. Anyhow, that was the way Bucky Connor had the big, hard-bitten Yankee figured, although he never

had seen Marshall until the arrival of the bedraggled army here on the 2nd.

The girl seemed to sense Connor's approach, for her hazel glance lifted over Marshall's tawny head and settled on the sergeant. There was a moment of attention given and received between them, which was natural. For she was a sight for any man and Bucky Connor, an even six feet with no spare flesh, was a competent shape, resolute, with his dragoon cap set on black hair at a cocky angle.

The girl's interest in something behind him caused Marshall to turn. His glance fell on Connor, at once showing resentment. Connor blandly looked past Marshall to the girl.

"We're marching at nine, Lily," he said. "I got Captain Moore to fix it up with General Kearny. You can go with us if you'll darn the General's socks."

"Lily's staying here," Marshall stated. "She'll not darn socks!"

Connor scowled. "That so, Lily?"

HER hazel eyes touched Connor, moved to Marshall, then going back to the sergeant again. At that moment a breech-clouted Indian had darted from one of the thatched huts near the house. He sprinted toward the hills, his movement arresting Marshall's attention.

Wheeling swiftly, Marshall bawled "Antone!" and strode to the post of a corral. He took a blacksnake whip from the post, walked swiftly toward the Indian boy, who stood rooted in his tracks.

Connor heard the girl's stifled gasp and he sauntered after the infuriated Marshall, who was bellowing: "Why aren't you with my horses?"

Antone did not answer, his stubborn silence raking Marshall more than an insolent answer would have done. The *major-domo* threw back his whip arm and lashed the lad across the small of his back. Antone cringed, but he held his lips pressed together, his black eyes pools of hate. Marshall raised a second red welt on the lad's dark skin, lifted his arm for another vicious cut at him.

"Stop it!" yelled Connor, the impact of his command bringing Marshall about.

They faced each other across a bare five feet, Marshall's gray eyes as bleak and brittle as granite. He snarled: "Keep your nib out of my affairs. That goes for Lily, too!"

"Don't hit him again. If you do I'll use that whip on you."

Marshall's cheeks shaded purple and veins made a dark etching on his forehead. He swore foully, snapped: "Shuck that gun and I'll beat your lights out."

Connor did not speak again but unbuckled his belt, laid it and the Walker Model Colt .44 on the dust, and walked into Marshall. Still swearing, Marshall, with a speed remarkable for so huge a man, reversed the whip and struck at Connor with the butt.

The crushing blow glanced off Connor's left shoulder, sent him staggering backward on his heels. Then Marshall was at him, throwing a sledging blow with his left. It caught Connor high on the head, knocked him rolling. Marshall laughed; then he quit laughing.

Coming swiftly to his feet, the white-faced soldier rushed at Marshall, swayed, causing Marshall to miss with a wild swing with the whip. Before the big Yankee could strike again, Connor let fly with a smashing left. It plastered Marshall's upper lip between his teeth, sent him reeling, the whip flying from his grip. He howled out his pain, tried to close with Connor and lock the sergeant in his bear arms. Connor danced away, seeking to draw Marshall from the gun.

Marshall followed, spitting blood and roaring furiously. Suddenly Connor rushed him, let go with a right, a left, another right, all of them to the Yankee's middle. Marshall grunted, tried to guard his belly, now badly battered. Connor measured him, hit him with a right on the jaw that would have broken the neck of a less burly man. Marshall dropped like a felled tree. And then for the first time in a life sprinkled with brawls, Bucky Connor saw pure will bring a mauled man to his feet.

Marshall was up, half blinded, his arms out. He staggered toward Connor, who had his moment's admiration for the other's brute strength. Measuring the swaying, lumbering hulk, Connor let a right go from the heels. It struck Marshall full on the chin.

There was a crack like the snapping of a dry stick. Marshall went over backward and landed flat on his back and rolled over onto his face. Bucky Connor stood there with lingering admiration for his foe in his blue-black eyes. Panting, sweat streaking his face, Connor licked a bleeding knuckle, picked up his belt and gun. He turned, to find Antone, his face devoid of expression, holding the whip.

Buckling his gunbelt, Connor said "Come with me," and walked toward the covered wagon.

THE girl was standing beside the wagon now, her face unsmiling. She waited until Connor had stopped, then she said: "You're a hard man, Bucky Connor."

Irritation showed in his eyes. "You coming or staying?"

"Why should I go with you?"

"You got folks around here?"

"My folks are dead—I think. There was a wreck off San Pedro when I was a baby. My uncle saved me. He was a peddler until this last trouble broke out. We were going to Tucson."

"What happened to him? Killed?"

She nodded. "Bandits. They left the wagon and mules. I was hid in the brush."

He stood with his eyes studying her, his mind framing the future of this girl. This was a new land, yet an old land. But raw and hard, without sympathy for an unaccompanied girl. He said: "Well, we're marching pretty soon. You coming?"

She was unafraid. Her voice was cool, the fatalism in it taking away all color: "I'll be hitched up and ready when you march."

His lips laughed and a rashness showed in his words. "All right, Lily." He turned to Antone. "Hitch up for her, lad. You ride inside the wagon till night."

The Indian lad said in Spanish: "Señor Beel Marshall will kill you. He is a bad man."

Connor shrugged his shoulders. "Others have tried to kill me. Go quickly and fetch her mules."

Antone, still gripping the blacksnake whip, ran toward the corral. Connor looked at Marshall, who was still stretched on his stomach, afterward bringing his glance back to the girl. Her hands were tucked into pockets of her flimsy coat, her eyes darker than before, her lips long and sober.

"I didn't ask you for anything," he stated, in a defensive tone.

Her lips twitched and she spoke in a direct, patient way as though she fully understood: "You don't need to apologize or explain, Bucky. I don't have to go." His bright glance kept constant, which made her shoulders lift in resignation. "Why did you say that?"

He said gruffly: "Anyone bothers you and I'll beat hell out of him. Why shouldn't I say that? I didn't, did I?"

Her expression broke and her lips parted and her eyes, quick and puzzled, showed an inner glow. She said in a deep breath: "No. No, Bucky, you didn't ask for anything."

Antone came up with the mules. He and Connor hitched them to the wagon and the girl, climbing up to the seat, turned to look at Connor once more, her glance so somber, and then slid across the seat and took the reins.

"Crawl inside, son, and stay there till I get you," Connor said, waited until the Indian lad was concealed, and struck off toward the camp. He glanced back, once and briefly, and saw the wagon and Lily following.

BOOTS and saddles was a long and clear call through the camp and dragoons swung up to saddles and the Army of the West moved in a straggling line toward the southwest. The previous day Kit Carson and Lieutenant Davidson had returned from a sortie with captured horses, most of them too wild for use. Yet now each officer and men and civilian had a mount of sorts, either horse or mule.

Kearny and his chief-of-staff, Captain Turner, with Captain Johnston, the General's aid, and Major Swords, quartermaster, rode ahead. Captain Moore and Lieutenant Hammond, commanding the dragoons, stayed with their men, while Lieutenant Davidson, having the two mountain howitzers in charge, brought up the rear. Lieutenants Emory and Warner of the Topographical Engineers, having several Mountain Men in their party, frequently left the column to observe strange flora or matters of scientific interest.

The army wagons having been left in New Mexico, Lily's covered wagon presented a strange contrast to the mounted soldiers. More than one dragoon found excuse to ride to the rear, his bold or shy glance, according to his nature, feasting on the pretty girl. Shortly after nine rain began to strike steadily at the column and Carson, riding beside Connor, predicted it would last all day.

At noon the army pulled up for hardtack, fresh beef, and coffee. General Kearny took his holey socks to Lily, stayed longer than necessary, and ordered the column to push on before Bucky Connor had a chance to speak to the girl.

The route lay chiefly through narrow valleys between brown hills topped with live oaks. Carson observed to Connor: "We're gittin' down to whar the yellerbellies is like to show, Bucky. You oughter see that gal stays a-tween Davidson's men 'n' Company K. Safest for a woman thar."

Connor dropped back, told her to close up. "Keep between us and the howitzers, Lily."

She nodded, tightened the reins, her hazel glance showing so definite an interest in him. "Bill Marshall will be out to get you, Bucky. Keep a hard watch out for him when we camp."

"He's thinking about you more than me. We pitch camp at Stokes' ranch in about an hour, Carson says. You know the ranch?"

"I know this country pretty well. Stokes' rancho is at the old Santa Ysabel Mission. He's an Englishman."

"Yeah, I know. Kearny had Marshall fetch him to camp day before yesterday. He said he was going to San Diego. Kearny gave him a letter for Commodore Stockton."

"Maybe he'd deliver it."

"Well, you stay right where you are," Connor cautioned, wheeled his mule, and rejoined Kit Carson.

Around mid-afternoon the column wound out of a canyon, found the rancho of Mister Stokes before them. A hard lump of a man, known as Blimey Bill, came from the old mission chapel to extend welcome. He was a deserter from an English merchantman, had lived in the country ten years, and apologized for the absence of Stokes in San Diego by offering food and drink for the entire army.

Drenched to the skin, officers, dragoons, and civilians looked forward to plenty of wine, warm food, and a blazing fire. Blimey Bill satisfied them to the utmost as to drink and eats, but the sole fire available was in the kitchen. Before the army had finished eating the rain stopped. By dusk company streets were marked off, picket lines formed. Soon tents sprang up and here and there sputtering fires began to dot the flats.

Captain Moore relieved Connor from his duties, told him to see that Lily's team and wagon were housed and the girl, herself, quartered in the bedroom of absent Stokes. This done, Connor watered his mule, enjoyed mutton and claret in the kitchen beside the girl, who chatted with Blimey Bill and several of the dragoons. After mess she excused herself and when Connor came out to a night filled with stars he found her waiting in shadow of the chapel.

He took her arm in a possessive way and turned her along the adobe wall to the rear of the building. Already fires in the camp were dying and through the growing stillness drifted the sawing of a tired dragoon's snoring. Beyond the chapel a grove of oaks stood pale against blackness. Beside a vast tree he stopped. She stood looking up to him, waiting for him to speak, as though she knew just what it would be. So she was not surprised when he drew her to him and kissed her.

The crush of his arms hurt her. But she offered neither objection nor cooperation. She knew. This was how a man acted when he wanted a woman, when he thought he needed her. He pulled her around until her back was against the oak and kissed her on the throat, forcing her head back. She put a hand to his cheek, pushed, and shoved him away with her shoulders.

He muttered, his irritation showing how baffled he was: "You ought to have stayed with Marshall."

She said, "We better go back."

His temper came out on his words: "What'd you let me kiss you for?"

"I didn't mind the kiss," she murmured. "Good night." She made a sharp turn and took two steps. She stopped so sud-

denly that his attention ran past her and took up the trail of her interest. Something was stirring in darkness banking the high walls of an abandoned building between the chapel and the hills.

She moved silently to him, whispered: "Horses, Bucky. It's an old trick of Californians to—"

A yell in Spanish shut off her voice, this followed by the flat report of a carbine and the alarm of a sentry. "Corporal of the guard! Post four!"

On the heels of the alarm, came the report of a musket, this drowned in the broken rumble beat up by running hoofs. A deep and broad wave of horses, wildly racing forward, broke from about the abandoned building. The shapes of several riders showed to the horses' flanks and rear. Somewhere a man yelled shrilly and a pistol flamed blue-red among the terrified horses. They broke for freedom, surged across the flats, and hit the camp on the dead run.

CONNOR grabbed Lily's hand, hauled her flying along the chapel wall, and turned a corner to see tents being knocked flat by the horses. He heard Captain Moore bawling for Company K to fall in. And above all other sounds cracked the rattle of carbines. Connor shouted, "Get in there!" and gave Lily a shove toward the wide chapel doorway.

She shouted something he didn't understand, nor did it check his speed toward the camp. Dragoons were out of their tents, or under fallen canvas, and the horses, met by gunfire from sentries and others on the farther side of the camp, were milling, some of them screaming and plunging in panic. From the mass poured a white stallion, followed by a dozen or more horses.

They swept directly at Connor, who whipped up his Colt and fired into the bunch, yet bringing down none save a bony roan. Then he was caught in the flood of brutes. A shoulder hit him, knocked him around. Another horse brushed him, sent him sprawling. He got up, pressed the Colt trigger and, swearing, put the empty gun away. Out of the loosening pack emerged a rider and Connor got a clear look at Bill Marshall's evil face.

Marshall, yelling, pouring out oaths at

Connor, tried to ride him down. But Connor stumbled aside, dimly aware of Lily's scream. Her voice brought Marshall wheeling back. He fired point-blank at Connor, sent the bullet past him with a little howl, and raced toward the girl.

Connor, running after Marshall, saw Lily was cut off from the chapel door. She had her back to the adobe wall, in her hands a long pole, and this she crashed across the withers of Marshall's horse as he swerved the animal and tried to catch her waist in the circle of his arm. However, while the blow sent the horse into a series of pitches, the pole snapped off close to her grip. Marshall, as good a horseman as Connor had ever seen, brought the brute under control, wheeled, and raced after Lily, who was running for the chapel doorway.

Yelling at Marshall, Connor drew his attention long enough for the *major-domo* to whip up his pistol, take aim. A deafening explosion erupted in the sergeant's face and flame poured heat against his cheeks and eyes. He had a glimpse of Marshall's twisted face. Then he had his grip on the horse's bridle. The horse reared and flung him about.

Marshall lifted his gun and struck with the barrel. White flame seared Connor's brain and a million red stars filled the night. Yet, even as he fell, he was vaguely aware of seeing Antone lashing at Marshall with the blacksnake whip. Then Bucky Connor was dead to the world. . . .

A VOICE said: "*Señor* Bucky. Please *Señor* Bucky!"

Seargeant Bucky Connor struggled out of deep darkness, into a gray light, his head throbbing and the salty taste of blood on his lips. A hand hauled at his arm, pulled him to a sitting position. Then his vision cleared and he looked directly into the face of Antone.

"Where is she?" mumbled Connor.

"*Señor* Beel, He is got her," Antone groaned.

Connor never had been sick in his life, never afraid of anything. But now his stomach was weak and his legs were shaking. He was thinking of Lily. He began to understand why Sergeant Cox, who had left a bride at Fort Leavenworth, was always worrying and stewing about some-thing happening to her while he was on campaign.

Antone was pulling at Connor's arm again. A dragoon hurried up and aided the Indian lad. Then Connor was on his feet, held erect by the dragoon, who asked: "Where you hit?"

"I ain't," growled Connor. He braced his legs, which were shaking. He took a step, would have fallen if the dragoon had not supported him. He sent his glance about.

The horses and Marshall and the Californians were gone. Flares gushed here and there among the troops, showing tents being erected. Somewhere General Kearny was swearing and Captain Moore was bawling for Company K to fall in.

Connor kept thinking of Lily and Marshall and what the girl's capture meant to her. He moved away from the dragoon and he would have fallen again if the dragoon hadn't caught him. The most jarring thought of his life shook Connor and he was again seeing Marshall and the evil face of the Yankee, so clearly expressing his want for the girl.

Captain Moore's huge yells kept breaking about Connor, who moved toward the chapel, the dragoon following and asking: "Where you going? We got to fall in."

"I'm going to get her," Connor growled.

"Hell, you don't know where she is," the dragoon said. He reached and pulled Connor about. "Listen, Sarge! You're out of your head. We got to fall in."

Connor licked his lips which were dry and hot. He spit blood from his mouth. He asked: "Which way'd they go, Antone?"

"I do not see, *Señor* Bucky. Antone is knocked down by *Señor* Beel's horse."

"Like huntin' for a needle in a haystack, to find her," the dragoon said. "Anyways, we got to fall in. Com'n!"

The dragoon was talking sense, Connor thought. He hauled his body about and set off for camp. His head was still dizzy and it pulsed above the right temple. He kept thinking of Marshall and Lily; and he understood something that he hadn't clearly understood before. He wanted the girl. He had wanted her there by the live oak tree. But this was different. He hadn't asked for anything then. He wouldn't ask for anything. Some things you couldn't get by asking; and some things you couldn't just take. They had to be given to you without any asking or they weren't worth anything. That was the way of it.

That was the way he wanted Lily. He knew it now. But knowing it didn't do him any good. Bill Marshall had her. That thought kept hammering at him, making him strong and weak by turns. Then he was on K's street and somebody was shouting at him to call the roll of dragoons and he was hearing Captain Moore say there was a captured Californian in General Kearny's tent.

Somebody yelled: "Hey, Sarge!" and Connor felt his legs give way. He tried to remain erect. But darkness folded about him in the space of a short breath. The last he remembered was somebody bawling for Assistant Surgeon Griffin.

CONNOR felt the lurching of a wagon er him. He pushed the blankets aside and sat up and looked forward. Antone was on the seat, driving, and this was Lily's wagon. Daylight was dead gray and streaked by rain. Connor was completely puzzled, although his head was clear enough and aches were gone from his body.

He pulled himself to the seat and planted his forearms beside Antone, who looked at him and came as near smiling as an Indian could.

"Where are we?" Connor asked.

"Near Rancho Santa Maria, *Señor* Bucky."

Kit Carson rode up beside the seat, his thin, brown face peering at Connor. "You all right, Bucky?"

"Sure. Sure, I'm all right. Where are we?"

"Pullin' up to Rancho Santa Maria. Hain't no grass thar. We're gonna camp two miles beyant, eff'n ol' Kearny's got sense. Captain Gillespie, Leftenant Beale, an' Midshipman Duncan with thirty-five men is jined us. Stockton sent 'em out. So I reckon thet English feller, Stokes, delivered ol' Kearny's letter. Captain Gibson come too."

"Seen any more Californians?"

"Nah. I rid back to Warner's, figgerin' Marshall mought a-took the gal thar. But he hain't. Seed an Injun whut said her

an' Marshall is with Andreas Pico's yeller-bellies 'round here somewhar. They hain't fur off."

"Going to give us a fight?"

"Mought be," Carson replied. He rode away.

"*Señor* Beel is a bad man. He does not mean good to the *Señorita* 'Leelee," Antone remarked.

"You ain't telling me nothing new," Connor growled, He crawled back to the blankets, between them, and remained there until the army stopped to pitch camp in a little valley through which twisted the still dry bed of the San Barnardo River. Mess call brought him out to K's street and he found he could depend on his legs.

Night, thick with rain, was spotted here and there by sputtering fires, although one of the scouts advised Kearny to extinguish the blazes. The enemy was reported to be encamped near at hand and another attack in force, preceded by a driven band of wild horses, might prove disastrous.

Kearny resented the suggestion, ordered Lieutenant Hammond and a detail to reconnoiter, even though Kit Carson objected. Connor sought permission to accompany the party, hoping to learn something about Lily. This request Kearny bluntly denied.

Connor returned to the covered wagon, pulled himself over the tail gate, and sat hunched up, with his arms around his knees. Antone's voice came from the front end of the wagon bed: "It is good the *Señorita* Leelee is with Don Andreas Pico, *Señor* Bucky. Don Andreas is a *caballero.*"

"He's a damn'd yellow-belly," growled Connor. "So's Marshall, if he is a Yank. I'd like to get my hands on him." He was silent a time, then asked: "What's a *caballero?*"

"A fine gentleman, *Señor* Bucky. Don Andreas is know *Señor* Beel is have the Indian wife."

"What's that? Marshall's got an Indian wife?"

"He is married to the daughter of Antonio Garra, chief of my people, the Aguas Calientes. Don Andreas is very strict. He will not like it for *Señor* Beel to steal the *Señorita* Leelee. I do not think *Señor* Beel is very smart when he join Don Andreas. A Pico is just."

"Pico's a yelly-belly," grumbled Connor and lapsed into silence.

The night wore on and the rain stopped. Connor heard Lieutenant Hammond and the scouting detail return. At once a candle showed in Kearny's tent and shortly after, around two o'clock, the call to horse sounded through the camp.

Dragoons poured from tents and presently Kearny, with Captain Johnston and others of his staff, headed the column on a forced march, leaving the howitzers under Lieutenant Davidson and the baggage under Major Swords to bring up the rear.

NINE miles lay behind them when, before day-break, the advance guard under Captain Johnston sighted the fires of the enemy, a short mile distant on the valley flats. A dragoon wheeled and returned on the dead gallop. Reining before Kearny, he made his sharp salute and announced the immediate presence of the enemy.

Ahead was the advance guard under Johnston, reduced to eleven men by the return of the messenger. Behind the General and his staff, Companies C and K rode in a serpentine column of twos, pressed in by the crowding hills, followed by the howitzers and, at the very tail, Major Swords and the packs.

Kearny was itching for a fight. Had not Commodore Stockton gained fame by defeating Californians? Was not that upstart Fremont getting his name on many tongues? And what had he, Kearny, accomplished to gain the popular eye? Taken New Mexico without a battle. One did not become a hero by issuing proclamations. One must shoot down Californians by the hundreds. And here was a grand opportunity at hand. Here was a God-given chance to show up Stockton and Fremont. Here was a glorious chance to show them how to settle this silly rebellion; to show the world how to take California.

"Eff'n I was you, Gineral," Kit Carson broke into Kearny's dreams of glory, "I'd take it sorta keerful. Thar's an Injun village named San Pasqual right 'bout whar them yeller-bellies is at. Pico hain't no fool. This mought be a trap."

"When I wish your advice, Mister Carson," Kearny snapped, "I'll ask for it."

Carson spat, shifted his quid to his other cheek. Kearny went on to the messenger from Johnston's advance guard: "Tell Captain Johnston to proceed at a trot until close to the enemy. Then charge them. Lieutenants Emory and Warner with myself, Carson, Connor and three men of the sergeant's choosing will follow closely. Captain Moore and his men will join with some of the men sent by Commodore Stockton and support our advance. We shall wipe out the rebels at once. Forward!"

So they advanced on the Indian village of San Pasqual, Captain Johnston and twelve men going at a trot. Carson, riding beside Connor to the rear of Kearny, muttered: "Yore a-gonna see hell a-poppin' fer shore, Bucky."

Connor, his nerves tingling, strained his sight to see ahead into the rising daylight. Once—only once—he turned to look at the rear guard, already strung out too much for strong protection. Suddenly Carson exclaimed, "Thar they be!" and at once the order to charge rolled boldly from Kearny.

A defiant yell in Spanish lifted from the Californians drawn up on horses in the village ahead. Connor, riding full tilt, his sabre out, saw the enemy, perhaps eighty strong, armed with carbines and pistols and long lances. Johnston and his troop of twelve was charging pell-mell. A ragged volley poured from the Californians.

Johnston pitched from the saddle and the astonished men of his party rolled back upon the closely following squad riding with Kearny. A dragoon's horse, its saddle empty, wheeled and tore back through the disorganized Americans. No sooner had they fired than the Californians retreated, galloping easily, their very calmness bringing out Kearny's raging command for the Americans to ride the enemy down.

Dashing headlong toward the retreating foe, Connor saw Carson's horse stumble, saw the Mountain Man loop from the saddle, his rifle flying far ahead, to shatter on the road. His comrades strung out Connor drove through the village, seeing Captain Johnston beside the road, a bullet hole in his forehead.

Somewhere ahead a carbine let go, the slug knocking Connor's mule from under him. He threw himself clear as the dead animal fell, landing on his knees. Coming up fast, he ran forward, seized the carbine and cartridge box of a dead dragoon, and set out in pursuit of his straggled comrades. Suddenly he was aware of Carson off to his right. But before he could more than shout to the Mountain Man, they were both caught in Moore's charging dragoons.

Horses' shoulders kept grazing Bucky Connor, one finally striking him fully and knocking him in a long roll to one side of the road. The dragoons swept by and others were coming up. The Californians had halted again, but just long enough to tantalize the eager Americans. Then again the Californians retreated, in good order, beyond the village, their derisive yells stabbing at their pursuers.

Again running forward beside Carson on the road, Connor shouted: "Look, Kit! The yelly-bellys are wheeling back. By Heaven! Look! Their lances!"

"Ol' Kearny rid right into it!" roared Carson. He pulled Connor to one side of the road. From there they began to lay shots into the charging Californians, who had taken clever advantage of the stretched-out long line of the Americans.

BUCKY CONNOR, firing as rapidly as he could load, was horrified by the slaughter before him. Lances at the level, the Californians swept down on the scattered and demoralized Americans in wave after wave. Sabres were useless against the lances, each a long-bladed knife bound with rawhide to a nine-foot pole.

Carson flung aside the dragoon's carbine he had picked up, got a rifle and bullet pouch and powder horn from dead Francois Menard, one of the four Mountain Men whom had been ordered to the topographical engineers under Lieutenant Emory. Again Connor and Carson raced toward the slaughter ahead.

Vainly the dragoons batted with empty carbines at the deadly lances. Connor saw Sergeant Cox, the bridegroom, go down, a lance driven through his body. He saw Kearny and the other officers, all discipline gone now, using pistol and sabre in vain attempts to defend themselves. A big Californian on a magnificent palomino pierced Captain Moore with a lance and Bucky Connor, white of face and sick, lifted his carbine and sent a ball through the big

Californian's head. He toppled from his mount.

This was annihilation, Bucky Connor knew. He loaded the carbine, took another shot, and was shoved from the road by Carson. One of the howitzers, its mules running away, came bouncing up the road. It was useless, but the Californians, seeing the artillery, broke back. The second howitzer lumbered up, while the first, its gunners all lanced or shot, dashed pell-mell into the main body of the enemy. Having neither artillery nor gunners, the Californians did not give Lieutenant Davidson a chance to bring the one useful howitzer into play. They wheeled and, at the command of Andreas Pico, retreated along the San Barnardo River, to the southwest.

By the time Connor and Carson came up to the scene of the most intensive fighting, the danger of their position began to press darkly on Connor. Dead horses and mules and dragoons were scattered over the flats, on the near-by hills. Lieutenant Hammond, breathing his last, was being tenderly carried toward the rear. Captains Moore and Johnston were dead, while Kearny suffered from two wounds, Captains Gillespie and Gibson and Lieutenant Warner from one or more.

A body of Californians suddenly appeared to the rear of the defeated army and Kearny ordered Lieutenant Emory to take a party and hurry to the protection of Major Swords and the baggage. Connor, in response to Emory's command, gathered some of Company K dragoons and rode the mile to where Swords awaited aid. The Californians departed at approach of Connor and the dragoons. Later Lieutenant Emory was relieved. He took Connor and a detail and returned to assist in finding the wounded and dead.

Smell of powder smoke lay thick along the narrow valley, but as drab daylight spread over the hills the Americans began the sad duty of collecting the dead and wounded. Bucky Connor led a squad to the body of Captain Johnston, whom, given in charge of Sergeant Falls and four men, was carried into camp. The work went on; and at roll call in mid-forenoon the loss was found to be eighteen killed and fifteen wounded out of the approximately eighty Americans engaged. Captain Johnston and one dragoon were the only Americans killed by firearms and all the wounds had been inflicted by the lances.

Throughout the day Carson and a detail of Mountain Men, with a scattering of dragoons, concealed themselves among rocks on the surrounding hills, from there prepared to sound the alarm of an expected attack by the Californians. By mid-afternoon Assistant Surgeon Griffin had dressed the many wounds, Kearny's so painful that he ordered Captain Turner to assume command. Turner ordered the dead lashed to mules and conveyed to San Diego for burial. But lack of sufficient number of strong animals to convey both the dead and the wounded brought orders to bury the dead as secretly as possible that night and thus avoid the robbing of their bodies by either the Californians or Indians.

Ambulances for the wounded were lacking, nor could Lily's covered wagon serve the purpose. In San Diego, forty miles distant, were wheeled carriages; so Alexander Godey, a Mountain Man, with a few of his own picking, was dispatched by a circuitous route to seek aid from Commodore Stockton.

Connor saw the position of the battered army was defensible, but he harbored doubts as to the ability of the troop to withstand a prolonged siege. Little rest would be obtained by the well or the wounded on the knoll covered with rocks and cacti. Provisions were exhausted, many horses and mules dead, those still alive on their last legs. The army, now reduced to half its strength, was worn down to the core, emaciated, the nerves of the officers and men stretched to the snapping point. Yet these were not the darkest of his thoughts.

He was thinking of Lily and Marshall, whose face he had vainly sought for in the battle. As to the girl's fate he hadn't the slightest doubt and the more he dwelt upon it the greater became his lust for revenge. Night found him brooding on the covered wagon seat, his silent companion the Indian lad, Antone.

In darkness as thick as pitch, he aided in carrying the dead to a clump of willows east of the camp. There, beside the San Barnardo River, with no service save the yowling of coyotes attracted by the smell, the dead were buried. Two thousand miles over desert and mountains, community of privations, hardships, and dangers, had produced an understanding greater than that of brotherhood among the men of Kearny's command. Bitterness at their rash leader welled up in Connor and he returned to camp with full realization that civilians like Kit Carson were the proper type to issue orders rather than to obey those given by the blindly ambitious.

The night was cold and damp and Connor, tired to his bones, crept between blankets covering Antone in the bed of Lily's wagon. Long afterward he fell asleep.

REVEILLE broke the cold, black heart of morning. Connor crawled from the wagon, saw Company K falling into line, and heard his own voice automatically call the roll. He reported the company to Lieutenant Davidson, in command since the death of Hammond and Moore, and returned along the street, the smell of wood smoke and coffee rolling around him. He watered Lily's mules, his own killed, at the river and, at breakfast of hardtack and mule meat, heard Lieutenant Emory say:

"Day never dawned on as tattered and ill-fed a detachment of men as you see here mustered under the United States colors."

Connor glanced at Emory, wondering then if the lieutenant felt toward Kearny as did most of the men. The Californians, emboldened by their victory of the day before, showed a considerable force in a narrow neck between hills ahead, although careful to remain beyond effective carbine fire. One of them rode forward, his huge size at once catching Connor's attention.

Running forward, sure the object of his sight was Marshall, Connor whipped out his Colt. Lieutenant Emory bawled for the sergeant to stop, but his command fell on deaf ears. Marshall, his lance at the level, wheeled toward Connor and came on at a run. Boots and saddles was a steady and quick call behind Connor, but he ignored it. He lifted his revolver, steadied its barrel on his left arm, and let go.

Marshall yowled, dropped the lance,

clutched his right arm, and spun his horse. This was no single-shot dragoon pistol blazing at him, but a new-fangled gun with a range superior to any other small firearm. A second shot nicked his horse's rump and the brute fairly flew apart as it pitched, unseated Marshall, and tore on. The big Yankee demonstrated unbelievable speed in seeking shelter among rocks edging the narrow neck.

A carbine cut loose from among the rocks and a ball whistled past Connor's head. He turned, ran back to camp, there to confront Lieutenant Davidson, who began: "Any more of that, Connor, and I'll—" and finished with a grin.

"Yes, sir," Connor said, saluting.

"And next time hit him in the heart," Davidson ordered and hurried away.

The order to march was given and presently the ragged band moved forward to give the enemy battle.. Four of the most seriously wounded rode on blankets in Lily's wagon, Connor handling the reins. Other wounded, conveyed chiefly in. ambulances devised by Carson and the other Mountain Men, suffered distressingly, the ambulances frequently grating on the ground. Kearny's wounds were sufficiently healed to permit him to resume command. Experience had beaten something into his skull. He consolidated the dragoons into one company under Captain Turner and, with the packs and wounded in the center, took Carson's advice to follow the right-hand road over the hills, this leaving the San Barnardo River on the left. As the Americans advanced the Californians retreated.

Carson dropped back to Lily's wagon, said: "English feller named Snooks owns San Barnardo rancho down the road a few miles. Mebbe eff'n ol' Kearny's got sense 'nough to rest thar a while we kin make it to San Diego."

"I reckon he's learned his lesson," Connor said.

"Dunno. Kain't tell 'bout an army feller. Comes to fittin' Injuns, 'n us civilians usually gotta take holt 'n fix things up so's the ginerals kin git the glory. Yellerbellies is lots like Injuns when it comes to fittin'. Anyways, thet's the way I feel."

Connor chuckled. "I'm an army fellow, Kit."

"Nah, you hain't. Not no regular one.

You jes' got a uniform on. An' not much o' thet. You'd a-made a dang'd good mounting man."

AFTER a march of nine miles through the foothills, the army arrived at San Barnardo rancho. It was deserted save for a few Indians, with whom Antone immediately conversed. Chickens were killed for the wounded, the mules and horses watered, but, finding no graze, Kearny ordered cattle collected and driven before the column toward grass on the bottoms of the San Barnardo River. Scarcely a mile lay behind the trailing howitzers when mounted Californians burst from the hills to the rear and raced to obtain position on a low hill commanding the Americans' advance.

Lieutenant Davidson shouted for volunteers to attack the hill. Connor leaped from the wagon seat, flinging the reins to Antone, and vaulted to the back of a mule before its walking owner was aware of what had happened. He dug his heels into the mule's flanks and the long-eared beast lit out with a bray. Lieutenant Davidson and Connor in the lead, some seven or eight dragoons charged the hill, returning the Californians' fire and getting results more by luck than skill.

Connor, yelling as no Indian ever yelled, swept up the slope toward scattered oaks on the top. A Californian dashed into the open, took a pot-shot at Connor, and was rewarded with a slug between his ribs. He wheeled, bawled orders to retreat, and headed his forty men toward the river bottoms as swiftly as the magnificent horses could carry them.

Meanwhile Kearny, with his usual lack of foresight, had brought up the army on the run. Now their treasured cattle were scattered, completely lost to them, on the river bottoms, where already the Californians were rounding them up.

In spite of the enemy's heavy fire from the hill, not an American was so much as scratched. Connor, rounding an oak, came upon a Californian, his fear far more a likely cause of death than the bullet slash across his cheek. Leaping down, Connor covered the cringing Californian with his Colt, yelled at him:

"What'd Marshall do with Lily?"

From chattering teeth poured a torrent of Spanish, being chiefly, Connor guessed, a denial of ability to either understand or speak English intermixed with pleas for mercy. Seizing the captive by the neck, Connor yanked him erect and booted him all the way to where Carson was angrily telling Kearny that to attempt to go on meant inviting an attack, with almost certain loss of the baggage and death to many of the wounded.

"Eff'n you got sense, Gineral, use it!" Carson snorted and strode away.

Kearny, purple with rage, held his tongue. He was one to bide his time and his mind was far-reaching in the small matter of revenge. The scowling faces of dragoons and civilians around him told their own story, so he ordered a halt for the night and commanded Doctor Griffin to attend the wounded again.

Here on the hill defense against attack was no longer a matter of concern, even though they were outnumbered three to one. Yet as the day passed it became apparent that holes dug for water found a short supply for the men, none for the animals. There was little forage for the horses and mules, one of the latter supplying meat for the evening mess. Around dusk several of the mules broke their picket ropes and fled toward the river and water. Connor and Carson took out after them, but gave up when shots whistled up from below.

Angry, helpless, they watched the Californians gather in the mules and Connor returned to camp in a state of mind to beat the lights out of the lone captive. To his surprise, however, he found Antone and the captured Californian talking freely in Spanish.

"What's the yeller-belly say, Antone?" Connor asked.

"He say same as Indians at Rancho San Barnardo say. *Senorita* Leelee is with Don Andreas Pico and his men."

"You mean that Pico took her away from Marshall?"

Antone rattled Spanish at the captive, who shrugged, but made no reply, which even Connor knew was a denial of knowledge. "Wait till I get my hands on Pico," Connor growled. "I'll take the yeller-belly apart." He wheeled and stalked away, ignoring Antone's call.

Night settled on the hill, and the beleaguered Americans could see the camp fires of the enemy all around. Groans of the wounded, moaning of the famished animals, raked Connor's nerves. He paced back and forth beside Lily's wagon, his thoughts of her, his memory of her, striking through him, leaving true physical pain. Who she was, what she was, mattered nothing to him. He knew he wanted her; and the power of that wanting more than once turned him toward the downward slope. Yet each time he stopped, halted by realization that she might be a captive of Pico at any one of the many camp fires, that he might have taken her away long before now.

Fatigue began to take its heavy toll and shortly afterward he rolled up in his blankets under the covered wagon.

MORNING broke over as dejected a body of troops as ever the sun had seen. There was no reveille; there was no mess call. There was nothing to do but wait. Wait and hope that Godey would return, guiding a relief party of Stockton's men. Kearny had called his officers to his tent. He swore, and insisted on marching, cutting the way through to San Diego. Yet whereas the rash Kearny had learned nothing from experience, his officers had, and, backed by Carson and another Mountain Man, they virtually compelled the irate General to remain. While Kearny fumed in his tent, word came of the approach of a flag of truce.

Lieutenant Emory called to Connor, who accompanied the officer to meet the detail of Californians. Antone joined them, acted as interpreter, the Americans learning Don Andreas Pico had just captured four Americans whom he wished to exchange for a like number of Californians.

The Americans boasted but one prisoner, and, with this terrified Californian, Emory and Connor departed to meet Don Andreas Pico. Conner wondered if the four captured Americans were Godey and his men, all hope drying up in him at the thought.

The messengers from Pico led the way to willows banking the river, even as they advanced Connor's mind trying to scheme out a means for rescuing Lily, or at least getting a grip on Pico's throat. Yet when he came into the presence of the Californians' leader all Connor's hate of the man fell away.

Don Andreas Pico was handsome, middle-aged, with level black eyes, and very much a gentleman. At once Connor realized what Antone had meant when he had said Lily was fortunate in having the commander of the Californians take her from Marshall. Pico was no rake.

Only one of the captured Americans was in sight. He was Burgess, a dragoon who had accompanied Godey. Several Californians, not nearly so evil-looking as Connor had assumed, stood to the rear of their leader, their eyes absorbing the Americans. Suddenly Marshall strode from behind the willows, his voice snarling at once!

"That's him, Don Andreas. That Sergeant there. He stole the girl I rescued."

Connor stepped forward. "You're a damned liar! You stole her, you dirty dog!"

Marshall lunged across the space, but Don Andreas Pico cut between the two glaring men. "Quiet, *Señor* Marshall! There is a way to settle this." He turned to Emory. "You have but one captive, sir. For him you may have Burgess."

"I want Godey," Emory said.

Pico smiled. "No, we do not free a man of Godey's strength. One common soldier for another. You may have Burgess."

Burgess joined Emory; and the captured Californian lost no time in scooting across to his dark comrades. Pico chuckled, went on:

"Unfortunately you have nobody to exchange for the *Señorita*. But possibly her release to you can be arranged. May I suggest a joust for the lady? Let *Señor* Marshall and the *Señor* Sergeant meet in combat. In the way of you *Americanos*. With the fists. If *Señor* Marshall is victorious the *Señorita* shall remain the prisoner of my women, as she is now. If *Señor* Marshall is not fortunate—Ah, the *Señorita* shall accompany the *Señor* Sergeant, if she so desires. Is that not fair, *Señor* Lieutenant?"

Emory, seeing the twinkle in Pico's dark eyes, smiled and asked: "How about it, Connor?"

"I'll murder you!" put in Marshall, his face red with rage.

"I'll knock your block off!" yelled Connor, doubling up his fists into tight knots.

"Let us have less wind and more action," Pico said, grinning. He stepped back, indicated a grassy flat, pulled a silk kerchief from a pocket. "Prepare, *Señors*. When I drop my kerchief—Ah, as you *Americanos* say, may the best *Señor* come out in the front."

Connor shed his blue jacket, handed it to Emory, who murmured: "Right in the belly, Connor. And tuck your chin in."

Marshall, stripped to the waist, his big chest sharply rising and falling, looked glaringly at Connor. Deep in his opponent's eyes Connor caught a faint flash of doubt, drawn there, perhaps, by the memory of the beating administered by the soldier when first they had met. Connor passed his gunbelt and Colt to Emory.

Don Andreas Pico spoke swiftly in Spanish, lifted the kerchief, let it fall.

Marshall fairly bounded across the space, his mighty arms spread to lock the lighter Connor to him. Connor met that rush, his body in a crouch, as he closed in under the grasping arms catching Marshall with a ripping left-handed punch in the pit of the belly. It drove a solid gust from the Yankee. Then Connor knocked Marshall's face upward and slashed him solid-knuckled across the eyes and watched him drop.

Marshall squirmed on the grass. His eyes were open, but dead, and the working of his mouth was strange to see.

"Get up!" yelled Connor. "I'm going to kill you!"

Marshall rolled over and tried to get up, but fell back, using his elbows for props. He spat out blood and a tooth and mumbled thickly. He tried to rise again, and couldn't. Connor realized that his first punch had temporarily paralyzed the huge Yankee from hips to knees.

DON ANDREAS PICO turned to Connor, openly admiring the soldier. "It is enough, *Señor*. It is an art. So simple when one knows how and where to hit." He spoke to a Californian. "Pedro, you will please to bring the *Señorita*.. And you, Manuel and Lugo, carry the *Señor* Marshall to Doctor Fernandez." He bowed to Emory, smiling and saying: '*Adios. Vayan con Dios.*"

Then Don Andreas Pico had faded into the willows, on the heels of his men. Connor, buckling his gunbelt, asked: "What was that last he said?"

"Go with God," murmured Emory. "You know, Connor, I hate to fight a fellow like him. He's a gentleman."

"Here, yes. But he wasn't at San Pasqual. I figure he sort of wanted to see Marshall licked."

Just as he finished speaking, Lily came running from the willows. She was laughing and crying all at once and, before Connor was aware of her purpose, she was pulling at him, her face coloring, and her parted lips a frank invitation.

"Oh, Bucky!" she cried. "I was afraid! I didn't know if you were alive or dead."

Bucky Connor ran through several shades of pink, finally telling her that he was glad to see her again, and concluding matters by hurrying her up the hill ahead of the chuckling Burgess and Lieutenant Emory. From her he learned of Godey's safe arrival in San Diego, he and the others having been captured on the return journey.

His blue-black eyes considered her a moment before he asked: "Marshall get rough with you?"

Her expression remained unembarrassed and undisturbed. "No. He took me straight to Pico's camp. Don Andreas was furious at him. He sent me to stay with the women. Marshall raved, but that's all the good it did him."

"I'll beat the block off Marshall yet," growled Connor, his straight stare failing to see the quick break of a smile across her cheeks.

They entered the camp and went to where Antone waited beside the covered wagon, his black eyes glowing with an inner light. Kit Carson hurried from Kearny's tent, laughing and saying:

"How d'ye do, Miss. I'm shore happy t' see you ag'in."

"And I'm happy, too," Lily returned, smiling at Carson, then at Connor. "I'm not taking chances on getting captured again."

"Not by no yeller-bellies, you hain't. But my gran'pappy allus said thet th' sooner young folks gits married, th' sooner they hain't apt t' either of 'em git kotched by somebody else."

It was Lily's turn to blush, although Connor ran a strong second. Carson left them to join Emory and Burgess and shortly after he called to Connor. Leaving Lily at the covered wagon, Connor hurried to the little group of officers gathered around Burgess.

From Burgess they learned of the safe arrival of Godey and his men in San Diego, of the capture by Californians on the return trip. As to whether Commodore Stockton was sending aid Burgess had no knowledge. In a sense the mission of Godey had failed.

"We can't hold out here until the wounded have recovered," said Lieutenant Beale. "It would take half our fighting force to transport them. For one, I'll volunteer to get to San Diego and have the Commodore send relief at once."

"Now yo're talkin'!" exploded Carson. "I'm a-goin' with you."

"So'm I," declared Connor.

"We can cut our way through," declared Kearny.

"Gineral!" burst out Carson. "Eff'n thet's the way you wanta git disgraced fer life, jes' go ahead 'n' git yore army wiped out. Whut beats me is the way you kin walk smack-dab into hell."

"Why, you insolent—" Kearny began.

"Carson's right, sir," Lieutenant Beale interrupted.

Kearny glared at the navy lieutenant, grumbled, "All right, have it your way. Carson. You and Connor may go," and stalked into his tent.

Connor returned to Lily, finding her chatting and laughing with Antone. She turned at Connor's approach, and all the happiness in her died with the first look at his face. His lips were pulled to a long edge and there was a flashing gleam in his eyes.

"Bucky, what is it?" she cried, her body still and tight.

"Nothing—nothing at all. Carson and Beale and I are slipping through to San Diego to fetch help. We're leaving right after dark." His lips laughed and the rashness in him glowed hotter than before.

Lily dropped onto the wagon tongue, shaking her head. Then she was weeping, definitely. Her shoulders lifted and settled slowly and she got a grip on herself. She lifted her face to him, tears bright in her eyes. She murmured: "Please, Bucky, don't go. You won't ever come back."

He took her arm and said: "Sure, I will. Sure."

"You won't even get there. You know it." She noticed how blue-black his eyes were, flame burning so brilliantly in them. "You haven't asked for anything, Bucky. I know you wouldn't, but—"

"How do you know?"

"I do. It's just one of those things a girl knows. I didn't mind your kiss. I won't mind anything, Bucky. If - you'll not go."

"Aw, now, you oughtn't to talk like that. I'll be back."

She searched his face and, over a little catch in her throat, murmured: "Don't you love me?"

His answer came out swiftly: "Love you? You know I love you!"

"Then that's all there is to it. Please stay here."

He didn't speak, but something in her eyes sobered him and he looked at her as a man would look at a woman fresh and desirable. He put one hand on her shoulder and her expression showed defeat. He was thinking how life would beat her down, and knew that his going marked the end of a hope now so alive in her.

He said soberly: "You wait for me, Lily. I'll get there and back," and turned sharply and walked away.

Lily held her hands in her lap, the fingers interlaced and white under pressure. She glanced at Antone, seeing the stillness of the Indian lad's face. She said huskily: "If he goes, he'll never come back. I *can't* let him go!"

Antone studied her a time, murmured: "If Antone can do anything to help, *Señorita,* say so."

She reached and drew him to her. She whispered: "There is. Oh, so much you can do." A long minute afterward, she released the lad, climbed into the wagon, and motioned for him to follow.

WHEN Connor and Carson, along with Beale and the latter's Delaware Indian servant, crept down the westerly slope of the hill, night lay wild and deep across the flats and the barren hills beyond Snooks' rancho. Murky moonlight was a tarnished silver that touched but could not dissolve the earth's vast blackness. Connor was remembering, the parting kiss Lily had given him. It had gone through him like a shock, telling him more than anything the girl could have said. He had sought to tell Antone goodbye, but gave no particular thought to the lad's absence.

All around the hill rode the Californian sentries, lancers in lines three deep, the long, sharp blades swinging against the sky. Connor, trailing Carson through tawny grass, knew discovery would be the end of the messengers, and the Army of the West. At the slightest suspicion the alarm would sound and lancers would swarm about them like hornets. From somewhere ahead a voice called a challenge in Spanish, and at once came the sound of running hoofs. Through the pale dark two horsemen made rushing vague shapes and Connor, detained by Carson's backward reaching hand, saw the Californians swallowed by a dip in the land. Murmur of voices reached them. Then enormous quiet settled down.

Again Carson stole forward, leading the way to where the grass thinned out and was lost in a wide wash. Here gravel and rocks and brittle brush prevented silent movement forward in boots or shoes. Carson hunkered, motioning the others to him. He whispered.

"Thar's no sense tryin' to cross with shod feet. Injun thar's got moccasins. But us fellers is gotta shed leather. Tuck 'em in yore pants, or som'eres."

Connor removed his boots, loosened his belt and bound them to him. Presently Carson led out again, the Indian bringing up the rear. Sharp stones cut Connor's feet and once his canteen rattled against a rock. Instantly Carson stopped, the four of them frozen lumps on the gravelly surface. Carson discarded his canteen, the others following suit. Again they crawled forward, cactus spines stabbing their hands and knees. A lancer heaved his horse up the wash bank, not fifty feet from them. All four of them flattened out.

Connor held his breath, certain the Californian could hear his heart hammering. The lancer rode on, spoke laughingly to another, and received a soft answer.

"Por Dios, the *Yanqui* is a fool."

Once more Carson went forward,

squirming along on his belly, now and then stopping to listen. Connor, his hands raw and bleeding, his knees and legs stinging under the prick of collected cactus spines, hung close on the heels of the Mountain Man. After hours, it seemed, the first and inner line of sentries rode a circle behind them. But ahead was the more active second line, its lancers, having more ground to cover, riding swiftly to and fro.

Time and again Connor saw Carson stretch on the ground, the other three at once doing likewise. Frequently a lancer passed within a few yards of the party and Carson decided the possibility of at least one of their number getting through would be greater if they separated. Even as they considered this, Don Andreas Pico rode within earshot, his commands coming distinctly.

"Keep a sharp watch. *Señor* Carson is a wolf. If the fool *Americano* general sends for aid, Carson will carry the message. Scour the flats and the far hills."

"The Yanqui, Marshall, wishes to see you, Don Andreas," a lancer said.

"Marshall is a filthy dog," declared Pico. "He knows where to find me."

"But Don Andreas——" began the lancer.

"I do not wish to soil my hands with Marshall," Pico cut in. He galloped away.

The Californian sentries renewed their zeal. They rode everywhere, and Beale lost all hope of either advancing or retreating.

Carson cheered him up, told the lieutenant to take his Indian and work toward the river and, once it was reached, follow it to the sea. There was no fear in Beale, but he was a naval man, his instinct for direction on land poorly developed. So finally Carson set off with Beale and the Indian, after giving Connor a rough lay of the route to San Diego and suggesting the sergeant take a circuitous route by way of Snooks' rancho.

CONNOR waited until the others were some distance away. Then, worming forward on his belly, he inched his way between sentries. His chest was scratched. His elbows and knees, his now bare feet, were pincushions of cactus needles. Stones cut his flesh, thorns slashed him. But he

crept on, stopping, going forward, stopping again. A lancer galloped by, so closely that the odor of his cigarette was a distinct and tantalizing smell.

From a little depression he surveyed the hills ahead. Snooks' rancho lay hard against them, the third line of sentries between him and the dark lumps that were the buildings. Now, the wash to his rear, Connor found the going somewhat easier, although his feet were torturing him at each step. He sat down to pluck cactus spines from his flesh. And it was then that he heard the murmuring ahead.

A soft voice was indistinct, but an unmistakably masculine one answered: "You keep your promise, Lily. I'll see Pico don't kill him."

Connor was almost shocked into crying out. Lily! Through his mumbed brain one thought stabbed. She had got to Marshall some way; she had made a deal with the Yankee; she was trading herself for Marshall's promise to capture Connor and have Don Andreas Pico hold him a living prisoner. Then Connor heard Lily saying:

"I'll keep my promise, Bill. We'd better tell Don Andreas to have all his riders search the flats between here and the hill. I'm going to ask Don Andreas to spare Bucky. I just know he will."

"I'll kill him if you don't keep your promise," growled Marshall.

Connor could hear the resignation in her even, colorless words: "You do your part, Bill, and I'll do mine."

Marshall spoke again, too indistinctly for Connor to understand; but Lily's angry and muffled cry and the sound of a tussle drove all else from Connor's mind.

Heedless of lancers, Connor raced toward the girl struggling in Marshall's arms. She was fighting soundlessly, yet with the ferocity of a tigress. Marshall tried to wrestle her to the ground, but she sunk her teeth into his thumb.

Connor, as he ran limping across the space, pulled his Colt, lifted it, but did not fire. Not for fear of drawing the already alarmed sentinels; for fear of hitting Lily. Marshall was a grunting, swearing shape before him. He struck Lily with his fist, and shoved her sprawling.

"You damn'd wench!" he snarled, kicking at her.

Connor panted, "Marshall!" and brought

the big Yankee around with the word.

Marshall's mouth flew open, astonishment holding him in its grip for a split-second. His bellow started to raise an alarm. And then it was that Connor brought down the barrel of his Colt. It struck the huge Yankee's skull with a brutally crunching sound.

His bellow stifled in his throat, Marshall dropped as if struck on the head with a hammer. He lay on his back, his knees hauled up, too dazed for the moment to do more than groan. Connor ran on, grabbed Lily by the arm, yanked her to her feet. He ran toward the hills, hauling her after him.

She pulled back, cried, "Over here, Bucky!" and swung him to the left. He saw a horse, knew it was Marshall's, and put on a burst of speed neither cut feet nor the flying girl, her skirts lifted to her hips, could retard.

Marshall was bawling lustily now, thus momentarily diverting the lancers now racing up. Seizing the horse's reins, Connor boosted Lily to the saddle, swung up behind her. He wheeled the powerful, long-limbed palomino—then swore grimly.

Directly in front of him was a lancer, his lance lowered, charging straight at him.

CONNOR whipped up the Colt and let go, the explosion breaking about him enormously. The palomino lunged and swerved, clearing the smoke. The lancer was down on his face and his horse had wheeled and had lit out at a dead run for Snooks' rancho.

A long yell, in Spanish, filled the night and somewhere a carbine laid down its flat report. Connor shouted, "Hang on!" and dug his bare heels into the palomino's flanks. The great horse bunched up and unraveled and Bucky Connor was traveling at a speed new to him.

The wildly galloping horse ahead caught the attention of a racing Californian, who wheeled and pounded up from Connor's right. Behind the flying palomino confused sentinels were yelling, although none made a louder roar than Marshall. The Californian pouring in on the right gripped Connor's interest. If he could get a horse for Lily they might escape.

Connor lifted his Colt, sent a ball at the Californian, and saw the horse stumble and heard it scream. Down it went, the Californian jumping clear and at once shrieking for help. Conor swore, gouged the palomino's flanks, and put his dependence on the superb horse's speed. They passed through Snooks' rancho at a head-long run, hit the road for San Diego a short distance beyond, and went thundering down it. Ahead of them tore the wounded Californian's horse. Behind them pounded the yelling pursuers.

The road ran the length of a narrow valley, slashed through a pinch in the hills, and began to twist upward. Connor glanced to the rear, saw no pursuers, and took the one slim chance of escape. He wheeled the palomino, sent it plunging and sliding down a grassy slope, and pulled up behind a willow clump on the bank of a narrow water run. Leaning forward, he partly covered the palomino's nostrils, thus muffling its blowing.

From far up the road came back the hoofbeats of the wildly galloping horse. Connor grinned. Now the Californians were sweeping along the road in hot pursuit of a riderless horse. Connor let go a long sigh, turned and faced Lily.

He grinned. "Lily, you sure played hell."

She tried to smile, but it wasn't much of a success. Then she was rubbing her face on his shoulder and sobbing and clinging to him. His grin fell away, but his voice was wonderfully tender.

"Aw, I'm glad you did, Lily. It's all right. We'll get to San Diego."

"We must hide till tomorrow night, Bucky." She sniffled.

"Nope. I got to get word to Commodore Stockton."

"It is thirty miles. Every pass—and there are many on the road — will be guarded. We must hide till tomorrow night. Then ride over trails in the hills." Lily brushed a sleeve across her eyes.

"Where'd we hide?"

"Why not Snooks' rancho? They will never think of looking for us so close."

"That makes sense. But I don't dare go back by the road."

She reached around his waist, locked her arms. "One of the old San Luis Rey *asistencias*—one of its outlying chapels— is just over the hill to our right. We can hide there."

"Reckon we better chance it," Connor

mumbled, turned the palomino up the bank. He kept to thick darkness under oaks as much as possible and, after a half-hour of slow and cautious travel, came to the deserted chapel.

The church was a long, low building with a great oak door, the walls of adobe so thick that the narrow windows looked like tunnels. Having watered the horse at a near-by spring, Connor staked him out to graze. Later he found a broken piece of pottery, in which Lily pounded up willow bark, added water, and made a sort of raw bread.

They sat beside each other in the open church door, eating the rather bitter paste. She spoke out of her thinking: "I didn't try to betray you, Bucky. I didn't think you could get through."

His eyes rested on her pale face a moment, then: "I understand. But how'd you get word to Marshall?"

"I sent Antone. He got back right after you left camp." She released a long breath, waited for him to speak. He didn't; and she hurried on: "I stole a mule."

"Then that was you they challenged out there?"

"Yes," she murmured. "I guess I was crazy, Bucky."

Connor showed her a glance full of remote laughter. "I've known you three days, Lily. I don't even know your last name. Not that it matters. You're taking mine, anyway. You don't know anything about me, either. But I reckon we know each other about as well as folks need to." He laid the saddle blanket across her lap. "You turn in. I'll watch."

All the next day they kept the horse in the chapel. While Connor slept, Lily stood watch. Nothing disturbed them. At dusk they saddled up, took hill trails toward San Diego, only once on the slow journey seeing signs of the enemy. However, they circled the camp fires near the summit of a pass and, near daybreak, slipped through Californian sentries scattered about on the hillsides of San Diego.

They took the road between the hide houses and the bay, where a frigate and a sloop slept at anchor. False dawn had given way to murky gray when an American sentry barked his challenge.

Connor soon convinced the sentry as to his purpose, was told that Lieutenant Beale and the Delaware Indian had arrived during the night.

"Lieutenant Beale lost his shoes." The sentry shook his head. "His feet hain't nuthin' but raw meat. Injun had moccasins, so he hain't so tuckered. Lieutenant Beale's plum' out'n his head. I never seen a deader live man. How'n great grief he got through 'em yeller-bellies 'round here is more'n I can figger."

Connor had a faint inkling of what Beale and the Delaware had suffered. His own feet burned and hurt inside his boots and he was sure they would have to be cut off. "Kit Carson showed up?"

"Nah. Not that I've heard of." The sentry openly eyed Lily.

"He will," Connor promised and rode on.

They entered a muddy and littered plaza, were stopped by a corporal of the guard, from whom they learned that Lieutenant Gray with one hundred tars and eighty marines had left the previous day to rescue the Army of the West.

ALL the adobe buildings lining the plaza were of one story save a pretentious two-story structure on a corner. This masqueraded as a hotel and Connor, thinking to leave Lily as a guest while he reported to Commodore Stockton, turned the palomino toward the hotel.

He stopped, stared, Lily's startled gasp telling him that she, too, was astonished to see Bill Marshall.

The big Yankee, his gaze on the naval vessels, was crossing the plaza. Connor scowled, mumbled, "Wait," and slid from the saddle. Just as he did that, Kit Carson limped from an alley, his shoulders slumped, his thin body held erect by nerve alone. Carson paused, came to a halt, interest showing across his sagged cheeks.

Connor picked his way toward Marshall, the sucking sounds of mud releasing his heels bringing the huge Yankee around. His eyes grew vast and round and stayed that way, while his mouth opened wider and wider, yet no sound coming out.

Connor saw Marshall carried neither gun nor knife and he began to suspect the Yankee had surrendered himself to Stockton to save worse than imprisonment by Don Andreas Pico. Connor glanced back. Lily was close to him on the horse and

Carson had moved forward to a spot nearby, the Mountain Man's weariness somewhat given way to anticipation. Connor took off his gunbelt, handed it to Lily when she came up, murmuring, "He wanted something from you. I'm going to give him something."

Marshall glanced wildly about, saw Carson, grinning, his rifle in the crook of his arm. The big Yankee flung his coat to the mud, let out a bellow, and charged Connor. Closing in, he tried to catch the sergeant in that bear-like hug, but failing in this, he brought over a looping right. It crashed through Connor's guard, caught him on top of the head, and sent him skidding through the mud, to drop on his seat.

Instantly Marshall rushed him, lifted a boot, aimed it for the soldier's ribs. Slithering about, Connor flung out an arm, hooked Marshall's kicking leg, and heaved. Up flew Marshall's heels. He smacked both shoulders into the mud, scrambled over and up, his face a dark and dripping smear. Connor, coming swiftly to his feet, waded into the sputtering Yankee.

Marshall struck blindly, the blow taking Connor on the shoulder. It stayed him, turned him, a bit. That was all. He whipped over a left, nicked Marshall's chin, and crossed a right. Mud from Marshall's face flew one way, he the other. He hit a puddle with a squashy plop, got to his hands and knees, shook his head.

"Get up! Get up, you two-legged skunk!" bawled Connor.

A greasy Mexican yelled from a saloon doorway: "Hola! *Señor* Beel ees geet the hell beat out from heem. Garcia! Conchita! Come for to see eet the fon!" He clapped his hands. *"Viva Americano soldado! Viva Estados Unidos!"*

Connor suspected the Mexican was motivated more by diplomacy than loyalty. But he had little time to consider the greasy one's purpose. For Marshall was up, coming forward, again displaying the bull-dog tenacity that gave the Yankee his lone claim to worth. He came in cautiously, one arm guarding his belly.

From the tail of his vision, Connor glimpsed the white roundness of Lily's face. True Irishman, he spat on his palms, rubbed them together, and went in to finish the job. Marshall, desperate, came alive and fairly exploded.

Marshall hit Connor on the mouth, laughing hysterically. Before the sergeant could straighten, Marshall hit him again. Connor felt his lips cut against his teeth. He took the next punch on his head, skidded, hauled himself erect. Marshall bolted forward, throwing sledge-hammer wallops.

Connor ducked, drove a left wrist-deep into the huge Yankee's belly. Marshall, "whooshed!" and Connor ripped a right to his chin, slammed a left to his jaw, and planted a right squarely on the button.

Bill Marshall spun completely around, pitched onto his face, and didn't even squirm.

"Eff'n you'd got licked I'd've licked you ag'in," stated Carson.

"Well, everything's all right, Kit. Everything." Connor slipped into his jacket, took the palomino's reins. "When you get to Commodore Stockton's headquarters rout out the navy chaplain and send him to the hotel. Reckon we can find a Californian woman to stand up with Lily. I want you to stand up with me."

"I'll fetch the chaplain," Carson promised, chuckling, his eyes twinkling up to Lily's rose-tinted face. "I'm talkin' special to you, Miss. Seein' you, no man could lay Bucky blame. I seed it a-comin' when you two sot eyes on one 'nother. You'll git 'long all right with the yeller-bellies an' you won't never go back to the yander east. Come a few yars an' this is a-gonna be a fine land."

With that Kit Carson trudged off through the mud. Connor smiled up to Lily and saw her bright eyes and her restless lips. The whirl of emotions between them was like a gust of quick wind, carrying away all but the strong interest locking them.

Connor struck off toward the hotel, leading the horse. He glanced back at Bill Marshall without any particular feeling, went on. A few seconds ago he had wanted to kill the Yankee. Now it was different, although Bucky Connor had no reason to suspect then that four years later he would stand in this same plaza and see Bill Marshall hung by the sheriff for murder.

He stopped before the hotel, lifted his arms, and tightened them about Lily when she dropped from the saddle. Arm in arm they turned into the hotel.

The Pilgrim Pistolero

By JAMES P. OLSEN

Pilgrim was his name, this whang-leather, Colt-heeled trail hand. A Texas pilgrim, if there's any such a brand!

BILLY PILGRIM leaned back against the bar, one trim boot heel hooked over the brass rail. Sipping his drink, he seemed to be giving his whole attention to a friendly game of faro going on at the nearby table.

Outside, whoops and yells told of another trail herd crew that had been paid off. . . . Texas men, those, even though they didn't all hail originally from the Lone Star State. It was a badge of courage, toughness, gunplay, to be called a Texas man.

More than a hundred men had come in with that big trail herd. The rest of the morning, afternoon, night, and for days thereafter, they would drink and play—and kill. "Show the dam' Kansas law we ain't havin' no blab off of tin star toters," was the by-word.

Law . . . Billy Pilgrim's lips curled scornfully. Young, this six-footer who wore his pants outside his boots, dented his sombrero in the front and wore one ivory-handled .45 down low enough so that it showed it meant business. Billy's mind went back . . . Texas. . . . His lean face hardened and his greenish eyes smoldered as he thought.

There had been a crooked sheriff, held under the thumb of a fast gunman. Billy Pilgrim was promised the pen if he gunned the sheriff's "boss." And would have taken a killing if he hadn't. Pilgrim, being nobody's damned fool, pulled out. He attracted little or no attention there in Dango, where hell and free living were on the loose. He wanted to attract none. Some day, he figured, a certain gent might come along. And when he did, law or no law, it would be a gunsmoke proposition.

Someone jostled Billy, slopping his drink over his hand. He turned, to stare down at the man who had pushed in behind. A smallish sort of man, with a snub nose, wide mouth and plenty of freckles that ran clear up to the roots of his dull red hair.

"Sorry, *amigo*," the little ranny apologized. "Let me buy another one. I need some hombre to drink with, anyhow." Billy smiled slowly, then nodded. He studied the other, noted he carried no gun —and that he was dressed like an Eastern dude.

"My name," the little man said, "is Brick Doul. I'm sort of a sightseer, uh-huh."

"Name's Billy Pilgrim, an' I'm likewise uh pilgrim in uh strange land." Billy saw no reason for not giving his own name. For a moment, the little man squinted, frowned, his eyes narrowing. Billy wondered. . . .

"Sure," Brick continued to talk, as if he were lonesome and longed for the sound of a voice, even his own. "I come down from east an' north."

"Did?" Billy nodded politely. "Well, pard, I'd stop slingin' them Mex words around—if I wanted anybody to be'lieve that!" Billy grinned. Slowly Brick grinned back.

"Kittling's cut a-loose ag'in," somebody called from outside. "Rim an' Joe's hazin' some ranny out uh the Brown House." Shots sounded from down the street. Men pushed toward the door, carrying Billy Pilgrim and Brick with them.

DOWN the street, in front of a sagging three-story wooden hotel building, a man was backing into the street, slamming shots at the front door. Glass tinkled as someone shoved a shotgun through a front window. The bellowing blast of the heavy gauge gun drowned out the crack of the six-shooter. Little puffs of dust spouted from the clothes of the man in the street. He left his feet and rolled in the thick dust of the street.

Rim Kittling, shotgun in hand, stepped out through the broken window to stand on the porch of the Brown House. Younger of the two Kittlings, Rim was meaner than his older brother Joe, when it came to hasty shooting. But not as deadly when it came to long-drawn gunfare.

They had a following, those Kittlings. Dodge, Ellsworth, Caldwell—all the cow towns of a flaming frontier, they made, dealing poker and faro bank. And where they went, they ruled the roost. Cotton hair standing on end, piggy eyes blazing, Rim strutted up and down the porch, demanding to know if the dead man had any friends who wanted to take it up.

"Dam' right!" A tall man stepped into the street in front of the hotel. Another stepped out behind him. Nebraska hombres, these gents. Now the Kittling followers, at least a hundred of them, commenced to let their hands stray toward gun butts.

The two Nebraskans came toward the hotel steps. Without warning, a rifle cracked from the hotel door; a half dozen six-guns flared from both sides of the street. Joe Kittling, rifle in hand, leaned on the door and chewed his tobacco steadily. In the crowd, a half-dozen guns were slipped back into holsters.

Joe, pock-faced, glowering, like a huge ape, shambled out on the porch. "Listen!" he bellowed. "We aims to run this here dump to suit ourse's. *Sabe?* She's open season, right now. Any law that tries to take this up, I'm offerin' a hundred pesos apiece for their skelps!"

A cheer went up from the crowd. Some hellion whooped and flashed his iron. A paunchy town marshal dived headfirst around the livery building a few doors down the street. Lead riddled the corner of the building. The marshal made it in safety.

"Our game's still goin' on inside," Joe bellowed. He turned and went back into the hotel.

A man came out of the little mercantile store behind Billy Pilgrim. In his shirtsleeves, unarmed, he pushed past. Billy reached out and grabbed him by the arm, pulling him back. Of all the law force in this town, Billy respected the sheriff, who also owned the store. Not a gunfighter, but a courageous man, just the same. Billy knew him slightly.

"Ed, they'll kill yuh sure." Billy shook his head. "Best let them be. Ain't the first town they've treed, them Kittlings."

"No, by gosh!" Ed Dance pulled away. "I'm going to get them."

Billy shrugged. It was none of his business. He strolled down a few doors, watching the sheriff as he went steadily along the board sidewalk. Open season on lawmen, with a price on their hides, but Ed Dance was unarmed, and they weren't shooting at him.

Men stood and watched him. No one spoke. For all the noise, Dango might well have been a deserted ghost town.

Dance mounted the steps. He stopped on the porch and called, loud enough for those in the gambling hall on the first floor to hear:

"Joe, you and Rim come on out and give up. I'm taking you to jail."

Joe appeared in the door, eyes wide with amazement. "Better get your gun and come back, Ed," Joe growled.

"I don't use a gun. You know it," Dance retorted. "You coming?"

"No, we ain't coming!" Rim appeared at the broken front window again. His shotgun was in his hands. Without warning, he fired. Ed Dance staggered, swayed, pitched backward and rolled down the steps into the street.

SOMETHING snapped inside Billy Pilgrim then. A fine hombre. Ed Dance. And he'd been murdered. Not even armed. Billy ran forward and gathered Dance up in his arms. Joe eyed Billy narrowly, then turned to cuss Rim. The crowd fell back. Face bleak, Billy carried Dance into his little store. A deputy sheriff cowered by the counter. The marshal, still white and shaking, was ready to crawl under the counter.

"Lord!" he moaned. "This is awful!"

Billy laid Dance gently on the counter, whirled on the marshall and the deputy. "Yuh're right, she's awful!" he snarled. "Me—I'd shift muh hawg-laig an' bring them skunks in."

"Pilgrim!" whispered, that word. Billy whirled.

Dance had opened his eyes. Weakly, he plucked at the badge on his vest. "Take it," he muttered. "D-dam' rabbits!" Dance relaxed, then stiffened. Gently, Billy covered him with sacks. He stood looking at the badge in his hand; rubbed a spot of blood off on his trousers leg; looked at the shaking deputy and the marshal.

Suddenly, Billy saw why he should take up a fight that was not at all rightly his own. He pinned on the star.

"Got one for me, pard?" Billy looked up. Brick Doul was grinning at him. Brick Doul had his coat pulled back. A .45 said "hello" under both armpits. Without a word, Billy stepped up to the deputy, jerked the badge off his vest. The deputy was glad enough to be rid of it. Billy flipped it to Brick. Without a word, they stepped outside.

In the middle of the street, Joe Kittling was bringing up a horse toward the Brown House. Even their friends hadn't liked the deal Rim had pulled. Rim stood on the porch, cursing and begging someone to try to get him, waiting for Joe to bring up his horse.

Easily, neither walking slow nor fast, Billy Pilgrim, new law force leader of Dango, stepped into the middle of the street. Brick continued on down the sidewalk. Billy, oddly, wondered why this redhead had called for cards in this game. Wondered who and what he was.

The men who milled in the street paid no attention to the pair, unaware of the badges they now wore. Not until Billy called out to Joe Kittling to let go the reins of the horse.

"I'm takin' Ed Dance's job, Kittling," Billy called. "Either give up an' come tuh th' *juzgado*, or fight it out right here."

Joe had seen Billy Pilgrim several times, knew him by name, knew him for a silent young hombre who picked no quarrels, yet carried himself in such a way that no one else felt like picking them with him. Joe dropped the reins of the horse he led. In his right hand he carried a shotgun. Now he gripped the barrel with his left hand, holding the gun across his chest.

O N the porch, Rim had backed up against the side of the hotel. His eyes were wide, his mouth gaping. He stared in a mixture of amazement and rage at Brick Doul. Brick, eyes squinted to mere slits, hands folded across his chest, mounted the bottom step.

"Told you I'd foller you," Brick growled, taking another step up the short flight.

"Joe!" Rim yelled. As he yelled, both for help and to try to startle Brick Doul, he drew his six-gun. Like magic, six-guns appeared in the hands of Brick Doul. His right-hand gun crashed lead and smoke, his left gun . . . Right and left again. Rim Kittling sagged, buckled as the second slug hit him, whirled around at the third and plunged to the porch floor as the fourth slammed into him.

Joe Kittling forgot himself so much as to look up at the porch. Billy Pilgrim stepped swiftly toward him, stopping a scant six feet from him, hand on his gun butt. "All right, feller," he droned. "Do somethin', or give up."

Behind Joe, a hundred men who would trigger guns for him. But right now, with two smoking guns in his hands, covering one side, and already having showed he could use them, Brick was holding a good position. No man knew but what *he*, out of all that blood-mad mob, might be next. Too, there was that Pilgrim ranny, soft-spoken, a face that showed he meant business, ready to crack down on Joe.

"If I don't—" Joe began.

Billy did not look at his face. He kept his eyes on Joe's stomach, right at the top pants button. He watched Joe's wrists. If those wrists moved, showing that Joe was going to whirl that shotgun down, Billy Pilgrim figured he could bust that button first. Joe knew this. His stomach contracted. Billy Pilgrim chuckled.

"Drop 'er, Kittling," he grunted. Joe hesitated, then tossed the gun away.

"You win," he said gruffly.

B RICK came down the steps. Billy put Joe in front of him and headed toward the little wooden jail. Brick marched back of them both. Stunned the crowd for a moment. Before they could rouse, the jail door closed behind the three. Billy sent a man running for a justice, opened the door to admit him when he came in, setting up his court at the jail desk.

Joe rolled a cigaret and leaned back in a chair. He looked at Brick.

"You ain't gunnin' for me, then?" he questioned, seeming to hold no malice against Brick for killing his brother.

"No," Brick shrugged. "I never was. It was Rim that done shot my pard, down in Texas. Told you I'd get you for it—both of you. Well, Rim's dead. You can sweat on it."

"Not me," Joe shook his head. "That's Rim's hard luck. But you'll catch hell, if I can see to it. Texas Rangers ain't no business shootin' men in this State."

"I ain't a Ranger, time being," Brick grinned. "Happens I'm a deputy of this here place. I got plenty rights. I done her according to law. *Sabe?*"

"So that's why you pitched in?" Billy Pilgrim chuckled. "Wanted tuh do her all proper?"

"Same as you do," Brick answered.

Again Billy Pilgrim wondered . . . Brick had a tale to tell, later on.

Dirty Pringle, the justice, rapped on the desk with a gun butt. He had a poker game he wanted to get back to. "Charges?" he demanded truculently.

"Murder!" Billy snapped.

Dirty hesitated. Joe Kittling had winked at him. "Reckon not," Dirty declared angrily. " 'Twas Rim what killed them hombres. 'Rest him, 'fya wanta get a killer. I'm chargin' you with disturbin' the peace, Joe. Fine'll be twenty-five bucks."

"Got it right here in my pocket," Joe laughed, hauling out a roll of bills.

"I'm chargin' him with attempt tuh murder, then. I demand he be locked up," Billy snapped. "Yuh got *thet* in yuh pocket?"

Suddenly, Billy shut up. Brick was shaking his head and frowning at him. "Changed my mind," Billy declared.

"Thanks," Joe said dryly. "Better be careful, you two. Booger's liable to get-cha." He stalked out, Dirty after him.

"How come yuh throw yuh loop tuh say 'no'?" Billy demanded of Brick.

"Feller, you're the hombre that was crossed up by that law down in the Pan-handle, some time back," Brick said. "I happens to know, because I was one of the Rangers what was sent in to keep law when that sheriff was kicked out, few weeks back. I heard about you," Brick intoned softly.

"Also happens the Rangers want that Big Shade, too."

"Yuh ain't a Ranger, right now," Billy reminded him. "Yuh're just uh deputy tuh uh ex-cowpoke, trail herder an' saddle tramp."

"And gunman with plenty guts!" Brick added heartily. "But listen—I shook my head because I got an idea. I'm quittin' you. *Sabe?* Maybe, now, if somebody was to slip it to Joe that you'd run from a gunie called Big Shade, Joe might get this here gunie up here, just to make you crawl. Joe's afraid to gun you now. He wouldn't have his friends do it, hardly. He'd think Shade would make you get down on your belly and lick dirt."

Billy Pilgrim gripped Brick's hand. "If it would work . . ." he almost whispered the words. Brick looked at him queerly.

"They say they ain't no man faster'n Shade," he said.

"How do I know?" Billy snapped. "I ain't tried it, have I? Shade tried to make me fight, an' I didn't dare, right then. Wanted tuh make me crawl; figgered the whole thing out. He ain't sure uh himself, looks like."

"Then," Brick decided, "we try to keep the name quiet."

EVEN Dango had its fill of killing for a few days. Billy Pilgrim had nothing to do in his new job. A job he held down alone, since Brick had left him. Brick was sitting in the game at the Brown House, having sold his guns to Joe Kittling, making up for the man he'd killed.

And down in the Indian Territory, word reached Big Shade that there was a lawman in Dango who was posing as the kingpin of them all; also word to the effect that Joe Kittling would pay some good gunie a nice pile to rub him out.

Big Shade, a bull of a man, scar-faced, dark-complexioned, vicious as a blind rattler, cussed and raved as he rode north. No gunman in the world could stand against him. That is, all but one. Shade had never tried his hand against that one, the wanderer known as Pilgrim Billy Parks. He'd fixed it, when Pilgrim Billy Parks was in his neck of the country, so he wouldn't have to meet this Bill gunie.

Pride forced Shade to Dango; want of money furnished a further urge. He rode fast. He stopped to talk to no one on the trail. Those who knew or had heard of Big Shade would not have cared for his company, anyhow.

It was evening, getting dark, the day Shade hit Dango. He flopped out of his saddle in front of the Brown House. Hitching at his gun belt, he stalked in, calling out for a hombre named Joe Kittling. Joe tossed down a poker hand and pushed back his chair.

"I'm the guy," he announced. "You Shade?"

Shade didn't answer. He was staring, wide-mouthed, at the man who stood to one side, watching the game. Pilgrim Billy Parks! Billy was paying no attention to Shade, ostensibly. Under his sombrero brim, though, he saw every move Shade made. Shade swallowed hard, then pretended he hadn't seen Billy. Brick, sitting in the game, winked at Billy.

"Yeh, I'm Shade," the big man growled at Joe Kittling. "I rid up here to notch my gun with a bad lawman. You want him out of town tonight—in the mornin'—or just want me to kill him?"

This wasn't the way Kittling wanted it played. He cursed the luck that caused Billy to be in the Brown House when Shade pulled in. Nothing now, though, but to carry it through. "Any way suits me," Joe answered.

"Well, I'll give him a chance to tail—mebbe." Shade swelled out his chest and eyed those about him with open contempt—making sure he didn't look at Pilgrim. Shade wanted to get this job over with and get out of Dango. Shade had once seen this wandering gunie in action; the reason he had doubts. . . .

"Where's the skunk you want smoked out?" Shade growled.

"Right here, Shade." Billy stepped out to face Shade, letting his vest fall open so Slade could see his badge.

SHADE'S eyes strained wide. A sharp breath hissed through his teeth. Eyes all around him . . . Staring . . . Waiting.

He'd made his boast. If he crawled, a hundred lesser gunmen would ride his trail, knowing he'd lost his nerve. They'd get him.

Shade tried to make his voice sound strong. He leveled his finger at Billy. Maybe Pilgrim was also afraid. Maybe he wouldn't have to meet him.

"You be out of town before sunup," Shade warned. "If you ain't . . ." He patted the butt of his gun.

"I'll think it over, yuh mangy coyote." Billy looked at Shade closely, a thin, mocking smile on his lips. He turned and went out. A buzz of conversation ran through the crowd. It looked like their fine law officer was backsliding.

A thin sneer on his lips, Brick got up. "I'm quittin', Kittling," he announced. "And I'm bettin' five hundred that Pilgrim kills *that!*" He jabbed a finger at Shade. Shade made a move as if he would draw a gun. Joe shoved him back.

"He's trying to get you wound up with him, too," he warned. "Keep your iron cool until morning. I think this whole thing is framed! And I'll take that bet."

"Ain't bettin' you, Kittling. Something tells me you'll be dead, maybe, comes time to pay off that bet. Anybody else?"

A dozen men rushed to cover the bet. Leaving Joe and Shade staring curiously after him, Brick went out and joined Billy at the jail.

Shade went upstairs, undressed and tried to sleep. He couldn't. He tossed and

rolled, and wished he dared drink, but was afraid to. He vowed to kill Joe Kittling, if he downed Pilgrim. If . . . Shade cursed his doubt, got up and sat on the side of the bed and smoked nervously. Would Pilgrim show up in the morning? More doubt that made Shade almost sick at his stomach.

An hour before sunrise, Joe Kittling tapped on his door, shoving it open and coming in. He looked at Shade's half-wild appearance, then at the litter of cigaret stubs on the floor.

"Shade," he grunted, "if you don't get him, he'll get me for framing this on him. How—"

"You go to hell!" Shade snapped, tugging on his sombrero. "I'll get him—if he shows up."

"He'll show, don't worry," Joe remarked as they left the room.

"Who's worryin'?" Shade demanded. "Don't fergit who you're talkin' to." Joe eyed him keenly, shook his head.

DANGO ran wide open, even in that low hour before sunrise. No one had gone to bed. Men looked at Shade wonderingly as he went out with Joe and into the restaurant a few doors down the street. Other men were there, eating heartily, appetites whetted by excitement. Shade choked on his coffee. It seemed like his eggs and steak stuck in his throat. He wished he was back in The Territory. Other men could drink their coffee, eat their food, and think nothing of it maybe being their last meal. Shade pitied himself. He was sick.

Yet, he knew he was as good as Pilgrim. But was he *better?* That was the devil of it. Shade pushed back his food and rolled a smoke. His fingers trembled.

Men were standing out in front now. More stood down by the dinky jail. It grew gray outside.

Joe pulled a pint bottle out of his pocket and handed it to Shade. Shade growled, uncorked the bottle and drank deep. Felt better. Some of his confidence returned. He began to tell himself that Pilgrim had likely sloped in the night.

Another ten minutes. A streak of red over the Kansas plains. Five minutes. . . . Men were crowding into doors along the street.

It seemed to Shade that Joe Kittling's voice was funereal. "Come on and get him, Shade."

Shade, his heart seeming to be in the bottom of his stomach and hammering in his throat at the same time, walked slowly toward the door. Joe stepped back and went quickly out the back door of the restaurant. Another man, who'd been standing close to the restaurant door, slipped between two buildings, also quitting the street.

A rim of red that was the edge of the rising sun shot into sight. A roar welled up from the group at the jail. They scattered. Billy came out and carefully closed the jail door behind him, then stepped into the center of the street. Shade made strange whimpering noises in his throat, then stepped out into the street also.

His stumbling walk became a trot. Then, with a wild yell, he broke into a run, drawing his guns as he went along. Too far. His first bullet plowed dust to one side of Pilgrim, his next went wide. Then, quite suddenly, Billy stopped, dropped to one knee. His gun flicked out, the barrel rested on the raised left forearm. . . .

A GUN crackled; Billy went over backward, like he'd been kicked by a mule. Another gun. Men looked around, wondering. Billy rolled over, grabbed his gun. Prone, he thumbed the hammer, the shots blending in one long roll.

Big Shade pitched forward, fell, leaving puffs of dust in his wake as he skidded in the street. A man who has two bullets in his heart, and another in his head . . . doesn't get up . . . ever.

Billy dropped his gun, struggling to a sitting position. He was deathly pale; beads of cold sweat dewed his face. He clutched at his heart.

For the first time, those along the street had time to look for the cause of those other shots. Shade was dead; evidently Pilgrim was going fast. They looked and gasped. Joe Kittling reeled out from between two buildings, stumbled across the sidewalk and sat down hard.

He grunted, groaned with pain, trying to raise the gun clutched in a convulsive hand. Crouched, teeth bared, Brick Doul ran out after him, smoke wisping out of his two guns. He stood there, sobbing curses.

"Dirty coyote!" Brick choked. "Hid in that little alley and shot Billy. Wasn't Shade a-tall! I s'pected him, follered him. Damn you, get that gun up!"

Joe steeled himself for a last effort, jerked up his gun as he sat there beside the walk. A double roar of revolvers. Brick's hands jerked as the heavy sixes flamed again.

"Ha-a-uff!" Kittling moaned. One more shot. He fell over flat on his back, laid still, one leg drawn up under him.

"Shot Billy. . . . But Billy still got Shade," Brick cursed.

"Sh-shot—hell!"

Brick wheeled, cried out, running out to Billy, who had fallen over and now tried to sit up again. He grinned weakly at Brick and at the others who came yelling into the street. Even Kittling's friends were not sorry, after the stunt he pulled.

"Gosh, it hurts," Billy complained. He pulled back his shirt. Large as a man's hand, showed a swollen, angry red splotch over his heart. Bent, heavy dented, his badge fell from his shirt.

"Damn' nigh drove her through me." Billy got his first good breath in many minutes and wobbled to his feet. "Plumb paralyzed me, almost. But, huh, thet's once uh badge saved me."

"Anybody here want a nice job and a badge?" Brick inquired.

A half dozen men stepped forward. The Kittlings gone. . . . Sure, they'd welcome the easy job the Dango law business now offered. And it would be an honor to wear that badge.

"What we aimin' tuh do, Brick?" Billy inquired a little later as they sat in the restaurant. Billy winced as he moved his sore body.

"Glad you said 'we,' pard." Brick beamed. "An' if you leave it to me, I'd say we rolls our tails back Texas way. Rangers can use both of us."

Billy nodded emphatically. Texas sounded good.

"Just uh couple rovin' pilgrims," Billy declared, his mouth full of fried spuds.

Dango was willing to bet that pilgrim pistols were plenty medicine, no matter which way you took it.

FIRE BRAND

By WALT COBURN

Outlawed by outlaws! It was a lone and bitter trail that coyote-tagged Ross Tyler rode. But at its end was payment for the red-welted brand that only the grave could hide.

NOBODY knew how to tie a hangman's knot and this fact occasioned quite a lot of merriment among the crowd of men who had gathered there under the big tree. Even Ross Tyler, sitting his horse with his arms tied behind him, smiled faintly. It was sure comical that no man of all this lawless gang, most of whom were due to hang if ever caught by the law, knew how to tie that hangman's knot.

There was the rope slung over a low limb, its end dangling. It was a new hemp lariat that the owner said needed stretching. Its noose was fashioned with the regulation hondo knot.

There was Ross Tyler, tall, black headed, black eyed, sitting straight backed in his saddle, his arms tied behind his back. His lean, handsome face was a little pale, but otherwise he showed no emotion. There was a half smoked cigaret between his thin lips.

The man who held the bridle reins of Ross Tyler's big roan horse seemed more nervous than Tyler. He was younger than the rest of this outlaw pack. Scarcely more than a boy, though he had already killed two men in a gun fight. He had red cheeks and thick, curly yellow hair, and his eyes were as blue as a Montana sky after a thunder shower. His name, or the name that he used, was Gail Meadows.

Gail Meadows had come here to The Hole with a tall, sour-looking Texan. It was for the cold-blooded, brutal murder of the Texan that Ross Tyler was about to hang. The Texan and Ross Tyler had met before somewhere down south where they both hailed from. At first sight of one another in the saloon at The Hole, each had dropped his hand to his gun. But neither had drawn. By mutual consent, without a spoken word, they had let their grudge lie dormant. But every outlaw there at The Hole knew the signs. These two men were deadly enemies. When the time was ripe, they'd shoot it out.

Of Ross Tyler they knew little except that he was wanted somewhere in Texas for a killing or two. He had drifted up here to Montana with a cattle outfit, had been recognized and had sought safety at The Hole.

Of the Texan they knew but little more except that he had been mixed up in two train hold-ups down south and had killed a deputy sheriff.

L AST evening the Texan had gotten drunk. One of those sullen, surly, mean drunks. He had told the bartender that he aimed to kill Ross Tyler. Tyler had saddled up that morning and gone out after a deer. It had snowed and then cleared up so the tracking was good.

Before the afternoon sun had set behind the badlands the Texan had saddled up and quit The Hole, leaving Gail Meadows sitting in a poker game. The Texan had taken his guns. He had made the remark to the bartender that he aimed to bring in some big game and it wouldn't be deer either. He was drunk when he pulled out and had taken along a quart.

It was after dark when Ross Tyler got into camp. On his pack horse was tied a big blacktail buck. He made no mention of seeing the Texan.

The news had traveled that the Texan had set out to meet Ross Tyler and shoot it out with him. So when Tyler returned alone and when the Texan did not return at midnight, Gail Meadows, who had been drinking some, had tackled Tyler on the subject.

"If you killed my pardner, come out like a man and say so."

"I never killed the Texican son of a snake. If I had, I'd be proud tuh say so."

Gail Meadows had not pressed the question. But when daylight came he and two other men set out. They found the Texan's dead body in the drifts about five miles above The Hole. He had been shot twice in the back and brutally beaten around the face and head with a club. His pockets were empty of money. Even his jack-knife and watch were gone. But in the dead man's holster was his .45. It had never been drawn. The carbine in his saddle scabbard was clean of powdermarks. The man had been murdered without being given a chance.

A heavy snow had fallen during the night, obliterating all tracks. Only that the Texan's horse was near the spot, they might never have found the man's body until a Chinook had melted the snow.

Ross Tyler was, of course, under immediate suspicion. A thorough search of his bed in the bunkhouse had brought to light the dead man's watch. The jack-knife was also found under Tyler's tarp-covered bed.

Even there in The Hole where only outlaws live, cold-blooded murder is punished. Grudge fights should be settled openly. To kill a man as the Texan had been killed is to violate the outlaw code there at The

Hole. To rob his pockets is no less a crime.

So they had sat in judgment, those outlaws of The Hole. They had found Ross Tyler guilty and sentenced him to hang. Gail Meadows should have the honor of leading Tyler's horse out from under him, leaving him dangling there from the tree limb.

And now not a man among them knew how to tie a hangman's knot.

ROSS TYLER puffed on his cigaret and smiled thinly.

"That had oughta be done proper, boys. A man's entitled to the trimmin's. Cut my hands loose and I'll tie yore damn' knot."

This brought an appreciative grin from the crowd. They liked to see a man die game. Somebody loosened Tyler's arms and they lowered the rope for him to tie the knot. A man with a bottle handed it to the man about to be hanged and Ross Tyler took a big drink.

The sun had set and it was getting dark already there in The Hole. A raw wind was blowing and it was snowing a little. Ross Tyler's hands were numb with cold as he tied the knot. Then he adjusted the noose around his neck and put his hands behind him.

"Another drink, Tyler?"

"Don't care if I do."

He lifted the bottle. "Here's lookin' at yuh all, boys, for the last time."

His voice was not loud or blustering, nor was it trembling with fear. He might have been in the saloon, taking a casual drink. The crowd stirred uneasily. Tyler was acting almighty game for a low-down bushwhacking murderer. They liked his nerve.

"Just a minute, boys." It was Gail Meadows who broke the awkward silence. "Let's hold this thing off till tomorrow. I ain't satisfied."

There was a murmur of assent from the crowd. More than one man there wanted to believe that Ross Tyler was innocent.

Ross Tyler's face never changed expression when they took the noose from around his neck. Nor did he thank Gail Meadows by word or by glance. The black eyes under the level black brows were hard and opaque. The thin-lipped mouth never changed expression.

And that night, there in the saloon, the sentence of death was revoked. While Ross Tyler sat in the saloon under guard, the outlaws of The Hole gathered in a cabin nearby. When they returned to the saloon one of them carried a small branding iron. It was a bar-iron such as some of the big horse outfits used on their best blooded stock. The bar was a scant two inches long.

Ross Tyler, tied hand and foot to a big, heavy barroom chair, eyed the iron with narrowed eyes. His lean jaw muscles tightened. His smile was bitter, his eyes slitted and hard. For he read their purpose.

"I tied you sports a hangman's knot," he snarled. "Why don't yuh use it?"

"Because," said Gail Meadows, who was a little drunk, "we figgered this would suit yuh better. Yo're gettin' off lucky."

He took the little branding iron and, opening the door of the big barrel-bellied stove, shoved it in to heat.

"I'll live to kill the man that lays that iron on me," rasped Ross Tyler, his dark face livid now. "I'd sooner hang!"

Gail Meadows smiled, showing his even white teeth. "So we reckoned, Tyler."

II

THEY ripped off Ross Tyler's flannel shirt and the heavy undershirt beneath. The man fought them as best he could, but he was bound hand and foot to the heavy chair. Now he sat there, his eyes slitted and red-shot. His thin lips were pulled into a twisted, bitter line. His gaze never left Gail Meadows' face. That pink-cheeked, curly-headed, heavily built young giant grinned and took more drinks.

"Somebody in this outfit," said Ross Tyler savagely, "knows that I never killed that lousy Texican snake, though I aimed to kill him when the sign was right. One man here knows I'm innocent. I hope to some day find out who that snake is. When I do, I'll double the dose that I'm goin' to git. Have at it, men. Meadows, do yore brandin'."

He ended with a twisted grin.

The blue eyes of the cherubic-looking young outlaw were congested and ugly looking now. In his gloved hand he held the slender branding iron. His face was white, save for the red spots that stained his cheekbones. It gave him a clownish look, as if someone had daubed red paint on a white surface.

Ross Tyler lay back in his chair, his black eyes staring from under tightly pulled brows at this half-drunken young giant with the red-hot iron. The crowd had formed a circle now.

The bartender, an old-time outlaw and ex-convict, poured himself the first drink he had taken in a year. There was a queer look on his battered face. For the fraction of a moment his glance crossed that of the man about to be branded. He made a little signal. Ross Tyler's head shook sideways the fraction of an inch. The bartender with the battered, scarred face automatically poured a second drink into his empty glass.

Under the smoky kerosene lamp that swung from the ceiling, men's faces took on fantastic shapes in the shadows thrown by the lighted, untrimmed lamp-wick. Bearded, hard-eyed faces. Faces of men doomed to travel the outlaw trail forever. Faces of men condemned. Eyes watching to see how another man would stand torture.

A spur jingled with incongruous music. The heat of the stove from the opened door threw a reddish glow across that ring of faces. Like a stage setting for an act of "Faust."

The silence was broken only by the heavy breathing of those men.

There was the odor of sweaty, unbathed men who had come from the stables where they kept their horses. The stench of tobacco smoke gone stale, of bad whisky.

Grotesque shadows danced on the log walls. Shadows of men who would die by the gun or by the rope. Shadows of men marked for death.

The bartender with the scarred and battered face stood apart. His bleak eyes watched.

GAIL MEADOWS stood above the prisoner bound to the chair. Ross Tyler was naked to the waist. His chest, the chest of a fighter, moved up and down with slow regularity.

An ugly smile spread Gail Meadows' lips. The red-hot branding iron touched the tender flesh under that hairy chest.

There was a faint, sizzling sound. The man's torso twisted a little. Ross Tyler's face went white. The thin lips parted in a grimace that showed the strong white teeth that were clenched.

Gail Meadows grinned in a ghastly fashion. His congested eyes shot sidelong glances across the crowd. One or two of the men stepped back as if unwilling to witness more of this brutality.

A short, gritty laugh from Gail Meadows. Again the iron bit into the flesh.

Beads of sweat marked the face of the victim, but he gave no outcry. His eyes, terrible now in their reddish, slitted intensity, never left the face of Gail Meadows.

Letter by letter was stamped that word upon the chest of the man found guilty of murder.

Once the bartender with the scarred face reached for the gun under the bar. Ross Tyler's eyes intercepted the movement.

Now, across the chest of Ross Tyler, in flaming, blistering, torturous red, was branded the one word:

"THIEF"

Gail Meadows stepped to the rear door and threw the hot branding iron outside into the snow. The crowd of men, looking a little sick and avoiding each others' eyes, made for the bar.

It was the scar-faced bartender who cut Ross Tyler free. The tortured man thanked him with his eyes. His lips were pulled into a misshapen line. Not one groan, one cry for mercy, one curse or prayer or plea for aid had passed those tightly pulled lips.

Gail Meadows was with the others at the bar. He was drinking his whisky from the bottle without using a glass. The others stood a little apart from him.

The bartender tried to give Ross Tyler a drink. Tyler knocked it from his hand and then got to his feet. He stood there, naked to the waist, that red-lettered "THIEF" stamped on his chest. Then, walking steadily, he crossed the floor and opened the front door.

A gust of wind and snow halted him there. The snow from the storm-ridden night swept across him and in through the open door, sending its icy blast into the smoke-laden, hot room. For a long

moment Ross Tyler stood there, staring
out into the black storm that drove against
his naked chest. Then he stepped outside and pulled the door shut behind him.

III

ROSS TYLER rode alone into the raging blizzard. Out there in the swirling, snow-filled blackness, he bared his
tortured chest to the storm and moaned
through clenched teeth. The big, deep-
chested strawberry roan carried him on
along the drifted trail out of The Hole.

Minutes. . . . Hours. What was time
to this man who rode, half delirious with
pain, into a black, snow-swept night?
Ahead lay only that same kind of blackness that he had quitted at The Hole.
He was an outcast now. Even among the
outlaw pack that prowled along the dim
trails, he was a man unwanted. He was
branded by them with the iron of hate and
shame. He could ask no shelter among
outlaws. He was a man apart, a pariah.

There was a price on the head of Ross
Tyler. A price that made him shun the
towns and ranches where someone might
recognize him and turn him over to the
law that had put a bounty on his hide.
So he had roamed from Mexico to Canada along the outlaw trail. Sheltered,
fraternized, welcome to share their blankets
and their grub and their jug. Now that
was taken from him. The Hole, Brown's
Park, Lost Cabin, The Hideaway—all
were closed to him. Branded a thief by
his own kind, he was now alone. Alone,
half dead, his body afire and freezing at
the same time, at the mercy of the blizzard
that roared down out of the Canadian
Rockies.

They said that he had murdered a man
he hated and that he had robbed that
man's pockets. So they had told him to
go, after they had marked him with the
brand of shame. That brand would follow him to his grave.

Through gritted teeth he laughed into
the stormy blackness of the night. And
as he laughed he swore to himself that
before he was shot or hanged he would
repay that terrible debt the outlaws at The
Hole had placed upon him.

Who had killed that Texican? Who

had murdered that man from Texas
whose kinfolks had fought the Tyler tribe
through four generations? Who was the
murderer whose crime had been laid to
Ross Tyler? Not Gail Meadows. Because
that big, red-cheeked, curly-headed young
hellion had been sitting in that poker game.
But Ross Tyler knew that one of those
outlaws there at The Hole had murdered
the Texican.

How many men north of Texas knew
that Texican for what he was? How
many men, outlaw or sheriff, north of the
Mexican border, knew the name of that
man who had been murdered so brutally?
Not many. Not even a few men knew
that dead man's name. Did Gail Meadows
know? Not likely.

ONE man there at The Hole knew the
real identity of the murdered Texican. That one man was the scar-faced
bartender. That bartender knew, because
he was kinfolks to the dead man. A second or third or fourth cousin. They wore
the same name.

Ross Tyler thought back. Back fifteen years to a day when he had put on
his store clothes and had ridden into
San Angelo to the funeral of Colonel Jeff
Tyler, his father. There, at the barn,
when he stabled his horse, he had met a
man with a scarred face. A man in ragged
overalls and a hat that a tramp would
throw away.

"Yo're Ross Tyler?" this scarred,
ragged tramp had asked.

Ross had been in no humor to confab
with livery barn tramps. He had started
to give the derelict a short reply when he
met the eyes of the man. Eyes that had
once, perhaps, been blue, but seemed to
have been bleached out and faded, as if
they had stared too long in the sun. Or
else had been hidden too long from the
sunlight. Ross had paused, his hand in
his pocket. It was hard for Ross Tyler
to turn down a tramp.

"I'm Ross Tyler. What's the trouble, ol'
feller?"

"I bin a-waitin' fer yuh, Ross Tyler.
I'd like tuh attend yore pappy's funeral,
but I ain't dressed proper. A clean shirt
and overalls. I . . . Him and me went up
the trail together. Yo're young an' up-
standin'. I told yuh by the Tyler brand

on yore hoss. Me and yore ol' daddy was close friends, young man. Went up the trail together, him and me. Fifteen a month them days."

"Who are yuh?"

"Me?" And the bleak eyes seemed to take on a bitter sort of light that made Ross Tyler take a step backwards, although the older man had made no play for a gun.

"Yes. Who are you that knows Colonel Jeff Tyler? Name yore brand, old feller."

"I am Slocum. Jeff Slocum. Me and yore daddy was born on the same day and named after Tom Jefferson."

"Slocum?" Ross Tyler's black eyes had hardened. "Slocum?" he repeated.

"Jeff Slocum."

"My father," said Ross Tyler, dressed in his town clothes and come in from the ranch to attend his father's funeral, "was killed by a Slocum. A man named Zack Slocum. We're holdin' Zack's funeral when they fetch him in from down in Mexico. I ketched up with Zack last evenin'."

JEFF SLOCUM had shook his white head in a somewhat bewildered fashion. He pulled a skinny hand across the eyes that seemed to have lost their real color.

"I just got out last week," he explained in a monotone that seemed weary and colorless. "Just was turned loose. I been doin' twenty-five years in Federal prison. That Missouri train robbery, mind? I come here tuh San Angelo tuh look up my only friend, Colonel Jeff Tyler. Hell, son, me and him soldiered together with Quantrell. Yuh say Zack Slocum killed Colonel Jeff Tyler? Zack'd be Sarah's oldest?"

"Sarah's oldest, yes. Now I have to be goin'." Ross Tyler, bitter, his gun hardly cooled from the killing of his father's killer, started to turn away. But old Jeff Slocum had, with skinny hand, plucked at his coat sleeve.

"Me and yore dady soldiered together, son. I know nothin' of any quarrels. I . . . just got out uh the Federal prison. I'd be proud tuh go to Colonel Jeff's funeral if I had some decent clothes. I'll . . . I'll pay yuh back some day, son. Jeff was my best friend."

So Ross Tyler had met Jeff Slocum. Jeff Slocum, once an officer under the hard-riding, marauding Quantrell, went to the funeral of his old friend, Colonel Jeff Tyler, dressed in broadcloth and clean linen.

Jeff Slocum was the only Slocum at the funeral. He did not attend the funeral a few days later when they buried Zack Slocum. He had gone, even as Ross Tyler had gone, up the outlaw trail across New Mexico and Colorado and Utah, into Wyoming and from there into Montana to The Hole. And there, behind the pine bar, he had peddled his whisky, drinking hardly ever, living in his memories of other wilder and more prosperous days when the James boys were his friends and the West belonged to the hardest riders and the bravest fighters.

Now, as Ross Tyler pushed his roan through the black night, floundering, lunging ahead through the drift's, he thought of that day so long ago when he had given Jeff Slocum the money to buy a decent suit of clothes to go to the funeral of Colonel Jeff Tyler.

Ross knew that Jeff Slocum would find out who had killed that tall Texican named Bob Slocum. Jeff would find out just how and where that red-cheeked Gail Meadows stood. Because Jeff Slocum was a man. Twenty-five years in prison gives a man the deep wisdom of ten times that many years spent in freedom.

IV

SOMETIMES the big strawberry roan went down, floundering in a big drift, and Ross Tyler had to quit the saddle and wade through the heavy snow, hanging to the roan's tail.

The bite of the cold snow on his bare chest helped a little, for it cooled that searing pain where the branding iron had stamped in deep under the skin. The man's whole chest seemed afire, burning and throbbing. He gave the big roan its head and when he began to feel himself getting numb from the cold he took a chew of tobacco and swallowed it so that it would make him vomit and thus keep him awake. Easy enough for a man to freeze to death on a night like this.

He buttoned his shirt and coonskin coat and slapped his arms on his thighs. The roan horse kept on.

It must have been almost daylight when the roan horse stopped. Ross Tyler, more dead than alive, leaned across his saddle horn. The snow whirled around the horse and man. They were in the lee of a cow shed. Some winter line camp, no doubt. Ross Tyler slid from the saddle and stumbled through the heavy snow. It was pitch dark, but he managed to find the gate that led into the corral in front of the open shed. Luck favored him and he located the barn that joined the shed. He found a match and lit a lantern that hung from a wooden peg.

Two horses there in their stalls. There was a third stall that was empty and Ross Tyler unsaddled the roan with hands so numb that they could hardly untie the latigo. When the big roan had muzzled him with a cold, velvety nose, and when the man had rubbed that soft nose with his half frozen hands, the stout hearted animal went to eating hungrily.

The horse had saved the man's life. Some such thought was in the man's mind as he stood there in the stall. To him it seemed that this big roan gelding was his only real friend. He felt alone in a world that held nothing for him but punishment and grief. Punishment and grief and the hatred for the man or men who had caused that "THIEF" to be branded across his chest.

Sleep was impossible, but Ross Tyler dozed fitfully in the barn under saddle blankets that smelled of horse sweat. He kept his hand close to his six-shooter. The weapon was in his hand when a man entered the barn at dawn.

THE man was a cowpuncher who was staying at the line camp. At sight of this outlaw with a drawn gun, the cowpuncher's hands went up. It was just getting daylight and in that gray of dawn Ross Tyler's face, drawn with pain and fatigue, took on a ghastly appearance.

"What do yuh want?" asked the cowboy.

"Some hot coffee," muttered Tyler.

The cowboy grinned. "Listen, feller you don't need tuh throw down on a man here at this camp tuh git a cup uh java. Go on to the cabin, where my side kicker is gittin' breakfast. He'll take care uh yuh. Man, yuh look sick."

Ross Tyler put away his gun. "Sick? Yeah." He grinned in a grisly fashion.

"These ponies kin wait, feller. Foller me."

He led the way to the cabin. A tall, wide shouldered young cowboy in an old mackinaw. Their overshoes creaked on the dry snow. Smoke swirled from the cabin chimney. A lamp burned inside the cabin, lighting the frost coated window.

Ross Tyler stumbled across the threshold of the door on feet that were badly frost bitten. The man inside the cabin had gray whiskers and keen gray eyes. He had not lived in the badlands along the Missouri River for forty years for nothing. He knew Tyler for an outlaw from The Hole. But he made no mention of the fact. He looked at Ross Tyler's pinched, frost whitened face.

"But he'p this feller off with them boots and overshoes. His feet's been bad frost bit."

He filled a bucket with snow and brought it in. Then, with the air of a man who is about to make a supreme sacrifice, he reached under his tarp covered bed and brought out a gallon jug. Ross Tyler saw the look in the grizzled old cowpuncher's eyes and shook his head.

"I never use it," he lied flatly. "Coffee suits me."

The old cowpuncher glared at him and snorted. Then he proceeded to mix a steaming drink that was half whisky, half water.

The warmth of the fire sent pains into Ross Tyler's hands and feet and face. The two cowpunchers rubbed his feet and hands with snow. The older one made him take off his coat.

The hot drink was soothing. The pains were leaving his feet and hands. He felt almost drowsy. Exhausted, utterly weary from the pain and the exposure and the long ride, Ross Tyler dozed into a dead slumber. The older man nodded to his younger companion who went out to finish his chores at the barn.

The grizzled cowpuncher loosened the sleeping outlaw's shirt so that he might breath more easily.

Now he took a step backward, his keen old eyes tightening at their puckered corners. There, across the chest of the guest, was that angry red brand . . . THIEF.

EVEN as the man stepped back, Ross Tyler's eyes opened. His hand went to his bared chest. His black, bloodshot eyes glittered.

The outlaw got to his feet and reached his hand into the pocket of his blanket lined canvas overalls. He took out a crumpled handfull of banknotes and tossed one on the table without even looking at its denomination. Then he sat down and pulled on his boots and overshoes.

Neither man spoke. Ross Tyler put on his coonskin coat and his cap. The grizzled cowpuncher made no move to stop him.

"I'm obliged for what you done," said the outlaw. "There's some money to pay for it."

"To hell with yore money. Take it back."

"Just as you say."

Ross Tyler pocketed his money and let himself out of the cabin. The contemptuous eyes of the old cowpuncher followed him. At the barn the younger cowboy was whistling as he fed the horses.

"You ain't goin' so soon?"

"Gotta be on my way," said Ross Tyler flatly, and threw the saddle on the stout roan.

It was still storming when Ross Tyler left the line camp. The younger cowboy waved him farewell, but Ross Tyler did not even glance back. There was no sign of life at the cabin where the grizzled old cowboy was getting breakfast.

V

THE snow let up about noon and the wind quit blowing. The storm was over. Familiar landmarks stood out against a sky as gray as the wing of a goose.

Down the river was a place where an old reprobate sold whisky and ran a trading store. Ross Tyler felt the need of food and a slug of raw whisky in his stomach. He had stopped more than once at that saloon there on the river. It lay along the outlaw trail. By following the river down he avoided the heavy going of the drifted coulees and cutbanks. The river had been swept bare by the wind. The big roan was sharp shod and made good time. The ugly red welts on Tyler's chest had swollen and blistered so that the least touch of his heavy flannel undershirt was like the scraping of a sharp knife blade.

Tyler saw smoke coming from the cabin chimney as he rode up to the place there among the bare limbed cottonwoods on the river bank. He stabled his horse, eying with narrowed gaze the several saddle horses in the big log barn. He loosened his saddle cinch, but did not unsaddle his horse. A man could never tell just what sort of company he might meet here at what the breeds and cowboys called Whisky Tepee.

His six-shooter was in the outside right-hand pocket of his big coonskin coat. He kicked the snow from his overshoes and walked into the saloon.

Several men stood there at the bar that was made of rough pine boards. A short, white whiskered old man with round, wide shoulders passed out drinks with thick, freckled hands that needed washing. He nodded to Ross without calling him by name or showing any particular recognition. That was his way. It never paid to call men by their names here at Whisky Tepee. Especially when there is a stock detective standing at the bar.

"Whisky?"

Ross nodded. "Whisky. Give everybody a drink."

The four men at the bar had shed their overcoats and chaps and were evidently there for a while. The stock detective from Choteau County eyed Ross with more than passing curiosity. Strangers were always under suspicion down here on the river where beef steers had a habit of vanishing. With him was a cowman Ross Tyler recognized as one of the Bear Paw Pool owners. They had some horses down on CK Creek wintering them. Ross reckoned that maybe somebody had been stealing a horse or two.

The other two men were strangers. One of them, who looked and smelled like he might be a trapper, was half drunk. He wore a greasy buckskin shirt and moose-hide moccasins and had a Hudson's Bay sash knotted around his waist. He gave off the unmistakable odor of musk and skunk. The man with him was obviously a 'breed.

"COME far?" asked the stock detective, a big man with a long upper lip and pale blue eyes. He looked good natured and human. So did the cowman with him, who was short and fat paunched and red faced.

"Quite a ways. I'm goin' fu'ther. Don't know as I care about these snow drifts up north."

"Ain't run into anybody ridin' any CK horses?" asked the cattleman.

"No."

Ross Tyler was lying. Gail Meadows had two big stout CK horses there at The Hole. Bob Slocum had ridden in there on a CK horse. But it was not for Ross Tyler to tell about it.

"I'm out ten head of top horses," complained the cowman. "I have a reward posted. I'm betting that I'd find 'em at The Hole if we could get in there."

"Gettin' into The Hole is hard," said Ross Tyler grimly. "And mostly the gettin' out is harder. Here's luck."

"We'll be needin' it," grinned the stock detective.

They downed their drinks and the saloon man was buying another round when three men came into the place. Ross Tyler's thin lips tightened. For one of the three was Gail Meadows.

The stock detective and the cowman eyed the newcomers. The three outlaws stared back with bold insolence. Now they came up to the bar.

"I'm just settin' 'em up, fellers," drawled the saloon man.

"And we'll drink," said Gail Meadows, "when the place is cleared uh snakes."

Ross Tyler's face twisted sideways in a bitter, pain-racked grin. His hand was on the six-shooter in his coonskin coat.

"Meanin' me, I reckon." His voice was flat toned, dangerous. "Well, Meadows, have at 'er. I'm ready."

The stock detective, the cowman, and the other two stepped back out of range. The two men with Gail Meadows had their hands on their guns. Gail Meadows, his pink cheeked face a little white around the mouth, crouched forward, ready to draw his gun. Then he took his hand off the weapon and laughed shortly.

"Show these men what's wrote on yore chest, Tyler, and see if they'll drink with yuh. Show 'em the brand put on yuh at The Hole. Then try to git a drink or grub here. Show 'em all what that shirt hides, if yuh got the guts."

THE frost bitten fingers of Ross Tyler's left hand picked aimlessly at his flannel shirt. His face was bitter and terrible to look at.

"I'll kill you some day, Meadows. I'd kill you now if yuh had the sand tuh fill yore hand with a gun."

"I'd call yore play, Tyler, and kill yuh," said Meadows insolently, "only I want yuh to live a long time. Show the men here what's branded on yore chest, then try to buy a drink at the Whisky Tepee."

The eyes of every man there were fixed on Ross Tyler. Slowly, without taking his eyes from the face of Gail Meadows, he unbuttoned his shirt.

There, exposed to them all to see, was that damned "THIEF."

The stock detective grunted almost inaudibly. The little cowman with him gasped a whispered "I'm damned!"

The bearded saloon man stared at the brand that was now swollen and terribly blistered. The trapper and the half-breed said nothing, but there was a strange look in the trapper's eyes. Now the saloon keeper removed the bar bottle and glasses. Perhaps it was just a gesture born of long habit. But Gail Meadows took it otherwise.

"Yo're on the Injun list, Thief," he sneered. "Time to move on."

The white whiskered saloon man nodded silently. He had seen one other man who had worn that brand. The man had finally killed himself out there behind the barn.

Ross Tyler's bitter eyes traveled from one face to another. Every man there looked at him as if he were some sort of poisonous thing. The saloon keeper nodded toward the door. To serve a branded man a drink meant the loss of all the trade along the river.

A thin, twisted smile on his mouth, Ross Tyler buttoned his shirt. His eyes were glittering.

"I only wish you was man enough tuh pull yore gun, Meadows," he gritted, and walked out of the place and closed the door behind him.

He tightened the cinch on the big roan and was leading him out of the barn when the trapper in the buckskin shirt came up.

"My camp is at the mouth of Sand Crick. Use it. I'll be there by dark if I ain't too drunk."

A long-fingered hand with black, broken nails pulled open the greasy buckskin shirt, exposing a chest across which was stamped a red word, "THIEF."

"Brothers, eh?" He leered, and quickly buttoned the buckskin shirt.

VI

BROTHERS . . . That stinking, bearded, shifty-eyed trapper with his leering grin that was like the grin of a mangy wolf. Brothers. It struck Ross Tyler oddly. He wanted to hit the man across his mouth with its broken yellow fangs. Instead, he laughed. It was a harsh, ugly laugh that made the trapper recoil a step.

"I got mine in the Klondike. When the scurvy was bad and potatoes scarce. . . . I lived though, while them as branded me rotted of the scurvy. I had what I stole well cached. Damn 'em. . . . I'll fetch a jug, brother."

Ross Tyler forced himself away from that camp at the mouth of Sand Creek. He had no stomach for that stinking thief who bragged of his rotten thieving. He was cold, so cold that he wanted to get off and lie down in a deep drift and go to sleep. That last, white sleep. But he fought back that drowsiness, that numbing forerunner of death by freezing, and rubbed tobacco in his eyes to keep awake.

The pain of his brand was getting worse. One of the big water blisters broke and his wool undershirt against the raw flesh was stinging him. His undershirt was sticky with blood and the water from the broken blister. It clung to his flesh and froze.

His empty stomach seemed tied in a knot. He needed warm food and hot whisky and rest. There at the trapper's camp, food and shelter and whisky would be welcome. But he would not go. He was no thief. Pride, the pride of a Texan whose kinfolks fought at the Alamo, made him grit his teeth and ride on, swaying a little in his saddle, his eyes mere reddish slits, half alive, half asleep. And it was in the last graying light of that December evening that the stout-hearted roan horse carried him along a trail and into a Sioux camp on the south side of the Missouri.

These Assiniboine Sioux had come from the Fort Belknap Reservation on special permit to hunt wolves. But there was venison in camp and a quarter of beef traded to them by a cowpuncher in a nearby line camp. He had a buckskin shirt in payment.

Old Eyes in the Water. Iron Horn, and Black Dog, together with their squaws and their families, were camped there in the badlands. They helped this white man from his leg-weary horse and carried him into a log cabin that smelled of *kinni-kinnik* and drying pelts. But the dirt floor of the cabin was swept clean and the blankets they laid him on were the white-and-red blankets from the Hudson's Bay country, thick and warm and clean. There was strong black tea and meat and the cabin was warm. The big roan horse was taken care of. Ross Tyler's hand fumbled in his pocket for money to pay, but he fell asleep before he could withdraw the numbed hand.

ROSS TYLER awoke the next day some time to find himself lying on a pile of skins and blankets and covered with more blankets. Half a dozen round-eyed papooses of various ages and sizes stared at this strange *wasege kuzee* who was in their cabin. His six-shooter and saddle gun lay beside him. He was undressed save for his underwear, and there was some kind of a poultice on his burned chest. He shook off his drowsiness and tried to grin.

Three Indian bucks sat there in the cabin on the dirt floor smoking pipes with wooden stems. They grunted and talked among themselves. A fat squaw in a blue gingham dress and beaded squaw leggings padded across from the sheet-iron stove with a big tin cup filled with steaming soup made of beef and venison. His hands were too swollen and weak to hold the cup and she held it to his mouth for him to drink. It took a long time to sip down that steaming soup, but he managed it. Then he took to coughing and lay back weakly on the blankets.

The biggest of the Assiniboine bucks pushed forward a fawn-eyed girl of fourteen or fifteen. She was the interpreter.

She asked him who he was and where he came from and if he worked for the Circle C outfit. He told her to tell them that he was lost and would pay them for what he ate and for the bed and the roof that sheltered him. When she asked him why he had burned that word on his chest he told her that others had burned that there because they thought he was a thief and a man who had murdered another man. He might have lied, but he didn't. He wondered if they would put him out as he had been put out of the white man's cabins.

But they let him stay. Not only that, they treated him like he was welcome. And that night he was delirious with fever and Eyes in the Water and Black Dog had to hold him there on the blankets.

Ross Tyler never knew how long he was ill there at the Assiniboine camp. Perhaps it was pneumonia. They cared for him day and night, feeding him and watching him.

ROSS was weak and thin and a heavy beard covered his face when he was able to get up. He drank tea that was black and strong and hot, soup that had strength to it. He asked about his roan horse and a small Indian boy brought the horse to the open door so that he could see how fat and well taken care of the animal was. They gave him a pipe to smoke and Ross Tyler pretended to like the *kinni-kinnik* and tobacco mixed. He had picked up some of their words and they sat around and talked.

But they never once asked him about himself. He gave them money to buy canned stuff and spuds at the trading store. And when Iron Horn hinted of his fondness for minne-pate, Ross told him to get a jug. This they managed to do in spite of the fact that it is unlawful to sell whisky to an Indian. And when the jug came they had quite a pow-wow among themselves there in the cabin.

With the jug came news—old newspapers in which some of the grub had been wrapped. Ross Tyler spread open the newspapers and read them. He got quite a bit of satisfaction out of the first paper he read. Gail Meadows and one of the others who had been there at the saloon that day were out on bond. They had been caught at the trading post for having some stolen CK horses in their possession.

Ross Tyler laughed for the first time since they had tried and convicted him of the murder of Bob Slocum.

The Indians smiled in sympathy. But they knew nothing about that which had caused the white man such merriment, nor did they ask.

They grinned all the wider when Ross passed them the jug. Only Black Dog, tall, straight as an arrow, with the haughty, proud, bold-featured face of the Sioux, did not drink. He had never touched whisky. But when the others were mellowed, Black Dog told of the day when he had gone on a horse raiding foray into the Crow country and killed three Crow warriors in single combat.

Eyes in the Water and Iron Horn danced and sang. The squaws stood about, dancing their squaw steps and joining in the song. They gave Ross Tyler a Sioux name and made him a present of a pair of moccasins.

And so, among these Assiniboine Sioux people, Ross Tyler found a home that was his so long as he wished to stay. The red THIEF on his chest had not kept them from doing that which his own kind had refused him. And that added more gall to the bitterness that rankled in his heart against his own kind.

LATE one winter day when Ross Tyler sat there in the cabin smoking and whittling some toy for the round-eyed Indian youngsters, two men on horseback rode up. Ross heard the crunch of shod hoofs in the snow and had peered out through a slit he scratched in the heavy frost that covered the windowpane.

One of the riders was the trapper. With him rode the 'breed. Black Dog had also seen them. His proud face took on a look of hatred.

"Crees," he said. "One Cree. One white man. Both bad. Trap robbers. Thief."

Ross Tyler nodded. He wondered why they were paying this visit. He opened the door and stepped outside to meet them. The trapper grinned and looked sideways at the Cree 'breed.

"H'are ya, brother?" leered the trapper,

leaning across his saddle horn. There were a couple of fresh pelts tied to his saddle. "How's tricks?"

"Can't holler," was Ross Tyler's non-committal reply.

"Never knew you was a squawman," the trapper went on.

"I'm not. But there's worse things than bein' a squaw man. I'm just stayin' here with 'em, just for a short spell." Tyler was not starting any trouble.

An ugly glint crept into the greenish, whisky-reddened eyes of the trapper. He pointed to Black Dog, who had come outside now and sood there in front of the closed door, tall and straight and stern.

"That Injun and the other two is trappin' over on my territory. Tell 'em to git off and stay off or there'll be trouble."

"Just what kind uh trouble, mister?"

"One of 'em might git mistook fer a wolf." He patted his carbine.

"You own any uh that land where yore trap line is?" asked Ross.

"No. Don't need to."

"Then just where do you git yore right to say who'll set traps there?"

"What's that to you, anyhow?"

"Nothing much."

"Then keep yore damned mouth out of it!" The trapper was ugly now. He had seen this man from The Hole disgraced there at the Whisky Tepee. The man had not showed himself to be very tough. The trapper had his half-breed partner with him. Likewise he was half drunk and whisky made him brave.

Ross stepped to the door and called out a few words in Sioux. Now an Indian girl of perhaps fourteen came to the door.

"Are these the two men that stopped you?" he asked her in English.

The Indian girl nodded, pointing at the trapper, then at the 'breed.

"Them two men," she said, and her dark eyes were sullen with anger.

"Go back inside," Ross told her. And when she was inside, the bearded outlaw stepped up to where the trapper sat his horse.

Suddenly, even while the trapper's hand was on his gun, Ross Tyler jerked the man from his saddle. A quick twist sent the trapper's six-shooter spinning. As the fellow reached for his hunting knife, Ross knocked him down. He glanced at the 'breed, who now sat stiffly in his saddle, his arms raised. Ross grinned. Black Dog had the Cree covered with a single barrel ten gauge shotgun loaded with slugs.

Now the trapper was on his feet, his knife in his hand. He circled Ross like an animal about to spring.

VII

ROSS TYLER was still weak from his illness. He could have jerked his gun and finished the battle quickly enough. But when he remembered the terror stricken Indian girl the day she came back from the trap line, her clothes torn and with the ugly story of having been stopped by two men from whom she escaped by sheer luck, Ross determined that he was going to give this lanky trapper a whipping or else take one.

"I'll give you a knife the best of it, you stinkin' coyote," gritted Ross, "and beat yore dirty face in."

The trapper kept circling there in the snow. His bloodshot, greenish eyes were like the eyes of a lynx. Now he sprang, the long bladed skinning knife flashing as it swept downward.

Ross leaped to one side. The blade ripped his shirt from shoulder to wrist, leaving a thin line of blood on his arm. Ross lunged at the man, who was off-balance. His fist crashed squarely into the unwashed face with its snarled, tobacco stained yellow beard. Now they were in a locked embrace. The trapper was trying to free his knife arm, but Ross had the wrist in his grip. It was a question of how long he could hold that sinewy wrist. Beads of sweat burst out on the outlaw's face. He was weak, too weak to fight long. The trapper was lean and wiry and strong.

Ross gave a terrific twist to the man's wrist. The knife dropped in the snow. Ross grinned at the trapper, who cursed in grunts.

The trapper broke away. He dived for the knife, but the outlaw kicked him in the face. Then he fell on top of the trapper, his fists smashing into the other's face Blood spurted. Ross found the corded throat under the matted, yellow beard that was now blood smeared. His two hands clamped tightly on the white throat, gripping harder, until the fellow's eyes protruded from purplish white sockets. The lanky body quit threshing around.

Ross Tyler let the man get up, kicking him roughly to his feet. His gun covered the trapper now.

"You two skunks will pull out tomorrow from where yo're camped. I'd uh choked the life plumb outa you, you stinkin' skunk, only that once you offered me yore camp because you figgered me a thief like you are. That's why I'm lettin' yuh off so easy. Drag it now. Gather yore traps and move outa this part uh the country, you and the 'breed. Because if yuh don't I'll let these Sioux men take yuh apart like they aimed to. This is a big country, but it's too small to hold such skunks as you two. Drag it."

"You ain't won a thing by this," snarled the trapper. "I ain't the kind that forgits." His nose was broken and swelling fast. His throat bore the marks of Ross Tyler's fingers.

"Git!" growled Ross, and took a step forward. The two rode away.

ROSS stood there watching until they were out of sight. Then he put up his gun and turned toward the house. Black Dog gravely held out his hand. The little girl was his daughter.

That night when Iron Horn and Eyes in the Water returned home from their traps, Black Dog related, with a great deal of drama and gestures, the fight that had taken place. Iron Horn and Eyes in the Water shook hands solemnly with Ross. They had a few drinks from the jug.

When the others were asleep Ross lay awake for some time. He knew that the trapper had made no idle boast. He would get some sort of revenge for that thrashing.

Nor had Ross Tyler long to wait for that blow to strike. At an hour near daylight, Ross was awakened by the sound of horses coming. He slipped into his clothes and buckled on his six-shooter. His carbine in his hand, he looked out the cleared slit in the frostcoated window. Half a dozen riders were coming across the moonlit snow toward the camp. He let them get within twenty feet from the cabin, then called out to them to stand still.

Behind Ross stood the three Indians, silent, wondering perhaps, just what was to happen.

"Stand where yuh are," called Ross, shoving the barrel of his carbine through a porthole he had fashioned for just such an emergency.

"Come outa that, Ross Tyler," called one of the riders.

"So it's you, is it, Meadows? Thought you was in jail?"

"I ain't," came the caustic reply. "I'm here. Come out or we'll smoke yuh out."

"Just what's yore business with me, Gail Meadows?"

"You was told to quit the country. Yo're still here. We're havin' a little necktie party in yore honor. Come outa that squaw camp."

"You might smoke me out," said Ross Tyler grimly, "but while yo're doin' the smokin' process, I won't be in here sittin' on my hands. Fact is, Meadows, I got you covered right now. If any man in yore mob makes a move, I'll kill you deader than a rock. That goes as she lays."

There was a muttered conference out there. Ross made out the trapper and the 'breed and the two men from The Hole who had been with Gail Meadows at the Whisky Tepee.

Ross Tyler, in spite of the odds, had the advantage. The log cabin made an ideal fort. Its one door was made of heavy planks. An iron bar fastened it from the inside. There were heavy board shutters that could be fitted to the one window. Even now, Black Dog was slipping those shutters into place. The cabin had once been an outlaw retreat, hence the shutters and barred door.

Gail Meadows was raving mad. He had not reckoned on this cabin. The trapper had simply told him that Ross Tyler was living at an Injun camp back in the badlands. Meadows had pictured a camp of tepees and tents. Now he saw his game balked. There was nothing to do but retire. But before they rode away, Gail Meadows left his warning.

"Be outa this country in three days, Tyler, or it'll go hard with these Injun friends uh yourn. We'll be back."

"Look here, Meadows, it ain't yore play to hurt these Injuns. I'm pullin' out tomorrow. But on my way outa the country I'm stoppin' at the sub-agency. If any harm comes to these folks, you'll git yourn. If it's me yuh want, meet me somewhere along the trail. But don't lay a hand on these folks."

"Meet yuh along the trail, did yuh say, Tyler?" Gail Meadows laughed harshly. "I might just do that there little thing."

They rode away as suddenly as they had come. Ross scowled after them. They called themselves men, those renegades. Drunken skunks. Thieves and killers who despised the Indians. Ross swore softly and lit the lantern that stood on the table. From behind the canvas partitions that served as walls of the cabin, black heads appeared. There was little talk, however, save between the men.

B LACK DOG, who understood the white man's language enough to get an idea of what had passed, lit his pipe.

"Our time away from the reservation is almost up. Tomorrow we pack up and go to our homes. You are welcome there." He spoke in the Assiniboine tongue, slowly, so that Ross would understand. He then showed Ross the hunting permit.

True, the permit would expire within a few days, so Ross did not feel so badly about involving these friends of his in the trouble that hounded him. Meadows and the others would not dare harm these Indians once they left the badlands.

"Tomorrow," he told them, "I leave. My trail goes far to the south. Where there is never any snow. That is my home. Some day I come back and visit."

They sat on the floor and smoked. Ross brought out the jug and it was passed around with great solemnity. Then he gave them each money. In return they gave him presents. A buckskin shirt heavily fringed and decorated with colored porcupine quills. A skinning knife. A red Hudson's Bay blanket.

And when they had exchanged these presents they sat around and talked. And after a time Iron Horn told a tale that had Ross Tyler listening intently.

Iron Horn, the better to tell the tale, had called his oldest boy, Jesse, to interpret. And from somewhere among his belongings he brought forth a heavy canvas sack that was stamped with the United States seal across its red and white striped exterior. The sack was padlocked and had been ripped open at the bottom by a knife. It was a sack used in the United States Railway Mail Service for the transportation of registered mail. Iron Horn pointed to a dull stain on the sack.

"Blood," he said. "White man's blood."

"Where did he get this sack, Jesse?" asked Ross.

"Near what the white man calls The Hole. Where a white man was killed from the brush. The old man says the man who done that killin' was one of them fellers that come here tonight."

VIII

S LOWLY the tale unfolded. Iron Horn, talking deliberately, smoking slowly between sentences, told his story of how he had seen a white man murder another white man for this sack and what it contained. And the man who had done the killing was one of the two men who had accompanied Gail Meadows from The Hole. A man with red hair and one hand crippled.

Ross Tyler listened carefully. This red-headed outlaw, with a hand that had been partly crippled by a knife some time in the bygone days, had come to The Hole about the same time Bob Slocum and Gail Meadows had drifted in there. They called him Paint because on his freckled hands and face were large white blotches.

"Old man say it was the day you kill a black tail buck he's bin trailin' long time. You ride a roan horse. This man who is get killed follow behind you. Old man watch with the field-glass. This one that trail you stop by a big rimrock. He get this sack and cut it open. When he is cutting this sack that feller with red hair shoot him dead and then work on him some with a club. He's bad man, that redhead feller, old man says. When the red-haired feller ride away, old man go down there to look. He finds this dead feller is robbed. Only this empty sack which old man takes so that he can show it to Black Dog and Eyes in the Water."

Ross Tyer's fingers passed across the brand on his chest. The brand that this red-haired Paint should be wearing. The red brand of shame.

"Tell Iron Horn that he must not give away that sack. Tell him to hide it where nobody kin find it. Uncle Sam owns the sack and when the time comes, mebbyso, Iron Horn will get a train ride up to Helena to testify in the federal court. There was money in that sack that come from a big train hold-up. Kin you tell him that, Jesse?"

"You're damn' tootin'," nodded Jesse Iron Horn, who was rapidly learning the language of the cowboy.

Ross Tyler passed the jug again. Now the killing of Bob Slocum was solved. Gail Meadows and Slocum and this Paint gent had been three of the five mixed up in the train robbery. One of the gang had been killed by an express messenger who had paid with his life for his valor in defending that which was in his care. A second one of the gang had been gathered in and was being closely held in the jail at Cheyenne pending trial.

There had been some talk, there in The Hole, about the agreement made between them that they were not to open a registered sack until they all gathered there at The Hole. Then the sacks were to be cut open and the loot divided. Each of them had packed his share of the sacks. The outlaw who had been captured would be convicted because of the fact that he was caught with two unopened sacks of registered mail. The dead man's share had been taken by the others.

ROSS TYLER suddenly recalled a quarrel he had overheard between Slocum, Paint and Gail Meadows. It concerned a missing sack. That sack was supposed to contain a nice little fortune in currency. Paint and Gail Meadows had claimed that Bob Slocum had it. Slocum had hotly maintained that the outlaw who was captured had that particular sack.

Bob Slocum had talked the other two down. Slocum was an ugly devil, drunk or sober, and the other two were afraid of him. Slocum had cursed them and sneered at them, then made them buy drinks. That had been Bob Slocum's tough-mannered way.

Well, they had paid Bob Slocum off in his own coin. Slocum had used Ross that day for an excuse to quit The Hole for a few hours. He had gone to lift that sack he had cached. Paint had caught him. Paint, supposed to be dead drunk and sleeping it off in the barn, had followed Bob Slocum while Gail Meadows had covered him by sitting in that poker game. And they had shifted the burden of guilt to Ross Tyler, Bob Slocum's most bitter enemy.

Ross smiled thinly. The Indians listened gravely while he told them, through Jesse, that the THIEF branded on him had been burned there because of that crime.

Ross felt that he owed these Indians more than he could ever repay them. He had given them each a hundred dollars. He knew that to add to that sum now would insult Iron Horn. Those old warriors had pride. Pride as fierce and straight backed as ever a white man could boast of. They had fought the white man. They had smoked the peace pipe. They had watched the white man break his treaties. But never once had they broken a letter of their signed treaty that gathered dust there in Washington while shrewd, unscrupulous Indian Department officials robbed them with both hands.

These three old men were real Sioux. They had fought the white man with cruelty and cunning. But they had smoked the pipe of peace and had forever afterward kept their given word to the white man.

Ross Tyler had learned much during the weeks he had spent there at the camp of the Assiniboine Sioux. They had taken him in when his own kind shunned him and forced him into the blizzards to starve and freeze. They had given him their blankets and their grub. They had nursed him back to health. They had put poultices on that THIEF that branded him. The THIEF that had made him an outcast among white men.

They sat there and smoked for a long time. At dawn the Assiniboines would be packing and leaving for the reservation that they called home. And into that same dawn Ross Tyler would again ride alone.

Later he would get word to old scarred-face Jeff Slocum at The Hole to keep an eye on Paint and Gail Meadows. For Ross Tyler could not go back there. He had no real proof against Paint and Gail Meadows. He could never go back to The Hole until he had definitely cleared himself of that damned charge against him.

Then he would make that outlaw pack eat crow meat. But until that time came, he must still ride alone. Shunned, unwanted. Outlawed by the outlaw clan. Lower than the lowest killer who rode the outlaw trail.

AT daybreak Ross Tyler shook hands with the Indians who had been his friends. His saddle was on the stout roan. He shoved the last money he had into the plump, dimpled little hand of Iron Horn's youngest papoose and hit the trail.

Across his saddle was the red Hudson's Bay blanket that would be his bed in the snow drifts. Warmed against his body, under the buckskin shirt that was hidden by the coonskin coat, was a string of cheap little trading-store beads.

And as he rode along the trail, headed for the Whisky Tepee on the river bank, he kept his hand on the six-shooter in the pocket of his fur coat.

Gail Meadows had told him that he'd meet him along the trail. Ross Tyler wondered how many men would be with Meadows. Paint, anyhow, would be with the apple-cheeked, blue-eyed Meadows. Paint would be there to do the killin'. Ross Tyler grinned crookedly and quit the main trail.

He followed a bare ridge down into the scrub pines. Among the presents exchanged the night before had been a pair of army field-glasses.

Ross located the pinnacle that Iron Horn had described to him. Iron Horn had hunted deer in here forty-five years ago. He knew every pinnacle, every trail in the badlands between Larb Creek and Cow Island Crossing.

Ross, sheltered by the scrub pines, trained the powerful glasses on the country below. He could make out the Whisky Tepee. A man moving out there on the frozen river. Ross reckoned that would be the old man who owned the place. He was packing something on his back. Now he halted out there in the middle of the frozen river, on the ice that was three feet thick. The burden slipped from his shoulders and out of sight through an airhole in the ice.

"Another Circle C hide gone under the ice," was Ross Tyler's grim comment. "The old son's too lazy to git venison. Don't blame him, at that. Barrin' acci-dents, I'll have a hunk uh that same meat for supper."

Now his glasses swung along the trail that led to the Whisky Tepee from Sand Creek. He saw two men riding, one behind the other. Now they halted and Ross reckoned a bottle was being passed. Then they rode off on a side trail where they dismounted. Inside of half an hour two more riders joined them. Ross Tyler's thin lips parted in a snarl. He had recognized his men. Gail Meadows, Paint, the trapper, the Cree 'breed.

Ross Tyler stepped to his horse. There was an odd grin on his face as he pulled the .30-40 cavalry carbine from the saddle scabbard.

"There," he told himself, raising the rear sight to its last notch, "is one ambush that is goin' to be badly scattered directly."

IX

THE range was long. Still, those leaden slugs plunked into the snow close enough to the four men to make them scatter. Ross pulled a fine bead and allowed for the wind. He had shoved in a couple of those sharp-nosed steel-jacket cartridges. It tickled him a lot when the four men broke for better cover. He dropped a few of those whining, snarling, droning slugs down among 'em.

Then, when he had scattered them, he shoved more cartridges in the box magazine of his cavalry carbine and put the gun back in its scabbard. He stepped up in the middle of his stout roan horse and took a short cut that would intercept Gail Meadows and the man Paint when they hit the trail for the Whisky Tepee.

But Ross Tyler had reckoned blindly. Gail Meadows and the man Paint were not going to the Whisky Tepee. And for good reasons. Meadows was jumping bond on that CK horse-stealing charge. It was cash bond, furnished by certain men in The Hole. One of the men who stood to lose money on that cash bond was this Paint outlaw.

Another who had laid cash money on the line was none other than the scarred-faced man who tended bar at The Hole. Nobody in The Hole except Ross Tyler knew the name of that whisky peddler with the scarred face. Not even Gail Meadows knew that he was a Slocum. Nor did Gail Meadows dream that this man with the battered face was going his bond for a reason known only to himself. The scarred-faced Jeff Slocum wanted Gail Meadows out in the open where he might make some kind of a blunder that would give Slocum a chance to hear more about Bob Slocum's murder. For Jeff Slocum, after the branding of Ross Tyler, was convinced that Gail Meadows and this Paint outlaw were badly involved in that killing.

There was, for instance, that money which was being squandered for poker and whisky by Meadows and Paint. Before the killing of Bob Slocum both Meadows and Paint had been nearly broke. They had both gambled heavily and lost. Then, without explanation, they had fat rolls again.

Jeff Slocum, wiping glasses behind the bar there at The Hole, missed but little that went on in the place. Sober, alert, tight mouthed, the old ex-convict did his work—set out drinks, took in money, and sprinkled fresh sawdust on the floor when some man's blood was spilled there. He remembered the face of every man who came and went. He knew the old-timers and where they had served time. He knew the wilder, younger gang that drifted in and out of The Hole.

Old Jeff Slocum was a hard man to fool. And so he had gone half of Gail Meadows' cash bond because he knew that Gail Meadows in jail would never make a break of any kind, whereas Gail Meadows free and half drunk might some day slip up in his talk.

AT the Whisky Tepee, under the bare-limbed giant cottonwoods on the banks of the frozen Missouri, a deputy sheriff who had once been foreman for the Bear Paw Pool was patiently waiting for this Gail Meadows to show up. Meadows was due to go back to Chinook for trial on that CK horse-stealing charge.

But this deputy had a notion that Gail Meadows had been mixed up in bigger deals. And he planned to have some serious talks with the young horse thief from The Hole. He reckoned that Gail Meadows might be pressed into talking under certain conditions that might be labeled under the head of third degree. He had seen more than one tough outlaw cave in after about three days on an empty belly and no tobacco. The odor of frying venison in the skillet, the pot of coffee simmering beside the camp-fire. Hot biscuits and beans. The tantalizing odor of tobacco. Two men alone in camp. One of them handcuffed to a sapling. The other eating and smoking. A bottle of good rye whisky.

"Did it ever occur to you," this deputy used to tell a prisoner who had coyote blood in him, "that I could save the State a lot uh money and trouble if I was tuh fetch you in dead? I'd shoot off this gun I taken away from yuh. Then I'd put a bullet in yore brisket. And I'd take yuh in dead and tell 'em how yuh made a break to run off from me. Just as easy as shootin' fish."

More than one tough outlaw had fallen for that bluff and had come clean with a confession. Perhaps it was not quite ethical, but this deputy was an old-timer and knew the men he had to handle.

Now he waited at the Whisky Tepee for Gail Meadows to show up. But old gray-bearded Jim Crowe, who owned and ran the place, had somehow gotten word out that the law was camped there at his place and that it was a good time for Gail Meadows and other such men from The Hole to stay away from the Whisky Tepee. Old Jim Crowe protected his trade as much as possible.

So it was that Ross Tyler waited in vain for Gail Meadows and Paint to come along the trail that led to the Whisky Tepee. And finally, tired of waiting, Ross had ridden down to the saloon. He had stabled his horse in the same barn that held the deputy sheriff's big brown. The brown gelding wore the CK iron.

THE white-whiskered saloon man stared at Ross Tyler through slitted eyes. Ross grinned thinly and nodded pleasantly to the deputy, with whom he had once worked at the Bear Paw Pool wagon.

"H'are yuh, Tom?"

"About the same, Ross. Yuh got quite a crop uh whiskers. Goin' tuh stuff a piller with 'em?"

Ross and the deputy shook hands. The

saloon man scowled. Now Ross ordered drinks which were served reluctantly. Ross leaned across the bar to stare hard into the saloon man's eyes.

"Yuh'll serve me, mister, whether yuh like it or not. Whether anybody likes it or not. If yuh don't serve me, I'll shoot so many holes in yore damned place that it won't be fit tuh live in when the rains come. Remember that, mister whisky peddler."

"What seems to be the defugalty, Ross?"

Ross Tyler unbuttoned his overcoat and tossed it over a chair. Then he opened his buckskin shirt and showed the deputy the brand on his chest. The big deputy whistled.

"They branded me there at The Hole, Tom. I come here tuh wait for the two skunks that is responsible. I don't call on the law to he'p me. This is just my own little affair and I'll handle 'er accordin'."

"Feel like tellin' me anything about it, Ross?"

"No. No, I don't, Tom. Me and you is friends. We worked together and you always treated me white, but this is personal business. But I tell yuh what I wish yuh would do. There's some Injun friends uh mine pullin' out for the Fort Belknap reservation — Iron Horn, Black Dog, and Eyes in the Water. They got a sack that they'll give to yuh. It'll come in handy some day. It's a sack that held gover'ment registered mail and it come from that Wind River train hold-up.

"Tom, I never yet sent a man up. I settled my fights outside the law. But there is two sons that is goin' to the pen unless they choose tuh die fightin'. That sack and the evidence I'll bring into court will convict 'em. Never mind their names, Tom, but when they git locked up you'll identify 'em by the brands I'll put on 'em. Give me some more whisky, Crowe."

ROSS faced the whisky peddler. "Look here, Crowe, you'll put out drinks for me whenever I call for 'em. If anybody puts up a holler, tell 'em I had a gun shoved in yore belly. I'm broke right now so you'll just put these drinks on the book. And speakin' uh money, Crowe, let's have a look at the money you have in yore pocket."

"What is this, a stick-up?" snarled Crowe.

"No. Just an inspection. Lay yore money on the bar. Tom, I hope tuh show yuh at least a few uh them banknotes that come from the Wind River train robbery. Come clean, Crowe. Yo're into 'er deep enough tuh take a twenty-five-year jolt. I know you plenty, yuh ol' wolf."

"A frame-up, is it?" snarled the whisky peddler. "You and the law here thinks tuh frame me, do yuh? Well, mister, just take another long guess."

But even as he jerked his gun, Ross Tyler was over the bar and on top of him. The gun was sent spinning into a corner. Ross quickly overpowered the man and from his overalls pockets took a thick roll of banknotes. These he tossed on the bar.

"Check them over, Tom, with the serial numbers on the money that come from that Wind River job. This old buzzard is in on the deal. He passes this dough along."

"Turned up, have yuh?" flared the saloon man.

"Nope. I'm just checkin' up. Damn you, Crowe, you know all about the job I'm on. You and Meadows and Paint all was in on it. It was you that heard I was at that Assiniboine camp. It was you that sent that trapper and his 'breed pardner to git me there. Don't deny it, you goat-whiskered old skunk, or I'll stuff yuh down in that air hole with that Circle C hide yuh shoved under the ice this mornin'. It's my deal now and I'm dealin' you and yore lousy layout misery a-plenty."

Now the front door opened and the trapper and his half-breed partner stepped inside. Their hands went up under the menace of Ross Tyler's gun.

"Where's Gail Meadows and Paint?" asked Ross harshly. Then he took a long guess. "And where," he finished, "did you plant Paint's dead pardner that was murdered between here and the Injun camp last night?"

X

IT had been a random guess, but it hit home like a bullet. The trapper winced as if struck across the face. The 'breed wet his dry lips and shifted his weight from one moccasin-clad foot to the other.

The deputy was watching the two men. Their eyes kept glancing covertly toward Jim Crowe, who glared at them from under his bushy white brows. The deputy looked inquiringly at Ross Tyler.

"A man was killed last night, Tom. That man was with these two polecats and Gail Meadows and a gent they call Paint. There was six in the gang, all told. One uh the six went back to The Hole. Meadows and Paint met these two burglars and they planned tuh bushwhack me. The other man out of that party of six is dead. Either he was shoved into that air hole by Crowe or else this trapper and his 'breed pardner hid his dead body. I've a notion it went down into the river along with that Circle C hide."

Again Ross was guessing. And again he had made a bulls-eye, for the whisky peddler let loose a string of profanity. The trapper and the half-breed stood their ground near the door.

The deputy lined them up facing the wall. He searched the trapper and his partner first, then went through the saloon man's clothes. Ross Tyler looked on interestedly, his gun in his hand. He was wishing that Gail Meadows and Paint would come.

But those two gentlemen were making tracks southward toward Gilt Edge. Their pockets were well filled with money. It was money that they had traded for. Honest money they had traded for here at Whisky Tepee. Jim Crowe had taken the money from the Wind River train stick-up and for every ten dollars of that Wind River money he had taken he had given five dollars of money that was safe currency.

Now, by a fluke, the saloon man was caught with that money. Not only that. He was thinking of the dead man whose body had been laced into that beef hide and shoved through the air hole out there on the frozen river. The body had been carefully laced inside the hide and had been weighted with the wheel off an old mowing machine. Gail Meadows and Paint had brought in the dead man.

"Shot accidental," explained Paint. "Mistook for a bear in that fur coat he was a-wearin'."

"Git shut of his carcass, Crowe," Gail Meadows had growled. "There's a hundred bucks in it for yuh."

They had come up on Crowe when he was butchering the Circle C beef. So Crowe had bargained with them. He had made a shroud of the beef hide. The wheel from the mower had been handy as an anchor. The air hole would no doubt freeze over in a day or so.

Jim Crowe, owner of the Whisky Tepee on the river bank, was a man who never threw away a scrap of anything that might be of use. And so he had taken the dead man's bearskin overcoat and after washing it free of blood, had hung it on a nail behind the stove, there in the saloon.

Bearskin coats are not common. Ross had immediately spotted the coat that was hanging there behind the big stove. From it came a faint odor of wet hair. And where the water had dripped down on the floor there was a pinkish stain. That coat of bearskin was damaging evidence. Ross saw Crowe glance at it from the corner of his eye, and smiled.

This Crowe, together with Gail Meadows and those other renegades from The Hole, had driven him one night from the warmth of the Whisky Tepee to die out in the snow drifts. Now he'd make them pay. He'd make every damned one of them pay the limit.

"I RECKON, Tom," Ross Tyler drawled, as the deputy looked over the money he had taken from the pockets of the trapper and the 'breed, "that these gentlemen will do a little talking after a while.

"Throw their guns away, Tom. They'll talk and talk plenty or they'll take a dive through that airhole out yonder on the river. Get the idea, Tom?"

"I had it before you ever mentioned it, Ross," came the grinning reply.

The deputy and Ross Tyler took the three men out to the edge of the airhole there in the middle of the frozen river. The arms of the three prisoners were tied behind them. They stood there, tight lipped, none too steady on their legs.

The water was green and deep enough to hide any secret. It lapped at the edge of the yard-thick ice. The ice there was rough and uneven on the surface because the current swirled and whipped around a buried snag that had once been a giant cottonwood. That opaque ice held its secrets well. And the secrets that the green, ice-cold water muttered to that ice were the secrets of Whisky Tepee. Whisky Tepee, the first saloon out of The Hole where lived men upon whose heads the law had put a price.

Even now it might be given another secret to hold in its turbulent bowels. There stood three men, their arms tied behind their backs. The two who watched over them were not soft men. One was the deputy who had a way of pulling secrets from the hard-bitten men he captured. With this law officer was an outlaw in whose heart rankled all the bitter hatred that a man can know for his kind.

Ross Tyler, condemned and convicted by an outlaw pack that had taken the word of a liar, knew how to hate. He was hating now. He was lusting for the bitterest kind of revenge upon the pack that had driven him forth into a blizzard to die. He knew how to hate, Ross Tyler. He came from a breed of men down in Texas whose blood had been spilled in the name of hatred and freedom. Ross Tyler's blood was Alamo blood. The blood of men who had died fighting. Men who had faced overwhelming odds back there in Texas and had fought until the last man of the Texans was dead.

From boyhood Ross Tyler had been taught how to hate. He had been raised with a gun in his hand, and his history was the history of the Texan. The Slocum-Tyler feud was another lesson in hatred. Another bit of history that was powder-scorched and blood-spattered. It had left its mark on Ross Tyler. And it was a mark that was now written in his black eyes and on his lean-jawed face that was pinched and ravaged by the past weeks of suffering.

THE trapper, the Cree breed, Jim Crowe of the Whisky Tepee saw no mercy in those opaque black eyes. Nor did they find much that might be called mercy in the cold ice-blue eyes of the big deputy. They stood there with bound arms on the edge of death and waited for some word to break that ice-cold spell.

Ross Tyler's black eyes watched them.

He wore no coat and the fringed and quill-adorned buckskin shirt was open halfway to his waist, so that those three men might read that branded word stamped on his chest. His eyes challenged them to deny their guilt. His thin-lipped smile was their death sentence.

Nor did the blue-eyed deputy, warming his hands in the pockets of the bearskin coat that had two bullet holes in its back, make a sign or speak a word. He stood there, cold eyed, unsmiling. The Law. The Law that had overtaken and pulled down a craven pack of mangy, inbred wolves who snarled and fought among themselves as beasts will fight over a hunk of red meat thrown to them. And the meat now thrown to those human wolves of an inbred pack was meat tainted with poison. Bait. Bait that one of them would snatch away from the others of that scurvy pack and then find in it that poison that would gripe him and leave him writhing in mortal agony.

Bait. Bait to be snatched from the snapping, snarling jaws of his fellow wolves. Wolves crossed with the yellow breed of the coyote. Not the gray wolf who fights to the death, but the half-breed wolf that snaps and snarls and lies on his back with tail curved between its hind legs. Not the wolf that stands alone on a snow-swept butte and howls its song to the cold stars, alone and unafraid. But the mongrel wolf whipped out of its pack and trailing with a cowardly breed of coyote that yaps and runs away.

Bait. Bait for a cowardly breed. That was what any one of these three would snap at and gulp down without as much as tasting.

The cold-eyed deputy stood there warming his gun in the pocket of a dead man's bearskin coat that was marked by the bullets of a coward. . . . A Texan whose black, merciless eyes watched. A Texan on whose chest was branded in red the word THIEF. . . . Three craven, gutless renegades from that cross-bred pack that had come from The Hole.

The cold ice, three feet thick, cracking up and down the river that was banked with crusted snow drifts. That ice cracked like pistol shots when the frost bit into it like a frozen blade of a knife.

and the muttering of the green water underneath. Water that drowned in its mysterious depths the secrets of Whisky Tepee and the men who had stopped there to drink its bad whisky and kill men they hated. Water that covered sins as black as the water at midnight.

It was the Cree 'breed who weakened. The Cree 'breed, who lacked the nerve that held the two white men tight lipped, afraid, yet not daring to talk of those things which haunted their sleep at night.

He dropped there on the ice, his shifting, dark-colored eyes red with fear of death. Words, part Cree, part the language of the white man who listened so coldly, spilled like unclean whisky from a broken jug.

XI

THE deputy took his three prisoners to town. The trapper, the Cree 'breed, Jim Crowe of the Whisky Tepee. Out of the snow-filled badlands and across the wind-swept prairies to Chinook. There to be held in jail, each one in a separate cell, each man with only his guilt as a cell mate. Charged informally with selling whisky and having in their possession stolen money. But the charge that would later be filed against them was the uncompromising charge of murder.

The Whisky Tepee was closed. Its doors were spiked shut, its windows boarded up. A barrel of whisky lay buried in the cellar under a mound of potatoes. Jim Crowe would never again stand behind the pine board bar in that badlands saloon. Never again would Jim Crowe make corn whisky back in the hills and fetch it in to sell to the men from The Hole. No more would he get men drunk and take money from their pockets while they slept. Half-breed, sheepherder, trapper, cowboy, outlaw. All had paid tribute to Jim Crowe at Whisky Tepee, squandering their hard-earned money and leaving Whisky Tepee with a stomach that was turned upside down, a head that throbbed and ached, and a parting gift of a pint or quart of rotgut whisky. Whisky Tepee was closed.

Snow, unmarked by print of a horse's sharp shod hoofs, now covered the trail

from The Hole to Whisky Tepee. Word had gone to The Hole that Whisky Tepee was no more. That Jim Crowe was in jail at Chinook and would later come up for murder. With Jim Crowe was a trapper who was wanted for murdering his wife in the Klondike country. He had been run out of that northern, snow-bound country for stealing the camp's supply of potatoes during a siege of scurvy. He was a British subject and would be deported to Canada to face murder charges there. The British law in the Dominion works swiftly and without faltering. The man would be hanged.

With him would hang the Cree half-breed who had killed two Sarcee Indians and one squaw when he was drunk.

Jim Crowe would be formally charged with murder. On him had been found nearly all the money that had come from the Wind River train robbery. He would draw life. Life or twenty-five years at least.

The airhole was frozen over now. Under the ragged ice the green water rushed past with its drowned secrets. The snow swirled and drifted around the log buildings there at Whisky Tepee. The wind from the north moaned through the bare limbs of the giant cottonwoods. Jim Crowe would never come back. Whisky Tepee was now but a name, a memory. Its log walls, pocked with bullets, were silent and cold, holding their dark tales of blood and powder smoke in the silence of the badlands.

Snow drifted against the spiked door. Snow sifted through the cracks and across the pine board floor that was worn and rutted by boot heels and dragging spurs.

The cheap glasses on the back bar gathered dust and cobwebs. There on the bar stood an empty bottle and some unwashed glasses. Rats scurried across the cloth-covered poker tables and across the sawdust-sprinkled floor. There was the musty odor of old tobacco smoke and spilled whisky. The big-bellied iron stove was cold and rusty looking. Some playing cards lay under a table. Dried tobacco lay caked in the two cuspidors. A big spider had spun a web across the picture of Custer's Last Stand that decorated the wall. There was ice in the tub behind the bar where Jim Crowe had once washed glasses.

The wind moaned and whimpered there at night. Whisky Tepee, where men had drunk and sung and talked and quarreled and died with their boots on, was no more. . . . The Law had passed its sentence.

Word had also gone to The Hole that Gail Meadows and Paint had quit Montana and hit the trail for a climate that was more healthy. Mexico, perhaps.

GAIL MEADOWS had jumped his bond on the horse-stealing charge and the scarred-faced Jeff Slocum was loser. He had antied five hundred dollars as part bond money.

The outlaws at The Hole sympathized with Slocum. They told him that they'd pass the hat and make up the five hundred. But he shook his head and grinned and said that it didn't matter, that he'd get it back some day.

"Some day when Kid Gabriel toots his tin horn," was the comment of one hard-bitten outlaw. "Meadows ain't the payin' kind. Hell, Slocum, looks like you'd uh copped onto a fist full uh that Wind River money."

"And got throwed in jail like Jim Crowe from the Whisky Tepee. No, thanks. I don't crave none uh that green money marked with numbers."

Which brought up the subject of Ross Tyler. They talked while the ex-convict listened.

Ross Tyler, branded as a thief, exiled from the outlaw clan, was more damned now than ever. They said that he was yellow and had run to the Law with his squealing tale. That it was because of Ross Tyler's squealing that the trapper would hang in Canada with his half-breed partner.

The trapper and the 'breed, because they were not the right kind of men, had never been admitted into that inner fraternity of outlawry that called The Hole their home. Nevertheless, they were men beyond the boundary of the law and now, because another outlaw had hollered too much to a damned deputy sheriff, those men would be deported and hanged in Canada. Ross Tyler had turned squealer.

Jim Crowe at Whisky Tepee had shoved a dead man through an airhole there at Whisky Tepee. He had handled stolen money, as he had, at other times, handled that kind of money. And now he stood to draw a life sentence at Deer Lodge. Because Ross Tyler had squealed.

At The Hole they called Ross Tyler a dirty, sneaking squealer and a thief and a bushwhacker. They claimed that he had double-crossed his own kind and that it was a damn shame they didn't make him stretch rope there at The Hole. Only for Gail Meadows, they argued, Ross Tyler would have swung. Gail Meadows had saved Tyler's life and now Tyler turned around and squealed like a rat. That and more was what they said there at The Hole about Ross Tyler.

JEFF SLOCUM'S scarred face had never changed expression. He had served them their whisky, made change, listened to every word that was spoken, watched the expression on every outlaw's face.

Old Jeff Slocum kept his thin lips shut. He had heard a thousand and one men talk as these men now talked. In outlaw camps, in jails where they herded criminals into the bull pen and the prisoners there held their kangaroo court. He had heard the same kind of talk in prison corridors, whispered from lips that never moved. He had listened and kept his mouth shut. Even as he kept it shut now when they maligned the man who was his friend.

It was hard to take, too. Hard to hear these outlaws condemn a man and class him with the lowest of the low. Jeff Slocum told himself that they were wrong, that Ross Tyler had never turned squealer. These men were all wrong. In spite of all the evidence to the contrary, they lied when they called Ross Tyler a snake.

He wiped the whisky glasses on a bar towel made from a flour sack and fed them more whisky. Perhaps they would do some more talking and after a while some one of them might forget and say something that was important. Jeff Slocum was waiting for news from Ross Tyler. He reckoned that Ross would somehow manage to send back word to The Hole that he was not a squealer and that he still belonged to the outlaw clan. But that word never came.

Ross Tyler was following the trail made by Gail Meadows and the man Paint. He had turned those three renegades in to the law because he wanted them handy when the day came for Gail Meadows to face trial. He figured that Gail Meadows and Paint needed hanging. He vowed that he would take them alive and brand them as they had branded him. Then he would deliver them up to the law and would testify against them.

XII

RAGGED peaks jutted out of a desert land into the blue sky. This was Utah. Above those rocky peaks a timberland sheltered men upon whose heads the law had put a price. Gail Meadows and Paint had stopped there on their way South.

Now Ross Tyler rode into a camp that was hidden by the rocks and pines. Some men were sitting around a camp-fire. One was cooking over an open fire, lifting the heavy lids of the Dutch ovens with a pot hook. They were a cold-eyed, unshaven lot. There was snow on the ground and they sat as close to the fire as the cook would allow. There, where the warmth of the fire crept out, the snow had melted so that the cook, a one-eyed man in canvas pants and a heavy wool shirt and a pair of run-over boots, tramped around in muddy slush.

There was a demijohn with a wicker covering that passed around the circle of men. Their bellies and faces were flushed from the fire and the raw whisky. The chill of winter bit into their backs and made them shiver a little.

These men eyed Ross Tyler as he rode up. He stared back at them with eyes that were red rimmed and bloodshot. There had been a sun yesterday that had seared his eyeballs and he was almost snowblind. His face, above the matted beard, was frost blackened and scabbed. Under the cheek bones his whiskers could not hide the fact that he was gaunt.

"Light, stranger, and set in."

The roan horse was in good shape. Ross Tyler knew how to ride a horse and how to feed the animal. Even while there was no grub tied to Ross Tyler's saddle, there were always to be found these three good feeds of oats for the roan horse.

He had cut the fancy fringe and quills from the buckskin shirt. He had slid folded newspapers between the soles of his boots and the worn-out overshoes. He had sold his overcoat back in Colorado and had used the few dollars he got for it to sit in a poker game that had been unlucky. The grain in the seamless sack had been stolen. Ross Tyler's pockets were as empty as his belly. He had only his guns and cartridges and a jack-knife.

"They said yuh'd be comin' along," said one of the outlaw pack that smoked and drank and warmed themselves at the fire that was cooking their supper. "They said there'd be a feller in a buckskin shirt ridin' a roan geldin'."

"Who said?" asked Ross Tyler through frost-cracked lips that were black and bleeding.

"Gail Meadows and Paint. They 'lowed that Ross Tyler would be a-follerin'."

"Supposin' they lied?"

"Open yore shirt, feller, and that'll prove it."

"I'm Ross Tyler." His voice was dry and harsh and gritty. "I'm follerin' Gail Meadows and Paint. When I ketch 'em, I'll stamp my iron on 'em and turn 'em over to the law. Has any of you sons got any special objections?"

THEY looked at the bearded, red-eyed man on the roan horse. They looked at the six-shooter in his hand. And no man said a word.

"Spit out whatever is in yore craw, men," he said hotly.

"You know what yore trail is and where it goes," said a man in a heavy buffalo overcoat. "Travel it."

"I'll travel it to the end," snarled Ross Tyler. "I'll put Gail Meadows and his pardner under the ground or in the pen. And if any uh you lousy coyotes has anything to say on the subject, say it. Damn you all! I don't want yore slimy grub. I wouldn't take a drink outa that jug for fear I'd ketch hydrophobia. I don't want to warm my hands at yore fire.

"But if any damned one uh you tries to go for a gun, there'll be some killin'. What the hell do you know about me and why I'm follerin' Meadows? Who in hell are you that says I ain't right? Where did you gutless coyotes come from and what did you ever do that was brave? Listen, you damned tramps, I'll ketch Meadows and his Paint pardner and when I ketch 'em, they'll know they are damn well ketched. And if any lousy, mangy bum tries to he'p 'em git loose from me, I'll kill him like I'd kill a rattler.

"I ain't any law officer. I ain't any one of yore kind either. But I'm tellin' yuh all and makin' yuh like it, that I'd a damned sight rather be a two-bit cop than to be one of yore dirty, sheep-brained, coyote-bellied gang. Take that with yore mulligan and beans. Swaller that with yore hot grub. And like it, yuh mangy coyotes.

"I'm hungry. I ain't slept in forty-eight hours. I'm half froze. My belly is caved in and stickin' to my backbone. I'd give my left eyeball for a good slug of whisky. But I'd a damn' sight rather starve in a snowdrift than eat and drink at yore fire. And I'll kill the dirty son that tries tuh take up the argument. Swaller that, you brave and bold gents. Swaller that!"

XIII

FROM Utah to the Moggolones and then into Arizona on a timbered rim that seemed to Ross like a spot from where he could see the world. He meant the world that is a cowboy's world. Water and grass.

A thunder storm came lumbering up like a big black bear over the skyline. It broke while Ross Tyler was up there on the rim. Lightning ripped across a sky as black as the inside of a gambler's hat. Thunder rolled back and forth across the basin below. The rain fell in an opaque sheet that, inside of a minute, had soaked the man who sat under a scrub pine, trying desperately to keep his gun and tobacco dry.

There was the hind quarter of a yearling hung from a tree limb. Ross Tyler had gorged himself on beef meat that was roasted on a green stick over an open fire. He had a sack of salt and a jack-knife. He caught water in his hat and drank it up there on that timbered rim. And he welcomed the rain that was breaking a hot

twisting trail that had its beginning in a Montana blizzard and had led him into the sun-blasted deserts of Mexico. Half of a year had gone by and still he had never come within rifle range of the two men he had sworn to kill. Men who rode the outlaw trail had marked him for death, but there was not an outlaw camp between the Little Rockies in Montana and the Capitans in Mexico that he had not visited.

There were no snake tracks along the trail of Ross Tyler. He had ridden boldly into every outlaw camp where he figured he might run up against the men he wanted. He had ridden into spots where his life was wanted, and he had ridden away from those places with a snarling, bitter curse on his lips and a gun in his hand. He had gone on along his lone trail to find the men he sought.

More than once or twice or several times he had run into snags. There was that narrow trail in Utah where they had cut his sign and held him for a day and part of a night. Bullets smashing against the granite boulders. He had left two dead men there in that rocky pass. And on the forehead of each of those dead men there had been left a powder mark brass shell.

They had laid another trap in New Mexico into which Ross Tyler had ridden one moonlight night. But he had ridden away from there as boldly as he had entered that canyon that they used to call Skeleton Canyon.

"Too bad you fellers didn't know I was wise to yuh," he muttered through clenched teeth as he left his powder maked brass shells on each of their foreheads.

ROSS TYLER left three dead men there in Skeleton Canyon and robbed their pockets of the money Gail Meadows had paid them to kill a man on a roan horse. There was a third man who had been hit in the thigh and who told what he knew to the black-eyed killer. Ross Tyler loaded the man on a pack mule and took him to the nearest town.

In that same town, there at the Post Office, Ross Tyler had found tacked to the wall a reward notice. It bore his picture and the amount offered for him, dead or

Ross Tyler had taken a soft-nosed .45 cartridge from his belt and sharpened it with his jack-knife. With this crude pencil he had marked out the amount of the reward offered and had added a cryptic note at the bottom:

WHEN YOU GIT ME THERE WILL BE TWICE THAT AMOUNT IN THE BANK AND ON A CHECK YOU WILL FIND IN MY POCKET. MY CHECK IS GOOD. THE MAN THAT KILLS ME IS ENTITLED TO FIVE THOUSAND DOLLARS. HE'LL EARN IT WHEN HE SHOOTS ME.

YOURS TRULY,

ROSS TYLER.

He had mailed a letter to old Jeff Slocum from a little station along the Santa Fe line. The envelope was addressed to Gilt Edge, Montana, and the name on the envelope was not Bob Slocum. But Bob would get it.

The letter was brief and to the point. It told Bob Slocum that he was going to follow his two men until he ketched up with them. He aimed to go to Mexico, where he had heard Gail Meadows had a girl.

But the Mexico trip had netted Ross Tyler nothing except some knife scars on his back. Gail Meadows had posted the girl's brothers. Ross had been crowded into killing one of the brothers of the girl. And when he tried to cross the border, they had stopped him. A well-meaning but somewhat clumsy-handed border official had been rapped across the head with a gun and had come alive some hours later with a terrific pain in his head and the hazy memory of a cowboy astride a roan horse.

Now Ross Tyler lay on his back under a scrub pine on the big timbered rim above Pleasant Valley and let the rain drench him, washing clean the sweat and the dust and the dried blood that caked his flannel shirt.

THERE was a little cottontail rabbit crouched under a thick bush. Birds huddled on the limbs of the trees. There was the sweet odor of wet earth and pine needles. His tobacco and his gun were wrapped up securely in a blue denim jumper.

AND within ten miles of where Ross had sought shelter from the storm, Gail Meadows and Paint were camped with some renegades who handled stolen beef cattle from Mexico.

They were unaware of his presence in the Arizona country. But Ross had picked up their trail at Payson and had followed it as well as he could until he located their camp.

No need to hurry now. The two outlaws were camped there on the rim.

He hoped that the lightning would not strike their camp. Ross Tyler did not want God, the devil, or man to cheat him of his vengeance. The lives of these two belonged to him. They were his bear meat.

The storm gathered in its intensity, smashing, rolling, crashing its thunder across the timbered rim and down into the basin below. Every few minutes that black sky was ripped apart by jagged lightning. The basin below was hidden in the gray sheet of rain.

And it was when the storm was at its worst that the drenched Ross Tyler knew, beyond all shadow of a doubt, that he was sharing this meager shelter with another man.

XIV

HOW Ross knew that someone was near there, he could not tell. Call it instinct of the hunted or something like that. The timber there was thick and was hedged in by underbrush. There was no visible sign of man or horse. And yet Ross Tyler knew that a man was within gun range and that man was watching him.

Ross got to his feet carelessly, unhurriedly. Then he leaped suddenly sideways into a brush patch, his gun in his hand. A crouched, nerve-tightened figure, ready to kill.

A long, tense moment. The rain whipping down out of a black sky that was slitted with ragged flashes of chain lightning and filled with the ominous roar of thunder.

"Stand yore hand, Ross."

A man stepped into sight from a dense thicket. The man was Jeff Slocum. There was a queer smile on the scarred, battered face. A sort of lump choked

Ross Tyler's throat as he gripped the old outlaw's hand.

"Follered yuh, Ross," explained the ex-convict. "Times has changed too much fer me. Can't somehow make out with these new hands that follers the outlaw sign. Kids, half of 'em. Pistol kids that is mouthy and shore brainless. I got that letter yuh sent, sayin' you was a-headin' southwards. I trailed along behind. Man, you shore have covered considerable territory."

Ross grinned and nodded. He found a bottle in his saddle pocket and they pulled the cork with their jack-knives. The whisky warmed the thin blood of old Jeff Slocum and put new life in his chilled bones. They squatted there under a thick branched juniper and grinned at one another like two schoolboys playing hookey. After the third drink, old Jeff Slocum quit shivering. He started questioningly at Ross.

"Located ary sign uh Meadows and this Paint renegade, Ross?"

Ross Tyler nodded. "They're camped somewheres near here. Within ten-fifteen miles, I reckon. But I've been that close to 'em before and lost 'em."

The old outlaw with the scarred face nodded grimly. "They been leavin' yuh a nasty trail tuh foller, boy. I know, fer I come along behind yuh and heard 'em tell 'er scary. Rode my hoss past a grave or two that was fresh."

"They taken up Gail Meadows' fight, Jeff."

"And woke up in hell with a Ross Tyler slug in their briskit," was the older man's dry comment.

"That," agreed Ross bitterly, "is about the size of it, Jeff. Meadows had paid 'em money, I reckon. He's scared tuh make a real stand. Even with Paint backin' his play, he's scared tuh show himself. He hired men tuh kill me. That's how tough he is. He can't take up his own fight. Not even when he's got that bushwhackin' Paint with 'im. Take another drink, Jeff, and tell me the news."

"That trapper and the Cree 'breed was hung. They got Jim Crowe locked up fer keeps."

"And they tell it along the trail that I'm a snake and worse for givin' them three over to the law. Ain't that what they say, Jeff?"

JEFF SLOCUM shoved some plug tobacco into a corncob pipe and lit it. He said nothing. His eyes, eyes that had lost their color in behind the gray walls of a prison, looked into space.

"They tell it that I'm a damned stool pigeon," Ross went on. 'They tell it that I turned against my own kind and that I'm lower than a snake's belly. They tell it that I squealed and that I'm a yellow-bellied coyote. What do you say?"

Jeff Slocum puffed on his old cob pipe. He still looked off into space, thinking, remembering, perhaps trying to forget some things. Now a smile softened the scarred, battered features of the man who had done time in prison. There was a queer expression on his face as he looked at the exiled outlaw who was the son of the man who had been his friend.

"What do I say, Ross? Yuh don't need my answer to that question. If I didn't know they lied, I wouldn't be here.".

"The Paint feller killed Bob Slocum." said Ross.

"So I figgered."

"The Paint gent murdered Bob Slocum on account of the money that Bob Slocum had hid out on him and Gail Meadows."

"I'd figgered 'er thataway. Bob was ornery. Awful ornery. He'd rob his own grandmother."

Ross nodded. "He might do that, Jeff, but he'd never shoot a man in the back."

"Bob Slocum wa'nt no bushwhacker, Ross. I know that."

Ross Tyler nodded. "He deserved a better finish than he got, Jeff. When he come in there to The Hole, it was him or me, that was certain. The feud run back a good many years and when a Tyler met a Slocum there was powder burned. But whenever a Tyler killed a Slocum or a Slocum killed a Tyler, it was clean shootin'. It was game men that pulled the triggers and game men that bit the dirt."

Old Jeff Slocum nodded. "And now a Slocum and a Tyler shares the same grub and blankets, and drinks outa the same bottle. I wonder is there any of the families that is turnin' over in their graves?"

"I reckon not. They done rode out along the last long trail to the big range where there is understandin'. They done left their shootin' irons at ol' Saint Pete's gate and gone in clean. I bet they're glad that the last Slocum and the last Tyler is sittin' here under the same tree gittin' soppin' wet by the big rain."

"And," added old Jeff Slocum, lighting his pipe again, "that we are ridin' together from now on. And when we ketch up with that Paint thing and Gail Meadows, they'll have two men, instead uh one, tuh shoot at. Gimme a drink, son."

A TYLER and a Slocum slept under the same tarp that night there on the rim where the thunder rolled and crashed and the lightning popped around them. It was cold and wet and wholly miserable, but neither man voiced a word of complaint as they shivered under the wet blankets that old Jeff Slocum had fetched on a pack mule.

"It wouldn't su'prise me if it clouded up and rained," said old Jeff Slocum once during that black night when the rain was falling in torrents and their bed was soggy and cold and puddled in the water and mud.

"She looks like a sprinkle was due," Ross came back at him. "The country needs rain, all right."

So they passed the night, those two men left from the Tyler-Slocum clans. Wet, shivering, uncomplaining.

When daylight came, Ross made a fire that sputtered and smoked in the drizzle of dawn and finally gave forth enough warmth to cook some meat and make a pot of coffee.

They put whisky in their black coffee and smoked soggy cigarets there under the inadequate shelter of a tarpaulin hung to the branches of two trees.

They made jokes and joshed around and did those things that men do to keep from breaking. The rain and coldness had taken hold of old Jeff Slocum and he coughed quite a bit.

Ross Tyler knew that the old ex-convict was sick. A bad pair of lungs and a stomach that had been badly hurt by black mouldy bread and bad water in a solitary prison cell. Old Jeff Slocum had been a tough prisoner. The guards had beaten him and starved him and tried to kill him. Those long, gray-walled years had beaten the man from a husky, grinning, devil-take-care-of-me outlaw, into an old man who talked without moving his lips and whose bones and muscles and sinews were scarred by the blows of the prison screws, even as that face, once straight featured and handsome, had been beaten and smashed into a scarred mask.

JEFF SLOCUM was nearing his trail's end. He was giving his last that life allowed him to a Tyler because, a long time ago, Jeff Slocum had soldiered with a man named Jeff Tyler. Both of them named for Tom Jefferson. Both Texans. Both men of rawhide. They had slept in sleet and snow and rain together, those two men who had been named after Tom Jefferson. They had boiled coffee grounds in the same tin can. They had slept the sleep of the dead under soaking blankets and had shared together the songs and the curses of the long march that had taken them back south and into the hard-riding, hard-fighting band of Quantrell.

Outlawed together, Jeff Tyler and Jeff Slocum had ridden, on sore-backed horses, back to Texas. And they had followed the outlaw trail mapped out for them by Quantrell. Kansas, Missouri, Texas, The Indian Territory. Riding fast horses now. Leading reckless men into the jaws of death and fighting on through. Robbing the rich to feed the poor. Taking, giving. Winning, losing. Riding on and riding back from blood and burned powder.

So they had gone, Jeff Tyler and Jeff Slocum. Until the law picked up Jeff Slocum in Missouri. And then it was, after a few years spent in jails, that Jeff Tyler, with a bullet lodged against his spine, had returned to his wife and his son in Texas, there to live along a few years and then die in peace. But Fate had turned up the joker of the pack and Jeff Tyler had died with a Slocum bullet in him. All on account of some fool thing that should have been laughed about and forgotten.

There are Slocums and Tylers in every part of the cow country. Hard men, hard riders, hard fighters. Nursing the bitterness of a blood feud. Killing. Riding on.

"Damn this wet terbacker, Ross."

"I bin toastin' me some in the skillet. She's about dry. Natural leaf, Jeff."

Jeff filled his pipe with the dried tobaco and lit it, nodding his approval.

"She smokes, so."

Ross was wiping the rain from his guns and cartridges. He looked across the camp-fire at the old ex-convict who had ridden the hardest trails that were ever blazed.

"I'm aimin' tuh Injun up on Gail Meadows and that Paint feller. You better stay here at camp, Jeff. That cough uh yourn is bad."

Jeff Slocum looked at the younger man from eyes that were puckered and faded. He puffed a few times on his corn-cob pipe and said nothing. Then he picked up the empty skillet and scoured it with wet sand. Ross buckled on his bullhide chaps.

"I might have a kind of a ticklin' in my neck that you'd call a cough," said old Jeff Slocum, "but I got some medicine in the bottle that'll ease 'er."

Ross grinned and fastened the last snap of his chaps. "Make 'er easy on yorese'f, Jeff."

"I always did have a taste fer skunk huntin', Ross." Old Jeff wiped his six-shooter across his damp undershirt and shoved the gun in a holster that was kept dry by a homely looking bit of slicker cloth.

XV

THERE was a reason behind Jeff Slocum's loyalty to Ross Tyler. A reason that few men could understand.

Ross Tyler knew that reason as he rode his roan horse away from the camp they had shared in a thunder storm that had left them cold and wet and wondering what tomorrow's night would hold.

Behind the fidelity of old Jeff Slocum lay a reason, a reason that only a Texan could savvy.

Jeff Slocum was traveling on to death. His trail was nearing its end. He was going to go out, even as Texans before him had gone out, with his boots on and a gun in his hand. That was the way Jeff Slocum wanted to make his last stand. Better, far better, an end like that than to die alone somewhere with a cough that racked a man's body and made him feel weak and afraid to die.

"I'll be a-follerin' yuh, Ross."

"Come along, Jeff, and listen to the music."

"I kin play the fiddle fer that kind uh music."

"Then th'ow in with the spread and we'll give what the Eastern dudes calls a concert."

Twice that early morning Joff Slocum took down with a fit of coughing. Ross fed him small drinks of whisky and talked to him about cattle and horses and cowboys they had rode with. Jeff Slocum was in bad shape.

"Yonder shows a smoke, Jeff."

"Take to 'em, Ross."

The smoke came from a camp fire some miles away. Old Jeff Slocum had to step down off his horse and cough. Ross told him to wait there, then rode on through the drizzling rain, toward the smoke that hung sluggishly above the tops of the pines in the basin below.

Now a shot ripped out through that rain-drenched grayness. Ross felt the hot, burning, stinging bite of a bullet that nicked his ribs. The roan horse jumped sideways into a brush thicket just as a second shot tore through the rain and missed its mark by a scant foot.

"Good horse," gritted Ross, and shoved the roan into some thicker brush, unlimbering his carbine as he quit the trail.

CROUCHED there in the brush, Ross Tyler wondered how far behind Jeff Slocum would be.

He waited for some movement that would betray the whereabouts of the bush-whacker, but could make out no sign of man or horse. Only the gray drizzle, the drip-drip of water from the wet trees, the whispering of a wind that drove the rain on.

The bullet that had grazed Ross Tyler's ribs had drawn blood that felt hot and sticky under his shirt. He swore at his unseen enemy in a montone that was like the growl of a terrier.

Now he slipped through the brush, his carbine in his hands, hoping to sight the would-be murderer. He knew the approximate location of the ambusher. He crept through the dripping brush, between the rocks, minus chaps and spurs, stalking an unseen man.

And down the trail Ross heard the sound of a horse coming. That would be old Jeff Slocum. Old Jeff, riding plumb into the trap, to be shot out of his saddle.

Ross Tyler did a reckless, foolhardy thing. With a wild cowboy yell, he quit the shelter of the brush and rocks, running, zig-zag fashion, through the trees and up the slope toward the spot where he reckoned the hiding murderer would be.

His ruse worked. Worked with a luck that favors the fearless. The man above, rattled by Ross Tyler's crazy move, opened up with his rifle. Bullets spattered like hot hail around Ross. Then the shots quit coming. Ross caught a swift glimpse of a man's head and shoulders. Halting abruptly, he blazed away at his human target, scarcely taking aim. He saw the man straighten up from behind the rocks, for all the world like a grotesque jack-in-the-box. Ross fired twice more and the man crumpled.

Just at that moment old Jeff Slocum came into view, spurring hard, a Winchester in his hand. Ross, now standing still, waved him to a halt.

"Take to the brush, quick."

"Brush, hell!" The old rascal spurred on along the trail. Now Ross was up there beside the man he had shot. The fellow was dead. He was a bearded, tough-looking man Ross Tyler had never before seen.

"Know 'im, Jeff?"

Jeff Slocum nodded. "A cow thief from over in the Moggolones. Never knowed his name, but crossed his trail two-three times. Kind of a coyote."

THE old ex-convict was still sitting his horse. He shoved his carbine back in the saddle scabbard and fumbled with cigaret papers and wet tobacco. He cussed petulantly.

"Damned terbaccer's wetter'n sop again. Ross, see was that dead 'un packin' ary dry smokin'."

Ross nodded and unbuttoned the man's slicker. In a shirt pocket under the denim jumper was a sack of dry tobacco and a package of papers. These Ross handed to the older man. Then he looked at the rifle there beside the dead man. It was a beautiful weapon, with its scroll work on the blued steel barrel and the half-pistol grip walnut stock. An automatic rifle with a shell jammed. That jammed shell had no doubt saved Ross Tyler's life. He slid it free from the ejector and put it in his jumper pocket.

Then Ross took an empty shell from his own gun and put it on the forehead of the dead man, whose white, beaded face was being washed free of blood by the rain.

"Reminds a man uh Tom Horne, up in Wyoming, Ross. He put a leetle rock on every man's forehead, didn't he? Or did he give 'em a rock fer a pillow? I fergit, never havin' bin in that Wyomin' war."

"That was before my time, Jeff. But I figgered this 'un out myse'f. I make a little mark on their foreheads with the empty shell. A little circle where I push the end of the shell in to their hide. Then I leave the empty shell there. It has kinda put a little fear into Gail Meadows and Paint. Yuh see, they've hired this pore son to kill me. Meadows is weakenin' and so is this Paint gent. I'm wonderin' how many more they have hired tuh . . . Duck, Jeff. Git tuh cover."

Even as the two hid themselves in the brush and rocks, three riders came along the trail at a long trot. Their guns were in their hands, their hats pulled across their eyes. Now they picked up the sign of Ross Tyler's horse and halted. Another located Jeff Slocum's sign. They looked around uneasily.

Ross Tyler barked out a hard bitten warning.

"The first man of yuh that makes a run for cover will git what yore pardner got about ten minutes ago. Stand where yuh are or we'll kill yuh like we'd kill skunks in a hen coop. Drop them guns, damn yuh, and drop 'em quick."

XVI

THE three riders obeyed sullenly. They glared at Ross Tyler and old Jeff Slocum, whose guns covered them.

"I need a new hat," said old Jeff Slocum. "Ask 'em, Ross, is there one of 'em that wears a size 7 sombrero. And see is there any of 'em with dry terbaccer."

A hat was duly collected, likewise tobacco and papers and an assortment of guns. Old Jeff Slocum tolled off the pedigrees of the three sullen, surly men.

"The skinny one with the funny nose is just a short sport that hangs around the pool halls in town, rollin' drunks and deal-in' crooked cards tuh drunk sheepherders. I bet a dollar yuh'll find a pair er two uh crooked dice on him.

"That big thing with the black slicker is a whisky maker from over around Fossil Creek. He's bin in jail a time er two and makes the worst rotgut likker ever sold to an Injun.

"That red muzzled freak is a half-witted cowboy that was run outa Globe fer robbin' a woman that had staked him to board and room when he was broke."

"Gail Meadows done hired hisse'f a fine crew," was Ross Tyler's contemptuous comment.

The three toughs looked at one another, then at the grim-faced two men who stood there in the rain with drawn six-shooters.

"Plant this gent that got killed," said Ross. "When yuh git him planted, ride back to yore camp and tell Gail Meadows and Paint that me and Jeff Slocum is com-in' to pay 'em a visit. We'll have our guns in our hands when we come and we'll be usin' 'em. Now dig a grave for this dead bushwhacker."

"We got no shovels," growled the big one.

"No? Yuh each got two hands, ain't yuh? The ground is soft from the rain. Dig with yore hands."

Ross Tyler and Jeff Slocum rode on in the gray drizzle. They had found a quart of corn whisky on one of the trio and Jeff nibbled at it as he rode, for the cold rain had bitten into his bones and he was humped across his saddle horn in a fashion that made Ross sick inside.

"Drink all yuh want, Jeff. Yuh look plumb peaked."

Slocum nodded.

"I feel all right, Ross. Just a mite shivery. Here's howdy."

Ross wondered how many more men Gail Meadows had hired. It was some-thing to know that he had Meadows on the run and that Meadows and Paint were scared.

"I got a hunch we'll be meetin' up with them two varmints," said old Jeff Slocum. "I know every foot uh this country. Was in here when you was a button of a kid. I reckon I kin figger about where they'll be hidin' out."

THEY halted on a rocky ledge and the older man indicated a heavily timbered strip down below the rim. With the field glasses, Ross made out a cabin in a tiny clearing.

"That's her, Ross," nodded Jeff Tyler. "Water and feed there and only one trail leadin' down. A bad trail, at that. I bet a dollar and six-bits that'll be where we'll come on 'em."

They rode single file down the rocky, precipitous trail. Now a white fog was drifting up toward them. They rode into its concealing dampness and were hidden.

Ross Tyler took the lead, Jeff Slocum following close. It was weird and eerie there in that white fog that billowed up like wet smoke. Only the crunching of shod hoofs on the rocks and the creak of saddle leather and the jingle of their spurs told of their presence in that fog-banked world through which the tall pines jutted.

Below was the cabin that held the two men Ross Tyler had sworn to bring to justice. Only one trail in or out of the place. There were tracks made by the dead bush-whacker and his three companions who had come too late to save him from Ross Tyler's bullets. Beyond those tracks, no more. Gail Meadows and Paint were down there at their hidden cabin, waiting for news from the men they had hired to kill Ross and his old stand-by. Let them wait there. Let them wait. It wouldn't be long now until those two renegades down yonder would be facing their fate.

Ross Tyler had in mind to capture Gail Meadows and Paint, brand them, then turn them over to the law. Gail Meadows had branded him, shamed him, made of him a damned outcast. He would put the same brand on Gail Meadows and he'd stamp it on Paint's chest. That was Ross Tyler's plan.

But old Jeff Slocum had other ideas. He was too old, too lacking in patience and strength to play a game like that. Old Jeff Slocum had decided to write his last verdict in bullets. He'd kill 'em when he caught up with 'em, and he'd let the buz-zards pick their bones clean.

Down through that white fog, a young man with bullet-scarred ribs that stabbed pain through his chest with every breath. An old ex-convict with a hacking cough that sometimes seemed to tear that skinny frame apart. Down through a thick white fog to meet the men they hated. Down through that blanket of white fog to meet fate.

XVII

IN the log cabin, hidden there in the pines, shrouded in the dense fog, Gail Meadows passed a jug of whisky to Paint, who tilted it up but drank sparingly.

"I don't feel good, Gail. I tell yuh, it's in my bones that some damn' thing is goin' to happen."

"Yuh scared, Paint?"

"No. Just cautious."

"Same thing. Hell, take a drink and grin."

"I ain't exactly in the drinkin' mood," said Paint, "and I ain't doin' any grinnin' But when the time comes, I'll do my end uh the fightin'. I'm leary, I tell yuh. This here fog. . . ."

"Yuh taken on a few too many last night. Nerves, feller, just old jumpin' nerves."

"Mebby. Mebby not. I tell yuh, I don't like this place. One trail out, that's all. It's a pocket. I've felt trapped ever since we come here."

"Safe as a jail, here." Gail Meadows stretched his big chest and took a drink from the jug.

"And just about as hard tuh break out of it, if yuh ask me."

"The boys up on the rim will be guardin' the trail. What the hell yuh worried about?"

"About Ross Tyler and old Slocum. About them men that Ross Tayler left dead along the trail. He's a curly wolf."

"Say, Paint, just how wide is that yellow streak that runs up yore backbone?"

Paint whirled on the other man with an angry snarl, but found himself looking into the black hole of Gail Meadows' gun barrel.

"Sit down, Paint, and tuck in yore shirt tail. You ain't startin' anything, feller. Because if yuh do, I'll kill yuh deader than hell. You are a great gent in the bush, but here in this cabin you haven't the guts tuh fight. Have yuh, Paint?"

Gail Meadows passed his thumb carressingly along the drawn hammer of his single action .45. Paint stared into the eyes of a killer now. He wondered if Gail Meadows would pull the trigger.

"Yuh need me and my gun for a while yet, Gail. Better not pull the trigger."

"If I don't, you'll like as not murder me from behind," argued Gail Meadows cold-bloodedly. "Gimme one good reason why I shouldn't shoot yuh in the briskit."

"I'll do better than that, Meadows. I'll give yuh two damned good reasons."

"Name 'em, feller."

"Ross Tyler and old Jeff Slocum."

"We got them gents on guard up on the rim."

"But how good are they? Where did they ever go through a real fight?"

"I'll risk it. If I don't kill you, you'll kill me, Paint. I reckon I'll just play safe and let yuh have it."

THERE was a thin smile on Gail Meadows' face. His eyes were red and congested as they had been that night when he had branded Ross Tyler. Paint, his face yellow with fear, tried to grin. But his eyes were wide and bulging.

Then both men stiffened, their eyes twisting their slitted stare toward the outside. From up in that blanket of fog that hid the rim and the only trail away from the cabin, there had come a sound. The sound that began like the roll of thunder, then ended with a crashing, smashing noise.

"Rock slide," gritted Gail Meadows. "Rock slide on the trail. There where she cuts in under that old hangin' rock. God, that'll clog the trail so it'll take a week tuh dig out."

"Rock slide," said Paint in a voice that was harsh with a new terror. "It never started by itself. Somebody is comin' down the trail."

"It'll be the boys comin' back for a drink."

Paint shook his head. "Meadows, there's men comin' down the trail. We can't git out. Our only bet is tuh fight. A damn' good thing yuh didn't kill me a minute ago. I tell yuh, Meadows, Ross Tyler and old Jeff Slocum has ketched up with us. It's a fight."

"Take a drink, Paint, yuh look like a corpse. Then we'll step out and take on these fightin' men. Show some guts!"

Paint tipped up the jug. This time he swallowed enough whisky to make him brave. The two outlaws shoved cartridges into their pockets and quit the cabin that was hidden in the fog. They took along the whisky and their slickers. The timber was thick near the cabin. The white fog hung like silky moss from the branches of the pines. The rain drizzled through the fog, making it more opaque than ever.

They took their stand there in the pines, hidden behind the thick brush.

An hour passed. . . . Two hours. No sign of man or horse. The trail to the rim was blocked now. Gail Meadows and Paint huddled under their slickers where the brush was thickest.

Dusk and fog filled that pine pocket.

A sound on the trail told Gail Meadows and Paint they were not alone. Four men were there, trapped by the rock slide. Four men with guns in their hands.

Ross Tyler barked out his challenge:

"I've come for yuh, Gail Meadows."

XVIII

THE words shrilled through the white fog that now was taking on the gray and black of the coming night. That challenge had sent a shiver down the cold spine of Gail Meadows. Paint laughed shakily.

"I told yuh I had a bad hunch, Meadows."

"Go tuh hell, Paint. Fight, damn yuh."

"I'll fight. This is my meat."

"If it ain't baited with strychnine, Paint. Luck to us."

They were about fifty yards apart, there in that gray gloom of a fog filled twilight.

"Luck to me, Meadows. To hell with you."

Through that grayness that was filled with drizzle, there came the crack of guns. Red streaks of fire from the barrels of guns.

In that fog shrouded gloom, the whispering cough of a man badly hit.

"God, Jeff, they got yuh?"

"Got me, Ross. I . . . take care of yorese'f, son. They got me. Any dry terbaccer?"

Ross Tyler rolled a cigaret from the tobacco that old Jeff had taken from a dead man. He risked being shot when he struck the match to light the hand-made cigaret that he had shoved between the old ex-convict's bloodless lips. The lips that now were twisted in a pained, crooked grin.

"I got . . . the Paint feller," he whispered. He tried to pull smoke from the cigaret into his lungs that were now filled with blood.

The match in Ross Tyler's hand went out, leaving everything dark and filled with the black drizzle. Old Jeff Slocum was dead, his head pillowed now on Ross Tyler's jumper.

Jeff Slocum was dead. The last of the Slocums had pulled his last trigger. And it was a Tyler who covered the dead man's body and closed the puckered old eyes that had lost their color behind prison walls.

Tears, scalding hot tears that Ross Tyler could not understand stung his eyes as he left the dead Jeff Slocum and went to find the man he had sworn to brand.

OUT in that black fog, two men faced one another. Each with a gun in his hand. Each badly hit and bleeding.

Ross Tyler's six-shooter began spewing fire. The gun in the hand of Gail Meadows was belching flame. They were each shooting at queer shadows that took shape in a fog filled twilight. Shooting with deadly accuracy.

Meadows slumped to his knees, there in the black fog. He was using both hands to lift his .45. And walking through that black fog toward him was a man whose legs were unsteady. Ross Tyler, shot through the hip and through one shoulder, came on.

Step by step, faltering a little. His teeth showing white as he grinned hideously, Ross Tyler walked toward the fallen man.

Gail Meadows was half dead. Ross Tyler was staggering like a drunken man. But through his clenched teeth came a laugh that was like an echo from hell.

Slowly, painfully, laboriously, Ross Tyler dragged the half dead Gail Meadows into the cabin. Then he went back and groped around in the rain and mud and darkness until he located the body of Paint. He dragged the dead man into the cabin and lit the lamp.

He was stumbling badly when he left the cabin and made his way to some brush where his roan horse stood. With a tremendous effort he unsaddled the stout roan and pulled the headstall from the horse's head. The roan shoved a wet, velvety nose into the man's face and Ross Tyler laughed softly.

"Good horse. Good partner. We've found the end uh the trail, ol' timer."

From his saddle Ross Tyler took something in a buckskin sheath. It was a branding iron. The iron that Gail Meadows had used on him at The Hole, then tossed out in the snow. The day to use it again had come.

Ross Tyler, carrying the little branding iron, went back to the cabin. He threw some pine sticks on the fire and heated his branding iron. Then he cut away the shirts and undershirts of the two men who lay on the cabin floor. Gail Meadows and Paint were both stone dead.

The little branding iron grew cherry red. . . .

IT was three days later when the sheriff from Prescott broke that rock slide free and came down the trail with a deputy from Globe.

In the log cabin were three dead men. All three were outlaws. There was the dead body of an older outlaw not far from the cabin.

"But what gits me," said the deputy from Globe to the sheriff from Prescott. "Why in hell has two uh these men got their shirts and undershirts cut off and what in hell is that brandin' iron doin' in the other fellow's hand?"

The old sheriff from Prescott smiled grimly. Perhaps he had heard news that drifts down the outlaw trail from Montana to Mexico.

"Hard tuh say, son. Hard tuh say."

THE TRADING POST

FRONTIER is pleased to present another true reminiscence of the early days of the Old West. In EARLY DAYS IN NORTH TEXAS, Mrs. Anderson gives an interesting account of the problems besetting the pioneers who carved from Texas a new home and a new and mighty Empire.

Any old-timers wishing to yarn about their early experiences will always be welcome to the Trading Post. In fact, FRONTIER offers $10.00 to the mossy-horn who spins the most exciting, smokiest, yet authentic tale of early days. Each issue will print one or more of these reminiscences, but only the best will collect. Dig down into the warbags of your memory and give us a tale of the great old days. Mail your stories to THE TRADING POST, care of FRONTIER STORIES.

THE EDITOR.

Early Days in North Texas

By Mrs. JAMES ANDERSON

AT the close of the Civil war my husband and I left our home in Mississippi and accompanied by my father and several other relatives joined a wagon train going to Texas.

We reached Texas in the early fall after suffering many hardships on the trail and settled in Parker county. We went to work and by the time the first snow fell we had our new home built, and it was here that my first baby was born.

All went well till the following winter when raiding parties of Indians started crossing the Red River. As soon as it was known that the Indians were coming one of the settlers would ride ahead and give the warning and the settlers would all gather at one house for protection. But sometimes they would strike so swiftly we could only leave our homes and take refuge in the timber, and return after they

had gone, to find our home a smoking mass of ruins.

I shall never forget the night our home was destroyed. It was mid-winter and the weather was bitter cold. My father, who was making his home with us, was away at the time, having taken our only team and wagon on the long trip to Gainesville for a load of flour and salt.

My husband and I had just gone to bed when we heard a horse coming down the trail at breakneck speed. The Indians were coming and were less than a mile behind the rider. As soon as the boy had warned us he rode on to warn the other settlers. We knew we could never reach the nearest house so with no light at all we dressed as quickly as we could and I wrapped my baby in quilts while my husband was getting his guns. We quietly slipped out of the house and took refuge in a plum thicket where we crouched, waiting.

We did not have long to wait for soon we could hear them breaking in to our little home and in a few mintues it was in flames. As we lay there in the darkness we could see them as they rode round and round the burning cabin with our quilts and sheets tied to their ponies' tails. Finally tiring of their sport they left.

We stayed hidden in the thicket till daylight and then, half frozen, made our way five miles to our nearest neighbor where my father had stopped for the night.

While in Gainesville my father learned from a band of soldiers that my cousin who had come to Texas with us had been murdered and scalped by a band of Indians.

He also learned that the Texas government was selling land to settlers in Montague county for a dollar an acre and that they were being protected by a company of soldiers under Captain Rowland. So with our home burned and nothing to hold us where we were, we decided to settle there where we would have some protection from the troops.

With the exception of a few raids in which no one was hurt the Indians had given us no trouble at all in our new home and we had almost forgotten about them, but that fall they began raiding again. People in the south had started driving their cattle to the northern markets and the Indians were attacking their herds. As we lived near the river the cattlemen would often camp on our place for the night, with their herds, in order to make the crossing by daylight.

There was a spring on the northern end of our place where they would always camp and they would always kill a beef and after they were gone the wolves would come around the spring and eat what they had left. My father would often go there late in the evening and shoot them and sometimes a deer. He had been to the spring early one morning and found quite a few deer tracks, so late that afternoon he told us he thought he would go back and see if he could get one. So taking his gun and dog he walked off through the timber. That was the last time I ever saw him.

H E hadn't been gone long when we heard two shots almost together and then silence and we were sure he had gotten a deer and would soon be home, but when sundown came and he had not returned we knew something was wrong.

We waited all night as my husband was afraid to go look for him and leave the baby and I unprotected, but as soon as it grew daylight he blew his hunting horn and fired his gun and soon a group of neighbor men had gathered at our cabin and the search for my father was started. They found his body by the spring where he had told us he was going. The Indians had literally butchered him and taken his scalp. They even cut the throats of the dogs he had with him. His broken gun was found lying by his side.

A few days after my father's murder there was a general raid on the settlements but we were warned and this time we were ready for them. In the battle that followed two Indians and one soldier were killed.

I remember our last encounter with the Indians very well. We had been warned that a band of them had been seen near our place so we decided to go to a neighbor's for a few days for safety. After we had been there a couple of days and still no sign of them my husband began to grow impatient and decided to take his pony and ride back and see if they had been there. On arriving he could find nothing wrong, and decided there was no danger and that he would just cook himself something to eat before riding back. So turning his pony loose to graze he went into the cabin and built a fire in the stove. While waiting for the stove to get hot he glanced out of the window and saw a band of about twenty Indians riding up to the house. He ran and caught his pony and rode off with the Indians close behind him. They chased him to within sight of the house where we were staying, then turned and rode off into the timber. That was the last we ever saw of them.

As the years went by and more settlers came into the county, the raids finally stopped altogether and the troops were moved. Later, after his retirement, Captain and Mrs. Rowland came back and settled at Nocona, Texas, where my husband and I visited them quite often and recalled to each other our adventures of the past.

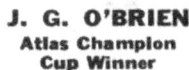

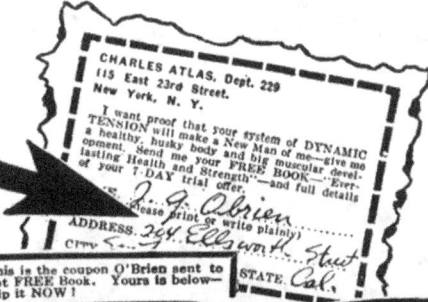

www.ingramcontent.com/pod-product-compliance
Lightning Source LLC
Chambersburg PA
CBHW080251280626
47159CB00019B/3406